CANTEEN CULTURE

Ike Eze-anyika was born in London in 1970. He joined the Metropolitan Police Service in 1992. *Canteen Culture* was written while he was serving in the Golders Green Division. Since writing the novel he has resigned from the police. *Canteen Culture* won the 1998 SAGA Prize for the best first novel by a black British or Irish writer.

The SAGA Prize was founded in 1994 by author and actress Marsha Hunt to encourage unpublished black novelists born in the UK and the Republic of Ireland. Sponsored by the SAGA Group, the award is £3,000 plus publication of the winning novel. Previous winners of the award are *Some Kind of Black* by Diran Adebayo, *Sister Josephine* by Joanna Traynor and *Bernard and the Cloth Monkey* by Judith Bryan.

Canteen Culture

IKE EZE-ANYIKA

First published in 2000
by Faber and Faber Limited
3 Queen Square London WC1N 3AU

Typeset by RefineCatch Limited, Bungay, Suffolk
Printed in England by Clays Limited, St Ives plc

A CIP record for this book
is available from the British Library

ISBN 0–571–20079–6

2 4 6 8 10 9 7 5 3 1

Dedicated to Sarah S. H. Miller and the beloved memory of my brother Odunze Eze-anyika

'CANTEEN CULTURE: the informal ethos of the lower ranks at the sharp end: often cynical, racist and aggressive in words, but not always in deeds.'

Glossary, *Talking Blues*, by Roger Graef, 1990

'Some things will never change . . . That's just the way it is!'

Tupac Shakur, 1999

PRELUDE

The green cell wall came gradually into focus as Lionel, one of the six occupants, stirred. He closed his eyes and drifted back to sleep. He was one of the three with the austere privilege of sleeping on the cement slab constituting the cell bed. Two other occupants lay on thick blue plastic mats on the floor. A third mat was vacant; its absent owner sat not too far away on a solitary Armitage Shanks toilet in the far left corner of the cell. His trousers and boxer shorts encircled his ankles; his white shirt was creased, unevenly buttoned and barely able to cover his paunch. It wore evidence of last night's frolic: a cocktail of chicken curry, beer and blood from a good old-fashioned punch-up outside their favourite Indian restaurant. He twitched as he tried to fold his arms over his chest, unable to link them at any point lower. The sounds of his laboured breathing and intermittent snoring filled the room. All of his eighteen stone was seated comfortably enough to remain in that position for the whole of the night.

Lionel stirred again. He twitched his nose in a subconscious response to the unpleasant odour oozing from the stale socks on the feet positioned only a few inches from his face. Overwhelmed by the smell, he broke into a frown and, without bothering to open his eyes, pushed the feet towards Speedy. Speedy stirred in silent protest and pushed them back towards Lionel.

The smell became unbearable.

'Saddam, your feet smell like a whore's underpants,' Lionel muttered as he painfully opened his eyes. He bent his left arm and strained to peer at his watch, then pushed the feet back to Speedy, who opened one eye and pushed them back towards Lionel.

'Piss off,' whispered Lionel, pushing the feet back towards Speedy.

'What's the time?' Speedy groaned.

'Time you looked at your own bloody watch to find out,' replied Lionel.

'I can't move my arm, it's stuck ... So what's the time?' Speedy asked.

'It's fucking six o'clock! Now shut up!' Lionel whispered, grimacing as though it pained him to speak.

'That means we've got forty-five minutes,' whispered Speedy.

'Then shut up! I need to get some sleep,' said Saddam.

'The only thing you need to get is a new pair of socks. Your feet fucking stink,' Speedy retorted.

'There's nothing wrong with my socks,' protested Saddam.

'They smell like they've been stuck up a camel's arse.'

'They can't smell that bad. I've only had them on for the past six months,' said Saddam jokingly.

They lay still for a while until Lionel, reacting disdainfully to the smell, got up. 'Fucking bollocks to both of you! I'm getting up. I can't sleep any more,' he said. He slid forward to the edge of the slab and set himself gently on his feet. He looked around the room to fix the position of the other occupants on the cell floor in order to make sure he did not step on them. Negotiating his way around Jazz and Sponge, lying on the floor, he reached the steel cell door, banged on it several times with his fists and waited for a response.

Disturbed by the noise, Jazz and Sponge stirred.

'What's the time?' Sponge asked in a weak voice.

'Six o'clock,' Speedy replied.

'What's that smell?' Sponge asked, half sitting up and trying to open his eyes. His left eye was sealed, bruised black and swollen shut as a result of a head-butt received during the brawl the night before.

The wick of the cell door suddenly opened and the face of the custody sergeant appeared.

'Room service,' he chirped. 'Until we fit in the telephones, can you ring the bell on the wall?'

'We need to get ready,' whispered Lionel, peering through the wick. 'We've got parade in thirty minutes.'

The keys jingled on the other side of the door and the key swivelled in the lock. Before the door was fully open, the custody sergeant was halfway down the corridor on the way back to his desk. 'The keys are in the cell door! And put my prisoners back in before you leave!' he shouted.

'Keep your voice down, skipper, I've got a splitting headache,' said Lionel as he hobbled out of the cell and followed him down the passage.

'Where the fuck do you think you're going?' the custody sergeant hissed at him. 'I said put my prisoners back.'

Four more occupants of the cell emerged, using the keys in the door to open the overcrowded adjoining cell. They ushered back in the original occupants, displaced the night before. Bubba had been deliberately left asleep on the lavatory when they shut the cell door behind the two new inmates.

'Don't wake him! He can get violent if you disturb him when he's having a shit,' Sponge said to them, peering through the wick.

As they filed out of the office, Sponge stopped to place the custody-suite keys on the sergeant's desk. The sergeant ignored them, biting into an apple as he concentrated on the Formula One racing on the portable television at the far end of his desk.

They filtered from the locker room up the three flights of stairs of Northwick police station to the team office for parade, held at the beginning of every shift. Northwick police station was a small division, located just on the border of the 2 Area section of the Metropolitan Police District of London.

Six officers and one sergeant constituted Team One, one of four designated uniformed teams that worked the division. The last to make it up to the team office had been Speedy; he lay on his back on one of the desks, his arms folded and his knees bent over the edge, drifting in and out of consciousness. Speedy was a Scotsman; dark-haired, with rough facial features and a crooked nose, he resembled a retired boxer.

Nobody had yet uttered a word as they sat in the team office.

'Right, ladies! Slippery isn't in yet. I suppose I'm going

to have to take parade again as no other fucker wants to do it,' said Lionel, breaking the silence. 'Who is driving what?'

'Which vehicles have we got available?' Speedy asked, without opening his eyes.

'How the hell should I know? I don't get paid to do this,' Lionel replied. 'Jazz, you've just passed your board – you should be APSing.'

'Is Slippery shown working today?' Jazz asked. 'He's the sergeant, he should be the one taking parade.'

Just as he finished speaking, the phone rang. They all sat and looked at it in silence for several seconds.

'Someone answer that thing,' said Lionel.

Nobody moved. The phone continued to ring.

'You're the youngest in service – you answer it,' Sponge said, looking at Lionel.

'Firstly, the phone's all the way across the room and all you have to do is stretch out your arm,' replied Lionel. 'Secondly,' he continued, 'I'm not the youngest in service in this shop, Jazz is.'

'I might have turned up at training school thirty minutes after you did, but according to you I'm supposed to be acting police sergeant now, remember,' said Jazz.

As if in answer to the argument, the answerphone came to life and a female tone, asking for a message to be left, responded to the caller. After the ensuing bleep, a croaky and angry voice came through on the speaker. 'Answer the phone, will you?' it said.

Sponge whipped up the receiver. 'Hello, sarge! I've only just walked into the room. How can I help you?' He listened. '. . . Fair enough, sarge,' he continued, 'Lionel's taking parade anyway. What are you sick with?' The call went on and then Sponge put down the receiver. 'Slippery's gone sick,' he announced.

'What's he sick with this time?' asked Lionel.

'He said we should use our initiative,' said Sponge.

'A stomach bug is the best I can think up,' said Jazz.

'He came to the Indian with us last night, but I can't remember seeing him leave,' said Sponge. 'Come to think of it, I can't remember anything past my eighth pint. I don't even know how I got a black eye.'

'You slagged off some bloke's good lady wife in the Indian and they waited for us to come out,' Jazz reminded him.

'Aye! The hallmark of what I call a bloody good night,' said Speedy.

'Slippery went home in a cab, fucking pissed as a village priest in a brothel, when we came out the pub,' said Saddam.

'Well, he's gone sick,' said Lionel, taking out the duties book. 'He's a lovely bloke but he runs this team like Boris Yeltsin would run a brewery.'

'You think our skipper's bad, what about our senior officers? They're about as useless as a one-legged man in an arse-kicking competition,' said Speedy sardonically.

Lionel began delegating the duties. 'I think we've got three vehicles. Speedy, you should be driving the area car; it says here you should have been at work an hour ago. Sponge, you're shown as operator. Saddam and I'll take the incident-response vehicle and Jazz can take the Panda.' He sat back with contentment and, looking at the binder, stretched back over the chair. 'That's it. Let's go, girls,' he said, concluding parade.

Jazz got up and walked to the radio cabinet. Selecting a radio, he attached it to his belt loop, took a battery out of the charger on the table and slotted it in.

'Get us an ESD while you're still there, Jazz, will you? I want to see if I'm still pissed,' said Lionel.

'You might as well be fucking for virginity, mate,' said Jazz. 'None of you have a fucking hope in hell of passing a breathalyser test.'

They each took turns to attach the white plastic tube to the device and blow long and hard into it. Each time the light ignored the green and, with only a fleeting hesitation at the amber, leapt to red.

'This isn't a matter of whether the light goes to red. It's a matter of counting how many seconds it takes to get there,' said Sponge. 'The only help it's given us is to find out who the least pissed of us are.'

'Right,' Lionel declared, 'there's no point re-doing the duties; we're still driving the same vehicles. Let's do the most important thing in a policeman's career: have a cup of tea.'

'I fancy some nosh as well, I'm famished,' said Jazz.

'The Underground Café for all of us, I think,' said Speedy, getting up from his seat.

'Oh, not there!' said Lionel.

'We're not going to stop going there just because you decided to hump the waitress,' said Speedy.

Shaking his head, Lionel followed them out.

*

The area car, a marked Vauxhall Cavalier, was parked close to the wall of the back court leading to the steps of the Underground Café, an obscure basement café frequented by builders, road sweepers and police. Behind the area car was the Panda, a marked Rover Metro, with only a token blue light on its roof to give it emergency-vehicle status.

Lionel looked at the abundance of parking space along the small service road as he sat at the wheel of the Irv. The Irv, or incident-response vehicle, was itself a marked police Vauxhall Astra, with blue lights and a siren. Lionel decided to park opposite the area car on the other side of the road. He turned to his operator, Saddam. 'You might as well get out. There isn't going to be any room for you to open the door after I've parked the car.'

'Don't flatter yourself,' replied Saddam, climbing out.

Lionel parked the car and got out. He shut the car door, took a self-approbatory look at his parking, put his baton through his belt loop and disappeared down the steps into the café.

Lionel drew a seat from an empty table and joined the members of his team. Sponge was playing on the pinball machine at the far end of the café, frantically pulling at its buttons.

They sat at the table with vacant expressions, waiting for a prompt.

'Do I take it this silence is about who's going to buy the coffees?' asked Lionel. Receiving no answer, he looked around at the other tables to find something to read. A daily newspaper lay two tables away. He half got up and stretched for it.

'Pass me the paper on that table, Lionel,' Speedy said as Lionel took hold of the newspaper.

'Piss off!' replied Lionel as he sat back in his seat.

'I don't think we're going to get served now you're here, Lionel,' said Saddam, nodding in the direction of a young mulatto girl who sat at the counter looking intently in the direction of the officers' table.

'Well, who's going to get the coffees in then?' Lionel enquired, flicking the corners of the newspaper.

'Sponge is,' said Saddam as Sponge walked back to the table from the pinball machine.

'Piss off,' hissed Sponge.

'You never buy the coffees,' protested Saddam. 'You haven't got a long slender dick from genetics.'

'What's that got to do with buying coffees?' Sponge asked.

'You're a tight-fisted wanker,' Saddam retorted.

Sensing they were ready to order, the girl left the counter and moved slowly across to their table, pen and notepad in hand. As she did so, both Sponge and Speedy smiled at her, evaluating her buxom figure, modestly disguised by a pair of jeans and a tight black top. 'Hello, Sophia,' they chorused as she arrived at the table.

She replied with just a smile and a nod. 'What can I get for you guys?' she asked.

They each ordered a coffee as she went round the group, deliberately leaving Lionel to last. Finally she looked at Lionel for his order; he had tried to remain oblivious to the proceedings by burying himself in the newspaper. 'Do you want one or are you waiting for me to ask?' she snapped at him.

'I'd rather have a coffee, please; white with no sugar, thank you,' replied Lionel in a quiet tone.

'Don't think I'm going to bring it over to you,' she replied waspishly.

'That's why I come here – to get insulted,' said Lionel without glancing up from the paper.

'You've got some cheek,' she replied. 'You're just a user.'

Lionel looked up at her. 'You're just like a bowling ball: picked up, fingered, rolled over, dropped, thrown in the gutter, and you still come back for more!'

'You're all piss and wind,' she said.

'Why don't you two bury the hatchet?' Jazz asked.

'I don't think I could trust myself with a hatchet,' she replied liverishly before walking off.

'You know, she reminds me of my ex-wife,' said Speedy, 'and, if she's anything like my ex-wife, you'd have been better off with a pot of Vaseline and a blow-up doll.'

'You were warned; you shouldn't have humped her, Lionel,' said Jazz.

'Oh shut up! Someone on this team had to do it; she was gagging for it. And I'm the only one here who goes out with black women,' replied Lionel.

Sponge got up and returned to the pinball machine.

'Now, I'd like to read my paper if I could, so keep your conversation down,' said Lionel, going back to the newspaper.

Sophia arrived with the coffees. She carefully placed each cup in front of each officer as she brought them in batches of two, quite obviously excluding Lionel from each delivery. She finally put the last two cups down on the table, one in Sponge's vacant place, the other in front of Lionel. 'Try and drink it all at once: rat poison starts to take effect straight away and kills you in thirty minutes. That gives me enough time to sit and have the pleasure of watching.'

'That happens every time we eat your cooking,' said Lionel, growing tired of the exchange. 'Can we get some food now?'

'Yes, of course. Now, what would you like to eat?' she replied sarcastically.

'Full English breakfast, another coffee and a diet Coke, please,' Speedy requested.

Sponge slowly made his way back from the machine and stood behind Lionel, reading over his shoulder.

'Anybody not having a full breakfast?'

The ensuing silence confirmed the order and Sophia walked back to the counter.

'Hey, Jazz, you're a black guy,' said Lionel, still looking down at his paper.

'Am I?' retorted Jazz.

'It says in here that Walt Disney are making an animated version of the O.J. Simpson trial. They say it'll have similar characters to the ones in *The Lion King*, only they're going to change the title slightly and call it *The Lying Coon*!'

Laughter erupted around the table and Jazz forced a lopsided smile. Lionel sipped his coffee and grimaced. 'Hey, Sophia, what is this stuff? It tastes like fucking shit,' he shouted.

'It is shit! I thought you needed topping up,' she shouted back.

'Have you guys heard about the eleven Scouser builders who invited a German au pair back to their place and started to rape her? She shouted, "*Nein, nein*, please *nein*," so two of them go home,' Sponge began. He received a lukewarm response.

Suddenly their radios burst into life as the first call of the shift came through.

'Any units available, please, to deal with a believed suspect on premises, 738 the Broadway. Call graded I, India. Any unit, please.'

Speedy looked at his operator, Sponge, with a forbidding stare. Unfortunately, Sponge had already picked up his radio and spoken. *'Yes, eh . . . November 1, we'll take a run over,'* he said.

'Yes, received . . . Any other units, please, to back up November 1?' the controller asked.

Lionel raised the mouthpiece of his radio to his mouth and hesitated deliberately, half bending his neck towards it for about ten seconds. *'Yeah, November X-ray, show November 21 as well,'* he said. He turned to the others in protest. 'This is what I hate about this job, it's shite. You can't even eat in peace without being called up. Ninety-five per cent of these are toilet anyway. Who the fuck is going to burgle a house this early in the morning? It's obvious they're builders.'

'If you don't like the job, bloody leave,' said Speedy.

'I can't at the moment; I'm too used to the money. I just wish I'd gone to university when I had the chance.'

'You wouldn't want to be a student, they're bloody

bums,' said Speedy. 'You're a student, aren't you?' he asked Sophia, who had come over to take their meals back into the kitchen to keep them warm.

'It's better than working with a bunch of drop-outs who want to wear a uniform because they were bullied at school,' replied Sophia, picking up the plates.

'You see! No respect for the uniform either,' complained Lionel.

'Oh, stop fucking whingeing, you took the call,' said Saddam, getting up.

'I'm only saying what everyone else is feeling,' replied Lionel.

'The sooner we go, the sooner we can come back,' said Saddam.

The four walked out of the café, up the stairs and got into their cars.

One of the inmates banged on the cell door. After a considerable delay, the wick opened. 'Yes, mate?' the custody sergeant asked, peering through.

'I'd like to have a piss, officer, and a cup of water,' the prisoner said, pointing at Bubba who was still asleep on the toilet bowl.

The wick slid shut. After a few minutes, the key turned in the lock and the cell door opened. The custody sergeant appeared with a cup of water in one hand and a clothes hanger with items of police uniform in the other. He stuck his hand into the cup, then violently flung water from his wet fingers into Bubba's face, making him flinch, stir and open his eyes.

'Sarge,' Bubba said blearily, recognizing the custody sergeant.

'Your team left this hanging in the utility room for you,' the custody sergeant said, throwing Bubba his uniform.

Bubba looked around the cell, surprised at the absence of his colleagues.

'Get your kit on and catch some thieves; the commissioner don't pay you to sit on the bog all day,' said the custody sergeant. He handed the inmate what remained of the cup of water and walked out, shutting the cell door behind him.

The prisoners sat bewildered as they watched a fellow cellmate transform himself into a uniformed officer of the law. Realizing his colleagues had forgotten to include his boots, Bubba put his white trainers back on and then gathered up his discarded garments. 'Got any water left? I'm fucking thirsty.' He looked at the inmate with the cup of water.

The inmate shook his head.

Bubba got up, walked across the cell and banged on the door.

About a minute later the cell door opened. 'Your missus phoned for you last night,' the custody sergeant informed Bubba. 'She wanted to know why you didn't come back home. The CAD room covered for you and told her you were dealing with a prisoner.'

'I couldn't fucking drink-drive, could I?' Bubba asked rhetorically. 'We decided to crash here because there was no point going home since we were on earlies.'

'Why you telling me? I'm not your fucking missus!'

exclaimed the custody sergeant with little interest. 'It's Saturday and the canteen doesn't open, get us a McDonald's, will you?'

'Yeah, sarge,' Bubba replied.

'And wash your face before you go out on to the street – you look as though you've been used as a sacrifice to the gods,' said the custody sergeant.

'Yeah, whatever,' said Bubba, too tired to argue.

'Wash your hands before you handle my food as well,' the sergeant shouted after Bubba as he sat back down again.

'See you in a minute, sarge,' said Bubba, opening the custody-suite door.

'One minute, Bubba,' the custody sergeant said, calling his attention. 'Change your footwear, will you. White trainers don't go with a black uniform.'

After the shift, they walked over to the Mason's Arms, the officers' local pub. They chatted in the beer garden for the greater part of three hours and, after the fifth pint, inebriation began to set in. Sponge sat astride a bench and rolled a joint while trying to use his back to shield his activities from the wind.

'I recognize that gear,' Speedy said. 'That's the skunk you took off those geezers last night duty. Do you have to smoke the shit you take off people in the street?'

'What do you want me to do, buy off a reputable dealer?' said Sponge. 'I'm a police officer, for fuck sake.'

'I think you've got an insect in your beer, boy.' Saddam pointed out a wasp wallowing in Sponge's pint.

Sponge leaned over and looked into his glass. He

extricated the insect with two fingers, then flicked it away. 'Go and buy your own,' he exclaimed jocularly to the wasp. 'It's your round,' he said to Speedy, realizing his drink was now somewhat depleted. 'Get the pints in, boy!'

'It's getting dark; we might as well go back in anyway,' said Speedy, picking up his half-full glass.

They stood up, followed Speedy in and selected a table at the rear of the pub but in front of the stage. The pub was busy; groups of men and women were squashed together at the tables and the staff worked frantically to serve the congested bar.

'Have you chaps ever thought what it would be like if we suddenly won the lottery?' asked Sponge as he seated himself.

'You've got to pay your contribution to the fucking syndicate first,' said Bubba. 'Besides, we've got a one-in-fourteen-million chance of winning, which is what's scientifically called an impossibility. Statistically speaking, we stand a fucking better chance of getting struck by lightning on a sunny day.'

'Well, if not the lottery, if you suddenly came across money, let's say,' Sponge theorized. 'Enough to pay off your mortgage and set you up in life, no matter what you wanted to do.'

'How much do you think would be enough to set you up outside the job?' Bubba questioned Sponge.

'Well over a hundred thousand pounds,' Sponge answered. 'How much would it cost to set you up outside the job?' he echoed, taking a drag from his joint.

'About a hundred and thirty grand. Buy myself a nice,

decent house and a restaurant somewhere in South Africa or Ireland,' Bubba replied.

'Why South Africa or Ireland?' Jazz asked.

'They're the countries I've got relatives in,' Bubba said. 'What would you do?' he asked Sponge.

'Open a whore house in the Philippines,' Sponge retorted jocularly. 'I don't know! Anything that wouldn't involve working shifts, I suppose, but meant shagging as many birds as possible.'

'Don't talk to me about shiftwork,' said Bubba, 'my marriage is on its last limb because of the shiftwork and the stress I get. If she leaves me, I'll never forgive the job.'

'What would you blokes do?' Sponge asked the others.

'I'd probably stay in the job,' said Jazz. 'Go for promotion.'

'I'd probably emigrate to Mexico and start up a business,' Saddam thought out loud.

'I'd go back to college and do a degree in Maritime Studies. I'm half Greek-Cypriot; shipping's in my blood,' said Lionel.

'What about you, Speedy?'

'I've put twenty-two years in, I've got my pension to think about. No matter how much money I came into, there's no way I'd leave all my fucking sweat and toil for someone else.'

'I don't believe you,' said Sponge. 'Stay in this job till you retire?'

'I don't know why you're always complaining. It gets on my fucking tits sometimes,' replied Speedy.

Having finished the round Speedy had bought, they

delegated the next one to Jazz, who duly rose to get the drinks in.

'Hey, Lionel! You like women with good legs, don't you? You'll like that bird behind you,' Sponge said, looking over at a girl who had stood up to go to the lavatory. She was one of a group of girls who were sitting on the other side of the pub.

'Why, how many legs has she got?' Lionel said, looking round.

'I'm going over to chat to them. I like the blonde one, she's the ugliest. The rest of you can scramble for what's left.'

'No thank you, mate! Wrong colour. You know I only go out with black birds,' said Lionel.

'Why do you always go for ugly birds?' Speedy asked Sponge.

'Why look at the mantelpiece when you only need to poke the fire?' said Sponge. He swaggered off in the girls' direction with a black left eye, a pint of lager in his right hand and a joint in his left. The others sat and watched, amused at his pot-valiance.

'There's no stopping him once he's had a few pints down his throat; he'd shag the crack of dawn if he knew where its legs were,' Joe shouted across to the officers as Sponge swanned across the room and sat himself in the seat the girl had just vacated for the lavatory.

The blonde sat bemused at his brazenness and looked at him enquiringly.

'Grab your coat, love, you've pulled!' he blurted out.

'Six months ago. Besides, you're pissed anyway,' she replied.

'If it weren't for alcohol, love, birds like you wouldn't get shagged,' Sponge retorted.

'I think you should stick to drinking on park benches; pubs are a bit too up-market for you,' said one of the other girls.

'Why don't you sit in the car and bark at strangers?' Sponge asked, half turning to dismiss her.

Sponge's original addressee looked up at her friend who had returned from the lavatory and seemed amused at seeing her seat occupied. 'Who is he?' she asked her friend as she sat down in a different chair.

'Just call me Sponge,' replied Sponge, introducing himself. 'Are you girls nurses?'

'Why, what do you do for a living?' she asked him.

'I'm an artist,' replied Sponge.

'Let me guess, a piss artist.'

'No. Painter and decorator, part-time musician, singer, songwriter and poet.'

'Really, what instruments do you play?' she enquired.

'The tambourine,' he replied. 'Anyway, enough of this smalltalk, which one of you girls fancies me?'

'None of us,' replied one of them. 'I'll tell you what, though, your friend looks quite nice,' she said, smiling over at Jazz. 'I wouldn't mind his boots under my bed.'

'Which one?' Sponge asked.

'The black guy; he looks quite familiar. I'm sure I've seen him somewhere before,' she said.

'What, down an alleyway trying to get your purse off you?' Sponge joked.

'I don't find that very funny,' she snapped.

'I'm only joking,' said Sponge.

'You've just punned a racist quip which I find offensive,' she said angrily.

'So you don't fancy a real man then,' sneered Sponge, ignoring her comment.

'I'm afraid you're not my type. I can see your ribs underneath your jumper; sleeping with you would be like shagging a bag of spanners,' she retorted.

'Listen, are you going to come over or shall I bring him over?' asked Sponge, getting up, his pride wounded. 'The band's going to start playing soon.'

CHAPTER 1

As was customary on Monday, the first day of a week of night duty, vehicles entered the yard quite early. The crew of the area car, Speedy and Sponge, came in at 9.30 p.m., an hour early, to cover the changeover.

When the others were fully assembled upstairs, Slippery, the team sergeant, took parade. 'Right, we've one van, one Irv, one Panda,' he said, assessing the situation. 'Speedy and Sponge are shown manning the area car. Grand recipe for disaster. Right,' he continued, 'Jazz, you take the Irv; Lionel, you're operator. Saddam, you take the Panda. Bubba, you can take the van . . . That's it,' he said, shutting the duties binder. 'Anything in the daily bulletin?'

Jazz leaned forward and opened the blue binder. 'No, only a few disqualified drivers and wanted persons.'

'Cup of tea time,' concluded Slippery. 'I'm custody officer tonight, which means no fucking prisoners unless you can help it. I need to catch up on my sleep.'

'Did you have a peaceful weekend off sick, then, skipper?' Saddam asked sarcastically as they rose from their chairs.

'I was visited by the duty officer at one in the afternoon on Wednesday. I got out of bed and answered the door in my underpants. I looked like shit because I only went to bed at seven that morning. Went to a 999 party and pulled some nurse,' said Slippery.

'Lucky he didn't come earlier,' said Saddam.

'If he had turned up at a few minutes before seven, he'd have seen me pulling up, music blaring out of the car, a bird on either arm, up to my eyeballs in whisky and coke, screaming at the neighbours,' joked Slippery.

The door opened and Musky, the team inspector, appeared.

A series of 'Hello, sir's' echoed through the room.

'Carry on,' Musky replied.

'We've just finished parade, sir,' Lionel said.

'Well, in that case, just a few things. Firstly, your team's been severely undermanned and I've been trying desperately to get more officers. The senior management have informed me you'll be getting two new officers off street duties tomorrow: a bloke and a plonk. I know you need more than that but they said that was the most they could give us at the moment – other divisions are just as desperate.'

'What's the plonk like, sir?' asked Lionel, with sudden interest.

'Ah, I knew you'd ask that. Apparently, she's a bit of all right.'

'Does she sit on our side of the church?' asked Lionel.

'According to her tutor at training school, she's already handled more cocks than Kentucky Fried Chicken since she arrived at Hendon.'

'Another station bicycle,' said Saddam.

'You know what the job's like: if a WPC goes out with a copper, she's branded a slapper and, if she doesn't, she's branded a lesbian,' replied the inspector. 'Another thing, the superintendent is off sick for the next week.'

'What with, sir?' asked Jazz.

'Something to do with his spine,' the inspector answered.

'He hasn't got one,' said Saddam cynically.

'Lastly, I'm sure you all know the canteen has been reopened.'

'Four weeks late,' said Saddam.

'Thank those bunch of cunts called senior officers. They find it so fucking hard to make a proper decision, they can't even fuck their own wives without calling a tasking meeting,' the inspector retorted.

With that, they resumed their ritual migration to the canteen. Bubba got there first, with a plastic bag full of various biscuits kept for those on night duty. He unlocked the tea cupboard and marked the cups with the names of his team members. The canteen had just been redecorated and still smelt of its bright blue paint.

'It looks like a fucking VD clinic,' said Saddam, placing his equipment on the nearest seat. 'Where are the biscuits?' he asked Bubba, searching for them.

'What do you mean, the biscuits?' replied Bubba. 'None of you fucking pay up when I ask you for the money.'

Saddam spotted the bag, went over to it and, wrenching it open, fastidiously selected a chocolate-coated digestive. The others pounced on the remainder of the biscuits, which he'd strewn across the table.

'When are we going to get Penguins?' Lionel asked with his mouth full.

'When you start paying what you owe to the tea club,' Bubba retorted.

Speedy hurtled into the yard in the area car and screeched

to a halt. Both he and Sponge jumped out of the vehicle and charged into the canteen. They stopped in their tracks when they saw their quarry – the biscuit-bag.

They were too late!

'This isn't fucking fair!' protested Speedy. 'We always miss out on the biscuits when we're on the area car.'

A call came over the radio. *'Any unit to deal, please, with a drunk causing a disturbance in the Broadway.'*

After a long pause, Lionel took the call.

'We'll go once we've finished our coffees,' Jazz said to Lionel, putting the car keys on the long wooden canteen table. He put his feet up and began to watch the television.

Bubba emerged from the utility room, sat down, folded his arms and then unexpectedly broke wind. 'Oops!' he exclaimed.

'You're not going to start this all night again, are you?' asked Saddam, moving his chair away.

'I'm sorry! I've got an emotionally temperamental arsehole tonight,' replied Bubba, letting out another stream of wind.

'And I thought "talking through your arse" was a figure of speech,' said Speedy.

Suddenly the radios crackled again. *'All units! All units! A theft from a motor vehicle! Two suspects seen to break into a red motor vehicle and now walking along Market Road.'*

Before the message was complete, all six of them were running through the canteen doors towards their vehicles. The yard was filled with the sound of rapidly reversing and accelerating cars as they attempted to make a precipitous exit. As they made towards the exit arch, the yard was turned into a dazzling brilliance of blue and white by the flashing blue lights.

'How far up is Market Road?' Jazz asked Lionel as he peered over the wheel of the Irv.

'It's the second turning on the left before Kent Lane, about three hundred yards up,' Lionel replied.

As they came within two hundred yards of the turning, Jazz switched off the sirens and, in another hundred yards, he switched off the blue lights and slowly decelerated. By the time they were within a few yards of Market Road, the vehicle was going at a slow crawl.

Bubba swung the van into another side road, in order to enter Market Road from its opposite end. The area car went down the side road before the Market Road turning.

Jazz slowly turned the Irv into Market Road. Both he and Lionel strained to see into the road, looking on both sides for signs of people concealing themselves. As they drove down Market Road, Lionel called up the control room on his radio. *'November 21 on scene, where's the informant?'* He hesitated as he saw two young boys walk up his side of the pavement. Tapping Jazz on the shoulder, he pointed towards them. *'Stand by, we've got two here. Can someone get hold of the informant while we deal with these two?'*

Jazz stopped the car and Lionel jumped out of the passenger's seat. Both boys saw Lionel, turned round and started to walk up the road in the direction from which they'd come. 'Oi! You two! Come here!' Lionel shouted after them.

They ignored him and continued to walk briskly. They passed the Market Road junction with College Lane and walked on. Suddenly, the area car appeared from the College Lane side road and skidded to a halt beside the two youths. Surprised by this, the youths stopped and watched as Sponge and Speedy jumped out of the car. All four officers surrounded the youths.

'Where the fuck did you two think you were going? Didn't you hear me shouting?' asked Lionel in an aggressive tone.

'Yeah, well we've got nothing to say to you,' said the elder and taller of the two.

'Who the fuck are you talking to like that? You gobby shit!' asked Speedy.

'Well, like we said, we've got nothing to say to you,' the elder one repeated.

'You shut the fuck up before you get slapped the fuck up!' said Sponge.

The younger of the two boys had a hooded top partly covering his face and had turned away from the officers. Jazz moved round to face him. 'What's your name?' he asked.

'We aren't answering any of your questions,' said the elder boy, answering for his confederate.

'Are you some sort of fucking ventriloquist?' Speedy asked him.

The boy ignored Speedy.

Bubba came over the radio. *'Lionel, free to speak, over?'*

The other officers clipped their radio mouthpieces so that

no transmissions could come through, as Lionel moved out of earshot. *'Yeah, I am now. Go ahead, Bubba.'*

'A car's been broken into and a radio's missing. It's got wires hanging out of the radio compartment. The informant says she just heard the sound of showering glass and saw two suspects moving off up Market Road towards the High Road, over.'

'How long ago, over?' Lionel asked.

After a silence, Bubba came over the radio. *'About eleven, over. My guess is that the two oiks you've stopped did it.'*

'Yes, received. We've got the Evett brothers here, who have obviously been at it. They don't look as though they've got anything as bulky as that on them, they'd have ditched it ages ago,' Lionel transmitted back.

'Well, someone's as good as seen them,' replied Bubba.

'They've both failed the attitude test. They know we know it's them, all right. They know the score,' replied Lionel. *'We'll take care of business from this angle.'* He moved back towards the group. 'Right!' he began in a loud voice. 'A car's been done and you two slags know about it. Which one of you is going to put his hands up to it?'

'You've got jack shit and know jack shit,' replied the youngest, with an air of arrogance.

'Right, empty your fucking pockets,' Jazz ordered.

They searched them and found nothing but a packet of Rizla papers, so decided to comb the surrounding shrubbery for evidence. Saddam arrived in the Panda and assisted in the hunt. Unable to find anything, Lionel returned to them. 'Right, lads. Are you going to tell us where you hid the radio?' he asked.

'We ain't telling you shit! We don't know what you're fucking talking about,' said the younger one.

'In that case,' said Speedy, 'I know it's not yet Christmas, but uncle has got some pressies for you boys. I'll just get our box of treats,' he said to the others. Walking to the rear of the area car, he opened the boot and returned with a small thick polythene bag. 'Right, boys, which one of these do you want?' He emptied out the contents of the bag on the pavement and picked up a screwdriver. 'We have the Fred West "where's my rent" floorboard and bathroom tile classic screwdriver.' He picked up a small six-inch bladed knife. 'We have here the Reggie Kray "who's the fucking grass" six-inch knife.' He then picked up a small carpenter's hammer. 'This is the Peter Sutcliffe "I fancy going clubbing tonight" hammer. Last but not least, the O.J. Simpson glove. I've only got one; one of my mates in the LAPD borrowed the other one.'

'By the way, you're both nicked for theft from a motor vehicle and for going equipped to steal,' said Sponge sarcastically.

'You're taking the piss,' the elder youth exclaimed.

'Have you got a specimen bottle on you?' Lionel asked him.

'No,' he replied.

'I haven't either. If I wanted to take the piss, I'd be carrying one about,' said Lionel.

'Look, mate, the radio's under the car you're standing behind,' said the elder youth.

'Good man,' lauded Speedy, 'I'm still going to throw in the screwdriver as a measure of goodwill.'

Jazz reached under the saloon car behind them and pulled out the car stereo.

Lionel spoke through his radio.

Speedy looked at the boys. 'Right, lads, let's go back to the factory.' Turning to Lionel, he said, 'We won't bother with the van; we might as well transport these vermin back ourselves. You take the gobshite and we'll take the other one.'

Sponge called up Bubba. *'289 receiving 308.'*

'Go ahead.'

'289, since you've got the zoo-wagon and you're with the witness, we might as well take them back and you can take statements.'

'Yes, received,' Bubba replied.

Sponge winked at the others. 'Something's up. Bubba wouldn't take a statement unless that witness was crumpet and he thought he was in with half a chance.'

Bubba was with the witness: a young woman clad modestly in a dressing gown. She stood next to her flatmate, still bleary-eyed and somewhat bemused by the turn of events.

Sponge had just instructed Bubba to take statements, which, by his calculations, would land him in the kitchen with a cup of tea and at least an hour or two to see whether or not he stood a chance. He gently slipped off his wedding ring, put it into his jacket and turned to the woman. 'Can I get a statement from you just detailing what you saw?' he asked.

'It's not going to take long, is it?' she asked.

'Only about ten to fifteen minutes,' he lied, fearful that if he told the truth she would ask him to come back another time. He knew it would be more than likely that a CID officer would take over the inquiry.

'Well, OK,' she replied.

Just as she finished speaking, Bubba's radio came to life again. Both she and her flatmate stopped to listen to the transmission. '*289 receiving 308.*'

'*Go ahead, Sponge,*' Bubba replied.

'*Can you do a car check on the car and take a statement from the owner as well?*' asked Sponge.

'It's my car,' said the woman.

Bubba nodded in comprehension. '*It belongs to the witness, over,*' he transmitted back.

'*Obviously a tasty piece of arse you think you can lay cable up.*'

'*I'm not free to speak! She can hear you!*' Bubba replied in embarrassment.

'*I know.*'

Bubba pulled the battery out of his radio to make sure nobody else could transmit any other comments, turned to the women and ushered them into their flat. He followed them into the kitchen and seated himself. He gratefully accepted a cup of coffee. Then he began. 'Right, before I begin taking a statement, I'm going to need some of your personal details.'

'Fine,' the witness replied, seating herself at the kitchen table.

'Firstly, your full name?' asked Bubba, unable to take his eyes away from her breasts, modestly concealed by her dressing gown.

'Terry Neal.'

'Date of birth?' he asked, trying to look casual.

'1 June 1974,' she replied, irritated by his ogling. 'Do you want your eyes back?'

'What?' asked Bubba, abashed.

'Look, officer, are you going to look at my tits all night or are you going to take this statement?' she snapped.

'Look at your tits all night,' Bubba replied jocularly.

'*What?*' she said.

'Only for thirty minutes,' said Bubba. 'I'm only joking!'

'If you worked as hard as your eyes do, I don't think my car would have been broken into in the first place. I think we'd better get on with the statement,' she said.

When Bubba entered the canteen, they were already seated and had almost finished writing up their notes. 'Sponge, you are as subtle as a mad cow with a bell around its neck!' he said.

'Did you get your leg over, then? Was she crumpet?' Sponge asked in reply.

'She was gorgeous and turned out to be a good laugh, actually. You should have seen her tits! They were fucking huge! And she only had a low-cut nightie on.' Bubba gestured as he spoke. 'When she laughed, they bounced about on her chest like two ferrets trapped in a sack.'

'No one would have thought you were married,' said Jazz.

'Hey, I love my wife, all right,' replied Bubba defensively. 'Big lions might kill people but a little pussy has never done anyone any harm.'

'We've just finished our notes; what was the witness statement like, then?' asked Lionel, changing the subject.

'It's not bad, actually,' replied Bubba. 'She heard them put the window in, saw the taller one reach into the car, take something out and walk off, towards the direction you stopped them.'

'We couldn't find the radio on them so we used the ways and means method,' said Sponge.

'They've been at it for fucking ages and had it coming for ages. I've given them the screwdriver,' said Speedy.

'Those two are thieving sacks of shit,' said Jazz. 'They'd steal anything that wasn't cemented or nailed to the ground.'

'Who's doing the case papers, then?' asked Bubba.

'Lionel will,' nominated Speedy.

'There you are then,' said Bubba, handing Lionel the witness statement. 'It's got her dates to avoid court on it.'

Lionel took it from him without complaint and stood up. 'Right, I'm going to time-stamp your notes.' He turned to Jazz. 'We've still got to deal with that drunk, you know. I'll meet you in the yard after I've done this.'

Lionel and Jazz drove out of the yard and set off for the Broadway on the border of their patch. One half of the Broadway, the southbound lane, belonged to Newpark Division; the other side, the northbound lane, belonged to Northwick Division. They pulled up by a phone booth and looked around without bothering to get out of the car.

They found the man lying on the pavement not far from the Parrot on the Moon pub, his head resting on a bread basket as he sang a slurred and drunken melody. Leaving the car, they walked slowly up to him. Lionel kicked him on the soles of his feet to get his attention. 'Hello, mate, had a drink, have we? Now, why can't we go home, eh?' he asked.

''Cos I'm pissed!' replied the man.

'What's your name?' asked Jazz.

'Douglas Bader, the legless ace!'

'It's Martin Summers,' said Jazz, recognizing him. 'You're becoming a bit of a regular, Martin, aren't you?'

'Will you do me a favour and hand me my booze?' the man asked Lionel.

'Why do you drink this shit? It's no good for you, you know,' Lionel advised him. 'You shouldn't do it.'

'I have to, I'm an alcoholic,' he replied.

Completely losing patience, they hoisted the man up and dragged him across the road on to Newpark Division's territory. 'He's not our problem any more,' said Lionel as they walked back across the road.

Jazz went over to the phone booth and dialled the Newpark Division control room to make an anonymous phone call. After a slight delay, he spoke to the controller. 'Hello, I was just walking home when I noticed this drunken man causing a disturbance on the Newpark side of the Broadway. Can you send some officers down to deal with him, please?'

The controller took details and promised to send someone there. Jazz thanked him and put his thumb up to Lionel.

Lionel spoke on the radio. *'No trace of the drunk on the Broadway. Area searched, no trace, over.'*

'Yes, received, I shall mark it up accordingly,' replied the controller.

They got into the vehicle and drove back to the station. No sooner had they arrived than the radio came to life again. *'November 21, your drunk seems to have returned and is causing a disturbance. Can you go back again, please?'*

'Yes, received,' replied Jazz.

'You'll have to bring him in if need be, over,' said the controller.

'Yes, received,' Lionel replied. He turned to Jazz. 'Those bastards on Newpark Division must have thrown him back on to our side of the road again. I've had enough for one night, I'm not nicking anyone else,' he said defiantly.

They drove back to the Broadway and found the man propped up by the phone box, singing away heartily in singular drunken revelry.

'I thought I told you to get lost!' exclaimed Jazz.

'Some coppers brought me here from across the road,' the man said in a paced slur.

'Well, you're not going to stay here, that's for sure,' said Lionel.

'I've got nowhere to go. My wife has kicked me out because she says I drink too much. So I decided to go out and get plastered. That can't be against the fucking law.'

'Well, next time marry a fucking alcoholic,' said Lionel and called up for the van.

After ten minutes, Bubba arrived. 'What's up?' he enquired.

'We just want to get this drunk off our patch and as far away as possible,' Lionel replied.

'I'm not fucking drunk,' the man replied truculently.

'You're making it all up. Just like the Birmingham Six and the Renault Five, I'm fucking innocent!'

'Shut up, you slag,' said Bubba.

They put him in the back of the van and both vehicles drove around the outskirts of their division for the greater part of fifteen minutes looking for somewhere to dump him. Eventually they decided to stop a lorry. They put on the blue lights and flashed the vehicle to a standstill just at the entrance to the motorway. The driver got out of the truck and joined them on the verge, bewildered and unsure of what he had done wrong.

'Do you speak English?' Lionel asked him.

'Not too well. I am Fraunch,' replied the man in a strong French accent.

'What have you got in the back?' Jazz asked.

'Nothing,' he replied.

'We'll just have a look anyway,' said Lionel.

'Sure,' said the man indifferently.

He lowered the doors of the vehicle. Lionel peered into the back while Jazz called the driver towards the front. With the driver out of the way, Lionel and Bubba took the drunk out of the van, tossed him into the rear of the lorry and closed the doors before the driver returned to secure them.

'Right, have a nice day,' Lionel said.

They sat in their vehicles and watched the driver get back into his truck and drive off. 'Where is he going?' Lionel asked Jazz.

'Home to France,' said Jazz.

'Fucking hell!' exclaimed Lionel.

'Well, it's too late now; the deed is done. He'll wake up

before they get to Dover anyway. Let's go back for a cup of tea.'

Just then Bubba spoke over the radio. '*Area searched, no trace of this drunk, over.*'

'*Yes, received,*' the controller concluded.

CHAPTER 2

Bubba

On Tuesday afternoon Bubba woke up at 2 p.m., an hour earlier than he normally did when he was on nights. His wife had taken the day off and he could hear her rummaging in the kitchen. Feeling hungry, he put on his dressing gown and went downstairs.

Bubba was thirty-one years old, with thirteen years' service and seven years of marriage. He was one of two on the team with children; two sons, three and five. He was experiencing problems in his marriage, torn between the demands of police work and the responsibilities of home life. He was a placid man who loved to cook and eat; he was unfit and obese, though this was extenuated to some extent by his height of six feet three inches.

'What's for breakfast?' he asked his wife, scratching his head and backside simultaneously.

'Good morning to you too,' she replied, without looking at him.

'Oh, don't start,' he said, sitting down at the table.

'What do you mean, don't start?' she said. 'You act as though you're not a part of this family. When was the last time we did anything together? We were supposed to see my mother over the weekend, and you spent the whole day with Sponge and the rest of those blokes in the pub. Some nights you don't even come home.'

'You don't understand, Maryann,' said Bubba timidly.

'I don't understand? When you always come home from the pub on your days off pissed!'

'I've got to have some reason to come home to you,' he replied, irritated by her nagging.

'Father Magnus phoned,' she said in a more sober tone, changing the topic.

'Yeah?' replied Bubba, uninterested.

'He said he hasn't seen you in church lately.'

'Tell him I haven't seen much of him in the pub lately,' replied Bubba.

'You see, there you go again. Father Magnus said –'

'There you go again, speaking to someone else about our marriage,' Bubba said, cutting her short.

'I need to speak to somebody about our problems.'

'We haven't got problems,' Bubba said, deliberately slowly.

'You see, you just don't care. This marriage is falling apart and you just don't care.'

'Well, what do you want me to do? I get enough grief at work without coming home for more.'

'You can leave that job of yours for a start! The shiftwork's most of the problem. If it weren't for that, at least we'd be able to plan our lives better.'

Bubba hesitated then spoke quietly. 'We've been down that road before,' he said. 'We can't afford the drop in pay. I'm not qualified to do anything else.'

'You do still love me?' she asked, looking for reassurance.

'Of course I do. I'm still fucking here, aren't I?' Bubba replied. Then, changing the subject, he said, 'I suppose I should pick the boys up from school. I promised them I would.'

'Remember we also promised to go and see my mum this weekend.'

Bubba didn't answer.

Jazz

Samuel Morrison was still asleep when his mother burst into his room. 'Samuel,' she shouted, 'why didn't you wash your plates?'

'Mum, I'm still asleep. I'm working nights.'

'I don't care, I'm fed up of tidying up after you and your father, I'm not a slave. You come in, use the plates, then leave them in the sink for your maid to wash up.'

'Mum, if you're not going to respect my privacy, I'm going to lock this door. I could have been naked.'

His mother turned round and stormed off.

He lay there, the intrusion leaving him unable to go back to sleep again.

He was Afro-Caribbean, of Jamaican extract, five feet ten with a stocky build. He had prominent winged eyebrows, chiselled facial features, full red lips and looked as though he had a permanent frown. Like Lionel, he had five years' service. At twenty-seven, he was still single and lived at home with his parents.

'I'm sick of this shit! I get no fucking respect in this house. In a few months' time, I'm moving out,' he muttered to himself as he walked downstairs to the kitchen.

He had lived at home all his life and had a love-hate

relationship with his mother. Born and bred in Burnt Oak, he had left school after his O levels and worked part time as a pizza delivery boy. He then worked in a local supermarket for three years before joining the Metropolitan Police at twenty-two. He was a reserved person who enjoyed his job. He had no real friends outside work and more or less socialized with his team members.

To stop his mother from nagging, he began to wash the plate he had left in the sink the night before. Satisfied he had done the chore, he went into the living room.

His father sat there with the television on reading a newspaper. 'Is your mother nagging again?' he asked without looking up.

'Yeah, I don't know how you could have survived being married to her so long,' said Jazz.

'I just try not to think about it,' his father replied.

'And they say married men are supposed to live longer.'

'It just seems longer, that's all.'

His mother burst into the room. 'Samuel, you came into the kitchen, just washed your plate and left all the others in the sink. You're a really selfish child, you know,' she shouted. 'I don't know what woman could put up with you. The sooner you meet a good woman, instead of all those nasty girls you meet in nightclubs, the better for your father and me. Mrs Patterson has a beautiful daughter, you know –'

'Leave the boy alone!' Jazz's father interjected.

'It's you who keeps encouraging him,' she began. 'I've told you not to do it but, like a typical man, it goes in through one ear and comes out the other.'

'And, like a typical woman, I tell you something, it goes

in through one ear and comes out your mouth when you're with Mrs Patterson.'

'Mum, I'm not interested in Mrs Patterson's daughter. I've told you before I can find my own women. I don't need you to match-make for me,' Jazz said.

'It's those police boys you go out with that are a bad influence on you. Taking you out to meet those horrible loose girls. Find yourself a nice black woman and settle down.'

'I'm going to the betting shop,' said Jazz's father, getting up.

'I've got to wash my shirts for work,' said Jazz, leaving the room too.

Sponge

Graham Sutton lived on his own in a one-bedroom basement flat. Never able to sleep off nights because he found it hard to adjust his physiological clock, he woke up at 2 p.m. He still wore the clothes he had come back from work in. He had slept in them, having drifted to sleep on the sofa after four cans of extra-strength lager.

Sponge was the shortest of the team, five feet eight inches tall, with short, mousy-coloured hair. He was slim in build, with protruding ears, no facial hair and boyish looks. He was a compulsive raconteur, friendly and jovial but with an element of recklessness to his nature. He drank frequently, his character seeming to alter with the intake of alcohol: the more he drank, the more brazen and aggressive he became. He was twenty-seven with seven years' service. He had originally joined the Metropolitan Police from Wales, where he had been born and bred.

Feeling hungry, he got up, went into the kitchen and opened the fridge. It was empty but for several cans of lager. He reached for one, opened it, took a gulp, then went back into the living room.

Sponge was an affable person with a tendency to get over-excited about things. He possessed an acerbic wit which, tempered with the alcohol, became excessive and cruel. He had no real ambitions and his tastes far outweighed his pocket.

He phoned for a pizza, then called his closest friend, Saddam.

Saddam

Simon Brookes was asleep when the telephone rang.

He was about five feet eleven inches tall, swarthy in complexion with dark, slightly greying hair. He had sagging cheeks, brown eyes and a rich, thick moustache, the reason why he had been nicknamed Saddam. He was thirty-seven years old, had sixteen years' service and had been married for fourteen years to a Mexican woman. He was Sponge's bosom friend and often influenced by his recklessness.

He leant across the bed and picked up the receiver. It was Sponge.

'What's the matter, mate?' Saddam asked in a sleepy voice.

'You coming round for a few bevvies? I'm bored.'

'You've just bloody woken me up,' said Saddam irritably.

'I've got that porno video, the one we found in the house where we dealt with that sudden death last week, and I've just ordered a pizza,' replied Sponge.

'Why didn't you bloody say so before?' said Saddam. 'I'll be round about five.'

Lionel

Matthew Flett woke up at 3 p.m. and, without wasting time, picked up his portable stereo, changed into his gym attire and walked through the section house to the gym.

He had gelled and heavily sculptured jet-black hair, a dark Mediterranean complexion and classic bushy eyebrows. Brawny and six feet one inch tall, he worked out regularly and prided himself on his physique. Lionel was a nickname he had acquired at training school as a result of his Cockney accent and his Friday-night-on-the-town wideboy looks. He was quick-witted and smooth, and loved women almost as much as he loved himself. He was twenty-six years old, had five years' service and, unsurprisingly, was single. Like Speedy, he lived in a section house, accommodation provided by the Metropolitan Police for some of its single officers.

After a forty-minute work-out, he had a shower, got dressed and drove to his favourite restaurant to eat. He loved Italian food and, when off night duty, preferred to treat himself to a lavish feast rather than the modest portion of a section-house meal.

He sat at a table behind two Greek-Cypriot men, who suddenly broke off their conversation but promptly resumed it after he gave his order. It was obvious they did not want him to hear what they were discussing, but Lionel's pronounced London accent seemed to relax them. As they lapsed into their own language again, Lionel strained to listen.

Three hours later, he was back at the section house knocking at Speedy's door.

Speedy

Hugh Donnolly was the oldest in service on the team and the most senior of the six officers.

At forty-three, he had twenty-two years' service behind him, having done the last eight on Northwick Division. Despite his age, he had an imposing and athletic stature: broad-shouldered, erect and tall. He spoke in a deep husky voice and a broad Scottish accent. He bore the sentiments and afflictions of an old sweat: bitter and twisted, racist, sexist, homophobic and divorced. His marriage had lasted fifteen years but crumbled five years ago as a result of the demands of police work, leaving him living in the section house.

'What the fuck do you want?' Speedy asked sleepily.

'You're not going to believe this,' said Lionel excitedly. He repeated what he had overheard in the restaurant.

Speedy took little convincing, and forty minutes later he and Lionel were discussing the finer details of a cunning and intricate ruse.

When Sponge came into work an hour early that night,

there was an unfamiliar uniformed officer with polished boots changing in the locker room.

'All right, mate?' Sponge said. 'You one of our new probationers?'

'Yes, I am,' the newcomer replied. He was about five feet eleven inches tall, with short black hair, an angular nose and a slightly protruding jaw. He was slender in build, twenty-three years of age and spoke with a Northern accent.

'What's your name, then?' asked Sponge.

'Richard Gail,' the probationer said, extending his hand to offer a handshake.

'I'm just called Sponge,' Sponge replied, ignoring the probationer's gesture and stooping to tie the laces of his shoes. 'How many of you are there?'

'Two. Me and a WPC,' replied the probationer, retracting his hand.

'Not bad. We've been desperately short over the last twelve months. With a bloke and a plonk, at least we can get some annual leave when we want time off instead of having to go sick,' said Sponge.

'Is it that bad?' the probationer asked.

'Don't look so surprised!' There's a lot you're going to learn about the way this job is run by that pile of shite we call senior management. They couldn't run a fucking bath.'

The probationer tried to secure his locker, twisting the key spasmodically. 'There's something wrong with my lock,' he said to Sponge, giving up.

'It's fucked,' Sponge said, 'just like everything else in this job.'

*

They congregated in the team office, with the two new probationers. The area car crew, Sponge and Speedy, had been called in to take part in parade.

Eventually Slippery assigned them to the various vehicles, pointedly not addressing the probationers directly. 'Speedy will take this bloke that looks like Rigsby from *Rising Damp*,' he said, nodding at Richard Gail without bothering to ask him his name. 'Speedy will be wiping his arse for the next couple of weeks.' He pointed at the female officer. 'You take her in the van,' he instructed Bubba. 'You and Jazz will chaperone her for the next couple of months as well. Lionel and Saddam in the Irv. I'm shown here as custody officer. Right, gents, parade's over.'

As the probationers followed the rest of the team out, Slippery called them aside. 'Before you go, I'd like to have a few words with you lot,' he said, 'what I say to any probationer that joins this team. There are two important things you need to know to survive your probation. The first is that I take three sugars in my tea. The second is that you should always remember the four Ps: prisoners, property, prostitutes and plonks. They'll get you out of the job faster than you can flick a switch.'

'Thanks for making us feel so welcome, sarge,' replied the male probationer.

'Welcome to the Met, the arsehole of the civil service,' Sponge said, patting him on the back.

Five minutes later, the team had reconvened in the canteen.

'Have any of you just received the new operational order

over the MSS this morning?' asked Slippery, picking up his cup of coffee.

'No, why?' Speedy answered.

'Apparently, we're doing AID downtown. You're policing the Gay and Lesbian Pride March in a couple of weeks on Saturday,' he informed them.

'I hate this job, I had something fucking planned that weekend. They don't seem to take the fact that we have families into consideration,' bemoaned Sponge. 'It does my fucking box in.'

'Does it fuck!' Speedy said. 'You don't have a fucking family.'

'Have you all had your fucking whinges?' Slippery asked. 'You're parading at 9.30 a.m., and Team Two are short of a skipper, so you'll be having another skipper on your serial.'

'Who?' asked Speedy.

'WPS Bell,' answered Bubba.

'Who? That plonk? She's a dike, isn't she?' exclaimed Speedy.

'What's wrong with that?' Jazz asked.

'Sometimes I worry about you and wonder which row of the choir you sing in,' retorted Speedy.

'Just because I don't mind working with a dike doesn't make me queer,' Jazz remonstrated.

'I fucking hate this job,' repeated Sponge.

'If you hate it so much, why don't you leave?' Speedy asked. 'All you do is fucking whine! You sound fucking worse than a vibrator on a low battery.'

'For the same reason you haven't,' said Sponge.

'Well, I don't whinge about it. Why don't you do something about it?' argued Speedy.

'Like I always say, one of these days something will come up and I will,' Sponge replied dreamily.

Speedy, Sponge and Rigsby got into the area car. 'Before we go out, first things first,' said Speedy. 'I've been asked to take you out,' he said to Rigsby, 'which means I've the task of breaking you in, so listen to everything I tell you. First lesson. What's my shoulder number?' Speedy asked, tilting his shoulder.

'204 TD,' replied Rigsby, reading the alphanumerics.

'Wrong,' said Speedy. He shifted round and showed Rigsby his right shoulder. 'What's my real shoulder number?'

'110 NX,' said Rigsby, confused.

'The left shoulder is what is called the complaint or oops shoulder. When you dip your hands into a black high court judge's pockets and try to stitch him up because he wouldn't tell you his name and then he does – that's when the left-shoulder number comes into play. You show him your left-shoulder number, let him write it down, get into the car and fuck off. That way, when things get a bit fucking moody when he comes in to complain, you can't be traced. They either think he's fucking making it up or doesn't know what he's fucking talking about.'

'Why not just change both shoulder numbers?' Rigsby asked.

'Intelligent question,' replied Speedy. 'Well, when someone wants to write a thank-you letter, you show your right shoulder. Besides, it's only on your outer garment; keep the correct shoulder numbers on other items of uniform. Now it's summer, your jumper should be your outer garment; when it's winter, it'll be your jacket. Just remember, before you do anything moody, put on your outer garment.' He left Rigsby to ruminate while he started up the engine and lit a cigarette. 'You've got a degree in wood-carving or something like that, haven't you?' Speedy asked, drawing languidly on his cigarette and looking at Rigsby through the rear-view mirror.

'It's in politics, philosophy and economics,' replied Rigsby.

'Fat lot of fucking use that's going to be when we're in the middle of a punch-up on a Friday night,' said Speedy.

They drove out of the yard, Rigsby in the back, barely able to contain his excitement at being part of the crew and on the streets for the first time. 'What's it like being in the police, then?' he asked curiously as they drove along the High Road.

'That's a fucking boring question,' replied Sponge.

'Like absolute shit!' replied Speedy. 'We'll go once round the block, then go in for din-dins.'

'We've only just come out. You must be one of those officers they call a canteen cowboy,' Rigsby joked.

'I tell the fucking jokes in this car. You don't fucking speak to me until I fucking speak to you,' rebuked Speedy. 'You get that?'

'Yes,' Rigsby replied, taken aback.

'Good. From now on, remember the only crack you're allowed to have in this car is the crack between your arse.'

They drove round three-quarters of the block in silence until Speedy finally spoke. 'What street are we in now?' he asked out loud.

Not sure whether the question was addressed to him, Rigsby ignored him.

'I asked you a question,' Speedy said louder.

'Sorry?' replied Rigsby.

'I said, which street are we in?'

'I don't know,' replied Rigsby candidly.

'So what would happen if something happened now and the control room were calling you up to find out where you were?'

'I don't know,' replied Rigsby.

'Exactly. Learn to fucking switch on. Having a university degree isn't going to be much fucking use to you on the streets,' said Speedy bitterly. 'I'll ask you again, so stay alert.'

Speedy parked the area car by the kerb so that they could observe their surroundings. A young black man walked down Northwick Road towards the tube station.

'Right, Cinderella! Get out and turn him over,' commanded Speedy.

'What for?' said Rigsby.

'What the fuck did you do for your eight weeks of street duties, scratch your arse and rub your balls?' said Speedy. 'This is the real fucking world, Jackie!'

'You'd better snap out of your fucking trance. Forget that shite you were taught at training school; it'll cost you the valuable seconds you need to save your life,' said Sponge.

'Watch how it's done and don't tell me you can't do it again,' said Speedy.

A blue Ford Fiesta XR2 pulled up at the 7-Eleven and two young black men got out. One headed for the Lloyds Bank cashpoint dispenser; the other walked into the 7-Eleven next door.

'Right, two IC3s in a flash motor. What do you think they do for a living?' asked Speedy.

'I don't know,' replied Rigsby.

'Aren't you fucking curious to know?' Speedy asked.

'I suppose so,' replied Rigsby, trying to give the right answer.

'Right then. Let's give them a tug,' said Speedy, releasing his seatbelt.

'I can't see our grounds for suspicion,' protested Rigsby.

'Are you normally this fucking stupid or is tonight a special occasion?' Speedy retorted. 'How many steps are there in your house?'

'I don't know.'

'Precisely! That's what you've got to fucking learn: not to fucking see, but observe. If you're going to work the streets successfully, then you've got to change wavelength. Now get out, we're going to have a chinwag,' instructed Speedy.

They got out of the car.

'Fetch the other bloke when he comes out of the 7-Eleven,' Speedy said to Rigsby. 'In the meantime, just watch me.'

Sponge and Speedy walked over to accost the man at the cashpoint. 'Excuse me, mate! Have a word?' Speedy said.

'Why? What have I done?' the man asked apprehensively.

'I'll explain in a minute,' Speedy answered, and waited for Rigsby and the other man to join them.

The young man was muttering to himself, annoyed at being stopped. 'What's going on?' he asked when he reached his friend standing by Sponge and Speedy.

'We want to know what you're up to and what you're doing here,' explained Speedy.

The man laughed nervously. 'So we're not allowed to come around this area? Have we done anything wrong?' he asked. 'I thought this was a free country.'

'It is a free country! Which means people are free to steal and commit crimes,' replied Sponge.

'So the car's stolen, is it? Or are you really stopping us because we're black?' said one of the youths.

'How did I know you were going to say that?' said Sponge. 'Even O.J. Simpson said that!'

'What do you do for a living?' asked Speedy.

'Student,' he replied.

'And I bet you strive to be really good. You work to get the best results you can, don't you?' asked Speedy.

'Yes,' he answered.

'Well, that's what I do. I'm a policeman and I try to the best of my ability to get the best results,' said Speedy.

'So why have you stopped us?' asked the driver.

Speedy looked at him as though he had asked a ridiculous question. 'Two guys get out of the car and walk in different directions. You, the driver, don't lock the door. I don't see you with any keys so it could have been hot-wired; the car's an XR2, which are frequently nicked.'

'Well, it's my car,' replied the driver.

'You might think I'm a lot of things, but one thing I'm not is psychic,' Speedy said. 'Have you got any documents to prove it?'

'No, not on me,' said the driver.

'We'll have a look in the car to see if there are any. Can you tell me what's in the boot?'

'Just a spare tyre.'

'Right, let's have a look.'

They searched the car for the benefit of instruction rather than genuine suspicion and found only the burnt ends of Rizla papers. Speedy turned his attention back to the men. 'Which of you smokes with the Rizlas, then?' he asked.

They both looked aloofly at him.

'I could search you, but I won't. A word of advice: I wouldn't skin up in the car. It just gives coppers like us a reason to search you.' With that, Speedy sent them on their way.

'How can you justify searching the car without reasonable grounds if we went to court?, asked Rigsby. 'We didn't have the power to search.'

'You can always work your way around that, by just asking them about things in the car and checking to see if they are there,' Speedy explained. He waited until they got into the car before continuing. 'Things are different when you work the streets. If half the fucking public and half the fucking blacks in this country knew their rights, we'd never be able to do our job. The job would be fucked.'

'And that means the whole fucking country would be fucked,' added Sponge.

'They say knowledge is power. That isn't fucking true.

What is true is that ignorance gives empowerment. Think about it. If you knew what I knew, no matter our level of knowledge, I haven't got the fucking superiority to commandeer a situation. What would give me superiority would be your ignorance,' Speedy said. 'Now, I know you've fucking learnt how to do things by the book at training school, but if you want to survive on the streets and on this team you'd better forget that stuff and watch and learn how it's really done, understand?'

'So what is the point of going to training school?' asked Rigsby.

'Well, a fucking cynical old hat like me would say that in order to bend the rules you've got to master them first.'

Rigsby nodded ruefully.

'I know you're keen,' Sponge said, detecting Rigsby's reservations. 'When I came out, I was so keen I'd have arrested my mother for arson for burning the Sunday roast. Give you eighteen months before you end up like everybody else.'

'I don't think I will,' retorted Rigsby with suppressed hostility.

Speedy spun round. 'Listen, sunshine! I've been policing these streets before you were a horny twinkle of mischief in your father's eye. I won't have gobshites like you just out of training school telling me what's what.'

They drove on without speaking for a few minutes.

'What's the divisional policy on parking offences?' asked Rigsby, in an attempt to break the silence.

'What fucking planet is this anorak on?' Sponge said to Speedy, sniggering.

'What sort of question is that?' said Speedy. 'There are people dying in Bosnia and you're asking about fucking parking offences.'

'Rigsby, has anybody ever told you you're boring?' Sponge said.

Rigsby remained silent.

'You're as interesting as a paper cup.'

CHAPTER 3

The week had slipped by and by Sunday night everybody was looking forward to changing over to day shifts again. They sat languidly in the team office. At Lionel's request, he and Speedy were the area car crew.

Slippery took parade. The Irv had ploughed into a bus while responding to an emergency call and been written off by the late-turn crew. 'Since Lionel's asked to be on the area car tonight, I'll put Sponge and Rigsby on the Irv. Speedy, you'll have to take Sponge to training school to pick up a spare Irv.'

'Will do,' replied Speedy.

'Jazz, you're with Doris in the Panda, Saddam with Bubba in the van.' Slippery tossed the duties binder to one side, then heaved a sigh and leant back in his chair. 'Anything on the daily briefing or is it the same as yesterday's?' he asked Lionel.

'No, sarge,' he replied.

'Right, gents, let's continue in the canteen,' said Slippery, rising from his seat. 'Run Sponge down to training school then come back for your tea,' he instructed Speedy.

'Wait for me in the canteen,' Sponge said to Rigsby, 'we should be back soon.'

The journey to training school took them along the A61

towards the intersection with the North Circular.

Sponge sat in the rear of the area car with his feet up on the seat, smoking the last remnants of a joint.

'Open the fucking window, will you, you'll get us all fucking stoned,' said Speedy. 'I don't know why you have to smoke that shite when you're in uniform. It's fucking unprofessional.'

Sponge ignored him and nestled further into the back seat out of sight.

The return journey brought them back along the North Circular. The area car led the way, followed by Sponge in the Irv. In front of both cars was a black Mercedes 600 SEL. As they pulled off at a set of traffic lights, the driver of the Mercedes seemed to hesitate.

'I think that's fucking him,' said Lionel, looking closely at the car.

'Are you sure?' asked Speedy.

'Yeah, that's fucking him. He's heading away from Cricklewood and he's running early.'

'What is he waiting for?' Speedy asked, angrily sounding his horn.

Rather than hastening the departure of the car in front, this made the driver brake suddenly and erratically. The Mercedes continued along the North Circular, trailed by the area car and Sponge in the Irv.

'We're still on Colindale Division's patch,' said Speedy.

'It doesn't matter,' said Lionel, 'follow him.'

They followed the North Circular until the junction with the A61 came into sight. With the police cars still behind, the Mercedes slowed to a mere crawl. By the time it got within thirty yards of the junction, they were fifteen yards behind. The traffic lights changed from green to amber and the Mercedes suddenly sped up in an obvious attempt to lose them. The ploy failed, resulting in a catastrophic four seconds of red light.

'Did you see that?' asked Speedy. 'The cheeky bastard! We're the only ones allowed to do that.' He switched on the blue lights, moved into the ahead-only lane, and drove through the red light in pursuit of his quarry along the North Circular.

Sponge was not in the mood to do any work until he had had a cup of tea. He stopped at the lights, not intending to follow his colleagues. After two minutes the lights changed to green and, just as he turned on to the A61, a sudden compulsion caused him to swing the car round on to the North Circular and off in support of Lionel and Speedy.

Speedy flashed his headlights twice. With no other vehicle in sight, it left the driver in no doubt as to who the signals were directed at. Compliantly, he pulled into a layby, a secluded part of the westbound lane of the North Circular. Getting out of the vehicle to speak to the driver, who made no attempt to move, Lionel drew parallel with the front window, stooped down and motioned to the driver to join him. Slowly the man got out, walked round the car and joined Lionel on the pavement. He was middle aged, of Mediterranean appearance, smartly but casually dressed in a loose chequered shirt and a pair of black trousers.

Speedy got out of the car to join them. 'What did you do that red light for, mate?' he asked.

The Mercedes driver appeared very nervous, his hands palpitating noticeably as he drew on a cigarette. In a sudden attempt to veil his trepidation, he threw the hardly smoked cigarette on to the pavement and stepped on it. Then he tucked his shirt into his trousers.

This behaviour did not go unnoticed by the two experienced officers standing beside him. 'What's the matter, mate?' asked Lionel.

'Nothing,' he replied in a foreign accent.

He looked at Lionel, trying desperately to remember where he might have seen his face before. Lionel walked around the car and peered through its tinted windows. The man nervously watched what he was doing. Speedy observed this and diverted his attention to the car. 'Is that your car?' he asked.

'Yes, it is.'

'Nice car,' Speedy complimented. 'Is there anything inside you're concerned about?'

'What do you mean?'

'Can you answer the question?' Speedy retorted. 'Have you got the keys on you?'

Reluctantly, the man produced the keys from his pocket.

Lionel opened the driver's door and began to explore. While Lionel was searching the inside, Speedy escorted the man to the boot of the car. 'Can you open the boot for me, mate?'

Slowly, the man inserted the key and turned the lock.

Speedy's attention was focused on the rising boot. At first the contents seemed like neatly stacked diaries in the dim light. Gradually they began to take on the guise of currency.

Speedy stood there, transfixed at the sight of bundles of notes, neatly arranged in the boot of the vehicle.

As the Irv pulled up, the man took advantage of Speedy's astonishment; within a second he was sprinting off into the bushes beside the pavement. Lionel came round to see how Speedy was getting on, the boot having obscured his view. He saw Speedy with an awe-stricken expression on his face. Lionel looked into the boot. Slowly it began to register.

Sponge jumped out of the Irv. He rushed up to his colleagues as the man ran into the bushes, leaving Speedy and Lionel still staring into the boot of the Mercedes. 'What the fuck are you letting him get away for?' he shouted at them. He was just about to run after the man when curiosity impelled him to take a quick peek in the boot. He was completely unprepared for what he was about to see.

Like his cohorts, Sponge stood dumbfounded by the amount of money before him. None of them noticed the green suitcase sitting in the far right corner of the boot.

'That's got to be about a million quid sitting there!' exclaimed Sponge.

'How the hell would you know?' asked Speedy.

'Because I used to work in a bank before I joined, remember?'

'I forgot,' replied Speedy, mesmerized.

'Whose money is it?' Sponge asked.

Speedy gave him a harsh glance. 'Don't ask stupid questions,' he said. He suddenly remembered the suspect and started for the trees.

Sponge grabbed him by the arm. 'Where are you going? He's long gone,' he said.

'You're right,' admitted Speedy. 'I might as well do a vehicle check on the car.' He was just about to press the transmitting button on his radio mouthpiece when Sponge grabbed hold of his arm again. Speedy noticed a glint of excitement in his eyes.

'Don't do that yet, no one knows we've stopped him. As far as we know, he might not be coming back to this car again,' Sponge blurted out. The first thing that had gone through Sponge's mind was to call up his boon friend Saddam. He called up the van on his radio and told Saddam and Bubba to meet them there.

'What the fuck are you talking about, Sponge?' asked Lionel.

'It's just clicked,' he said, talking at just about a comprehensible speed. 'You know I was asking you about what you'd do if you ever won the lottery?' he asked the other two. Without waiting for an answer, he continued. 'There's a one-in-fourteen-million chance we'll ever win the lottery. This is our chance in front of us here.'

'You're fucking mad,' exclaimed Lionel.

'Hold on, he's got a point, Lionel,' interrupted Speedy. 'Unless the car's been nicked, which I doubt it has, we've just come across a courier, who, if he was under surveillance, the Old Bill wouldn't have let us stop without attracting our attention.'

'I know that, but you blokes have got to understand that money isn't everything,' said Lionel.

'Money isn't everything, but the only things that money

isn't cost money,' said Sponge. 'Let me tell you something: we're at the bottom of the pile. We're coppers, all right, but who gives a toss? All we are are numerical quantities. You get shot today and, if they can't have anyone replace you with your shoulder numbers by the end of the shift, they'll get a circus monkey. Do you think they care about you?'

'I don't believe I'm hearing this,' said Lionel. 'Bend the rules a little bit to put a villain away is as far as I'm willing to go.'

'And you think anybody appreciates that? Let me tell you, the so-called public you bend the rules for would convict you on a jury faster than Fred West could bury a body under his bathroom sink,' said Sponge.

The van arrived and parked a few yards away, down a small side road. Bubba and Saddam joined them. 'Hello, boys!' What have we here?' asked Bubba.

'The fucking jackpot!' said Sponge.

'What are you talking about?' Saddam asked.

Sponge explained the situation.

'Do you know what you're saying?' asked Bubba in disbelief. 'You're a copper, for crying out loud. Besides, if we got caught we could go down for years.'

'That's the thing,' said Sponge. 'We won't get caught. He's obviously a one-man gang and he won't be coming back for his goods. Even if we take it, he's not going to come into a police station asking for it.'

'You've forgotten one important thing,' pointed out Lionel.

'What's that?' asked Sponge.

'We don't know where the money came from or who it belongs to,' said Lionel. 'What's in that suitcase?'

For the first time their attention was drawn to the large green suitcase lying at the far right of the boot. Sponge leant in and pulled the suitcase nearer. He unzipped the case and flicked open the lid. Neatly packaged in small transparent polythene food bags was a compact white substance. They stood in silence, gaping at the fresh discovery.

Sponge put his hand into his pocket and pulled out his keys. With a swift jab, he punctured one of the packets and dipped a finger into the opening. 'Anyone got any idea what this stuff is?' he asked the others, holding up a finger smattered with white powder.

'Why don't you taste it like in the movies?' asked Speedy.

'Because I still wouldn't know what it was,' replied Sponge.

'It's either coke or heroin,' said Saddam.

'Which is all the more reason why we should take it in,' said Bubba.

'Wrong,' barracked Speedy. 'That's all the more reason why he won't come back for it.'

'It makes no difference. I'll bung it into the Thames or something. I could destroy these drugs in less than twenty minutes,' said Sponge. 'Listen,' he said. 'We can't waste time. Let's carry this to a vote.'

'And what happens if I still refuse?' asked Bubba.

'You're part of the team and I expect that everything that goes on between us stays between us. That's the code. As far as this goes, you don't know about it,' said Sponge. 'Who's for?'

'I'm for,' said Saddam.

'Lionel?' Sponge enquired.

'I'm against.'

'Bubba?'

'I won't have anything to do with this.'

'That's two against two,' said Sponge. 'Speedy, you have the carrying vote.'

'Wait a second, what about Jazz? He's part of this team, isn't he?' asked Lionel.

'I think the less people that know about this the better,' replied Sponge.

'He's part of the team,' exclaimed Bubba.

'So is Slippery. We can't jeopardize this whole thing by bringing everyone into it. Too many cooks spoil the broth,' said Sponge.

'Well, I don't want to have anything to do with this,' said Bubba, again dissociating himself.

'Speedy?' asked Sponge. 'Your decision carries.'

Speedy stood silently for a while. 'You know, I've got twenty-two years of service and pension. I've come to realize that in all those years the job has taken and taken and never given me anything back. In fact right now, I owe the job nothing. You blokes get rid of the drugs immediately, though.'

'So, is that a yes or a no?' asked Sponge.

After a cup of tea Jazz and the female probationer, Sonia, had gone out in the Irv. Jazz drove aimlessly around the division, not in the mood to do any work. 'How are you finding the job?' he asked Sonia with idle interest.

'At the moment, I hate it,' she replied. 'I don't like the way they treat us probationers. You lot are sexist, crude and so cliquey.'

'You seem to be getting along pretty well. Just keep your head down and get on with it. Ignore any comments and don't answer back or you'll be labelled a gobby probby,' counselled Jazz.

'It just seems the only way to get ahead with the blokes on this team is to give them head,' complained Sonia.

'Listen, if what you want is sympathy from me, you're not going to get it. When I was a probationer, being a black guy I went through absolute hell. You're having it easy compared to what I saw. Just come into work, do your eight hours and go home.'

'That's an exciting attitude for a new starter like me to join the job with,' Sonia replied.

'So I take it you don't fancy any of us then?' said Jazz, changing the subject. 'There are a few blokes who'd definitely be interested.'

'Are you joking? I'd rather be gang-banged by Iraqi binmen than sleep with a policeman again,' she said.

'Just remember, if you can't take the jokes and pokes, don't work with blokes!'

Sponge had waited for Saddam and Speedy, who'd driven back in the Irv to pick up Sponge's car. Bubba went off in the van, taking Lionel with him, neither of them wanting to remain witness to the proceedings. Saddam and Speedy joined Sponge back at the Mercedes.

'I'll only be a part of this if we lie low for at least six

months,' warned Speedy. 'No one spends a penny of the dosh or leaves the job for six months, and we get rid of the drugs straight away. Is that agreed?'

'Yeah,' answered Sponge.

'Sweet,' replied Saddam.

'Just in case the others change their minds, we'll keep their shares for them for at least six months. That way no one gets pissed off they've been left out,' continued Speedy. 'You've got to understand how fucking important discretion is. No one does anything or says anything to give the game away.'

'Yeah, yeah,' said Sponge.

'Don't fucking yeah, yeah me, Sponge,' shouted Speedy. 'You've got to fucking understand how sensitive this is. Once we take this money, there's no going back.'

'We know that,' replied Saddam.

'Help me offload the gear,' Sponge said to Saddam.

They drove the Mercedes up a side road, which led to the grounds of a school on one side and those of a park on the other. They shifted the cash into the boot of Sponge's car. Because it was considerably smaller than that of the Mercedes, they put the remainder of the money into the rear foot-well. Zipping up the suitcase, they wedged it behind the front seat to cover the notes. They even took pains to count the bundles as they transferred them; the amount totalled nine hundred thousand pounds.

'If it's still quiet in the early morning, I'll drive straight home and get rid of the gear. I'll count the money, share it out and deliver it personally to you at home,' Sponge pledged.

'Don't come round to my house with stuff like that,' replied Speedy. 'I'll come and pick it up.'

'What should we do with the car?' Sponge asked.

'Leave it here. It's not on our ground so no one can trace it to us. As far as he's concerned, he was stopped by Colindale Division coppers,' said Speedy.

They left the keys in the ignition of the Mercedes and drove back to the police station.

Sponge parked his car down a quiet side road, locked it up and walked back to the canteen. Jazz and Sonia were not yet back. 'Go and wait for me in the Irv,' he said to Rigsby. 'You're supposed to monitor the main set. Make yourself useful for a change.'

Rigsby got up and left, leaving the others alone again. With Slippery in the custody suite, they were free to talk a few things over.

'We'll keep your shares for six months. If you change your minds, you'll get one hundred and eighty grand,' Sponge said.

'Let's get one thing right,' said Bubba. 'As long as we fucking work together, you don't mention what happened tonight ever again and we won't have a problem. Do you understand?'

'Just bear it in mind,' said Sponge.

'This just doesn't fucking feel right,' said Bubba.

'The Met's fucked and if only the public knew! There's no morale and the powers that be are far too busy sniffing each other's arses like dogs in a park to think about us,' said Sponge.

'How many times have we manned this fucking division on less than full strength?' added Saddam, corroborating Sponge's point.

'It's things like this that loses us the public's faith,' disputed Bubba. 'We're still coppers.'

'Do you really think anybody wants to do the mundane menial shite you deal with every day?' asked Sponge. 'We're fucking cannon fodder! Everybody in this job looks down on us. This is my chance to redress the fucking balance, stick a few fucking bob in my pocket to ease the daily knocks.'

'This is shite I can't handle,' said Bubba, getting up to make another sandwich.

Sponge left for home before the early-turn area car crew turned up. He'd been thinking about nothing but the cash and the drugs in his car. Suddenly the life he had been living, confining him to shiftwork and financial mediocrity, evanesced. Now he could afford to buy himself things and go to places he had always fantasized about. What surprised him was the lack of guilt or angst he was feeling. He was able to justify his actions by thinking of the number of times he had gone beyond the call of duty – for staying those extra minutes to comfort a burglary victim and going round after work to board her window, and for chasing an armed suspect at the risk of being shot. No one had ever thanked him. That was not why he did it, but they were acts of personal benevolence no one but the recipient would ever credit him for. It was a thankless job and he had just got his thanks. He wasn't sure about Speedy insisting on them remaining in the police for the next six months. He had always thought of what it would be like to own a business, not having to do quick changeovers, getting four hours' sleep and disorienting his physiological clock.

For the first time since he had been a probationer, he felt an uncontrollable hatred towards the police and those that represented its hierarchy. This was his chance and he had taken it without even thinking twice.

By the time he got home, it was not yet light. He used the cover of darkness to offload the booty into his flat. He stacked the money neatly on the centre table in the living room and left the suitcase in a corner. He drew the curtains, switched on the living-room light and again began to count the money. A sudden feeling of avarice swept through him. Why should he even bother with the others? He could take this money and disappear. That was the only time throughout the night that he felt any form of shame or guilt. No matter what, he would never betray the loyalty and trust that existed within the team. He was due back at work in less than seven hours and needed all the sleep he could get.

Saddam had sat with his own thoughts in the canteen, preoccupied with the knowledge that Sponge's car was filled with drugs and cash. He knew what he was going to do with his portion. He'd been to Mexico with his wife and had always hoped to be able to return there to live. Police shiftwork was not doing a great deal for his marriage, and the loyalty he had once believed the police service showed to its own no longer existed. They were on their own, left to police the streets by senior officers who knew nothing of the real world.

The moment the shift was over, he jumped into his car to go home and get some sleep, then on to Sponge's to get his money. His plan was to give it to his wife to dispose of. Once it was in a bank account and transferred to Mexico, even if the whole affair was exposed, his wife would be safe. He couldn't lose out. She was still asleep when he got home. She normally got up at about 8 a.m. and left, ready for work, by 9.30 a.m. They hardly saw each other when he worked nights, the short periods they had together in the evenings insufficient to amount to prime marital time.

He undressed and got into bed before trying to fall asleep, but sleep eluded him far into the night, his thoughts skirting from one subject to another but centring on a single recurring theme.

Money! Money!

An amount he'd never imagined he'd confront sat in Sponge's flat. What a comforting thought.

Saddam was still awake when his wife got up, dressed for work and gave him a kiss on the cheek. Money! he thought, as he heard the front door close. If they invested it properly, she wouldn't have to work in that smoke-filled solicitor's office. They'd be able to have the family they so affectionately talked of.

Money! Sitting in Sponge's flat. But wait a minute! What if Sponge absconded with it?

Sponge wouldn't betray him; Sponge was his best and closest friend. He thought of the ease with which Sponge had attempted to proselytize them. Sponge's scruples could incontrovertibly be classified as 'dubious'. Suddenly he did not feel as secure as he had before. A man he had habitually and unreservedly entrusted his life to, he now had no confidence in. He lay there deliberating. Finally, realizing there was no point lying there when he was due back at work in a few hours, he got up and dressed. He picked up the phone and dialled Sponge's number.

Speedy sat uncomfortably in the canteen. Things had not gone the way he and Lionel had planned and he knew he should have abandoned the whole operation the moment Sponge had jumped out of the car. However, as cautious as Lionel was not to involve anybody else, the sight of such a large amount of money was too much to ignore.

His twenty-two years hadn't all been bad. He had joined when things were not altogether unsalutary. The money was not great in the early 1970s, but there was still respect for the uniform and they were in overall control of the streets. Then came the Thatcher era, a rise in pay and overall conditions improved things; before that, the prevailing ethos of the job had been to look after its own. The miners' strike, the Brixton and the poll-tax riots, were protests he had sympathized with, being of working-class extraction himself. But he policed them and kicked arse merrily, because that was what he was getting heavily paid to do. He earned copious amounts of overtime and had quite an exciting life as well. He joined the SPG, a roving squad of officers who either dispensed law or dispensed with the law, depending on the merits of the occasion. Then things started to go horribly wrong. The economy faltered, public administration had its funding structurally adjusted and starved; inevitably the police suffered. The Met became intellectualized and fiscalized. The human element went out of policing, to be replaced by budget balancing, cost justifying and public imaging. Suddenly, you could read a book or get a degree and become a policeman overnight.

Twenty-two years of abuse, a broken arm, three beatings, being shot at twice, spat at numerous times, having televisions and fridges dropped on him from high-rise blocks.

This was his chance to have his say and he was going to take it. He was not going to allow it all to amount to nothing. So, no matter how much money he came across, he was going to stay in until he got his pension, because he'd worked for it, earned it and deserved it.

Did he feel guilty? A little. Because it had not all been bad. His excuse was not as cogent as Sponge's and Saddam's; they hadn't seen great times. After twenty-two years of shift-work, the funny thing was having given away his youngest, most virile and the best years of his life without one single day of thanks. He owed the police and the public nothing.

He was old, qualified in nothing and trained to do everything. No one would be interested in employing him at his age. The only thing he was waiting for were the results of his sergeant's exam; if he could be promoted before he retired he would get a better pension. Anything that would make his retirement more bearable was welcome, especially money. He drifted off to sleep and was woken later by noise in the yard below. The early-turn area car crew were conversing with the station garage man. He got changed and went home.

*

Lionel wavered between feelings of anger and resentment.

Nothing had gone according to plan. The only thing that pleased him was the performance he'd put on by the car. What had surprised him was the dexterity with which Sponge had improvised, as if he had no reservations. Saddam had concurred and Speedy agreed, despite his knowledge of Sponge's recklessness. Lionel had to admit it was tempting. The chances of getting away with it were good, so long as Sponge behaved.

He did have ambitions but they had evaporated with the reality of policing, once he had finished his probation. Competition had become fierce for the few specialized positions in the Met, and most posts had been civilianized because it was cheaper. He had always hoped to return to college to do a degree in Maritime Studies, but he knew he would find it difficult to live the frugal life of a student.

He and Speedy were the only ones supposed to be in the area car that day.

He thought back to when he'd been in the Italian restaurant on Tuesday afternoon. He had heard the two Greek-Cypriot men discussing meeting at 1 a.m. at the Greek Embassy – a drug deal set to occur in five days' time. They had discussed this in Greek behind him, not knowing that he understood the language. But his mother was a Greek-Cypriot and spoke only in Greek to him at home. He followed the conversation and, straining hard, heard most of it.

The Greek Embassy at 1 a.m. on Monday morning! He knew the restaurant: it was on the Edgware Road in Cricklewood. Further along the Edgware Road, in Burnt

Oak, was Jazz's house. He paid his bill and went outside, thinking to himself there was obviously some money involved and all he needed to do would be to wait in full uniform in a police car and waylay them.

He stayed in his car until both men came out of the restaurant, having put on his black bomber jacket to make sure that they did not recognize him. They crossed the road and got into a Mercedes 600 SEL. It was a while before they drove off with Lionel on their tail. He followed them to a detached house in Mill Hill, an opulent and well-groomed area of north-east London. He sat watching the house, not quite sure what strategy to adopt.

He remembered CID officers talking about the restaurant being one of the prime locations for drug deals in north-west London. At 1 a.m. on Monday something was going to happen; all he had to do was wait outside the restaurant and watch. He needed to get hold of one member of his team to drive him there and cover him. He was not interested in drugs but in any money that the men would be leaving the restaurant with.

They might not go straight home, thought Lionel, which would mean they would have to follow them immediately from the restaurant. Once the men moved off, they would be after them. All Lionel needed was an excuse for being off their ground around that time. He could not think up a good one at this point. He needed someone else in this. Speedy was the first person he thought of, given they lived in the section house together. Besides, he only had seven years to go till he left the force and any extra money would help him have a more comfortable retirement.

All Lionel wanted was to do a degree at university. He had joined the police the very week he was due to go to college and had thought it the right decision at the time, but, as the years had gone by, he had come to regret it. He had seen schoolfriends getting better jobs with greater prospects and after his years of service he had nothing.

He spoke to Speedy later that day. Speedy thought all they needed to do was sit outside the restaurant and wait. All Lionel had to do was change the postings that evening to get put on the area car with Speedy. This hadn't been difficult. Sunday night was normally quiet and they wouldn't need to tell anybody they were going off their ground. Things went smoothly but for the fact that they had to drop Sponge off at training school to pick up the spare Irv. Things went from bad to worse when the Mercedes turned up unexpectedly in front of them. He must have got the time wrong. They acted on impulse and decided to stop it. Sponge arrived in the Irv when they thought he was on his way back to the police station. He and Speedy had not intended it to be a joint enterprise with Sponge and Saddam and he, for one, was not going to be a part of it.

Bubba contented himself with a ham and banana sandwich, pasted with butter, marmalade and cheese. His marriage was in a sorry state; his wife was making demands which, owing to shiftwork, he could not meet. Going out with his team mates was the only way he could properly unwind and cope with the stress of the job. Only those he worked with really knew him. He who feels it knows it.

His marriage and his two sons were the only things he had outside the police. Police life was taking its toll on his family life and, like a majority of other police marriages, his was drifting towards its inevitable demise. He had always considered settling in Ireland and buying himself a small restaurant in Dublin, but he'd never had the capital to relocate.

The money would help, but not at the expense of compromised standards. He lounged about the utility room, making himself another sandwich before leaving for home.

His wife was up and getting the children ready for school. Now he was policing Gay Pride and unable to visit his mother-in-law as they'd discussed, he knew an argument was brewing. He was not going to tell her just yet; he could not afford another row right now. He went to bed.

Sponge stayed up for three hours, counting the money repeatedly before finally setting aside his portion: one hundred and eighty thousand pounds. He went into the kitchen, collected a roll of black bin liners and put his cash into one of the bags. The next task was to find somewhere to hide it until he could pay it into a bank account in another name. Such were his thoughts as he roamed about the flat looking for a place to stash the money.

Suddenly the phone rang, breaking his serenity and stopping him in his tracks. Panic overtook him. Should he answer it? He walked into the living room and watched it as it rang. It had to be someone he knew! One of the team. No one else would ring him at this time. If they'd been discovered, then he'd be having a knock on the door rather than a phone call. Taking a deep breath, he lifted the receiver. 'Hello, who is it?'

'It's me, Saddam.'

'What do you want?'

'I'm coming round to pick up my dosh, I can't get any sleep just thinking about it. I thought I'd phone up first in case you panicked if I knocked on your front door unexpectedly.'

'I'll have it waiting,' said Sponge.

'How much is it?'

'One hundred and eighty grand.'

It was 12.15 p.m. when Saddam turned up on Sponge's doorstep. The remainder of the money was still stacked neatly on the living-room table. Saddam's share had been apportioned and packed into a bin liner.

'I don't know what to do with the rest of the dosh,' Sponge said.

'Never mind that, where's mine?' asked Saddam.

'It's in the bin liner on the carpet,' replied Sponge. 'Fancy a coffee?'

'No thanks,' answered Saddam, overwhelmed by the sight of the money on the table and the size of the bag on the floor. 'What do you think the others are going to do? Do you think they'll change their minds?' he asked, looking at the pile, a sudden gust of greed overtaking him.

'Probably,' answered Sponge. 'What are you going to do with yours?'

'I wouldn't have minded emigrating to Mexico, but I

don't think this money will be enough to set up and forget the job pension.'

'I'll tell you what,' said Sponge. 'If that bloke had sold those drugs, we would have got a far more decent cut.'

'He obviously couldn't flog the whole stuff. Bit of a waste getting rid of it. There must be over a million quid's worth of gear,' said Saddam.

'You're joking?' said Sponge.

'No, seriously,' answered Saddam, looking at the suitcase in the corner. 'Shame we're going to get rid of it.'

'Let's not get rid of it yet,' said Sponge, a glint of mischief in his eyes. 'No one in this day and age would flush over a million quid down the bog.'

'We couldn't flog it,' said Saddam, making no attempt to challenge the proposal.

'I'll ask about. I'm sure there are loads of places we could flog it; it's just a matter of putting out some feelers,' said Sponge.

'This could get us into trouble,' said Saddam.

'We're already in trouble,' said Sponge. 'It'll be a one-off deal, over a million quid. We'll never need to work again.'

'OK, I'm game. What about the others?'

'We don't bring them into it. I'll stick the case in the back shed. You don't live far from Speedy. Take his dosh. I'll keep the rest. If they don't ask for it after we flog the gear, we'll keep that as well. I don't know what Speedy was on about when he was talking about staying in the job for six months,' said Sponge.

'What do we do with the car?'

'I'll go round and torch it,' suggested Sponge.

'Well, I won't hang around, I need some sleep,' said Saddam, picking up his bin bag.

Sponge had already started to count out Speedy's share of the money. 'Give us a hand to count Speedy's wad, will you?'

'Oh yeah,' said Saddam, remembering.

He sat down and began to count the money.

Sponge left the minute he had stowed away the suitcase in the shed and his money underneath his bed. If it leaked, no matter where he hid the money a search squad would find it anyway. He took along a pair of gloves to drive the car to a location where he could set it alight. He went to the spot where he had left the Mercedes the previous night.

To his consternation, it was no longer there. In disbelief, he drove up and down the road before searching the other side streets nearby. When this yielded no results, he went to the nearest phone box and telephoned Saddam.

'Yes,' Saddam answered in a sleepy voice.

'You asleep?' Sponge asked.

'Just fell asleep on the chair.'

'It's not there,' Sponge blurted out.

'What are you talking about?'

'The car. It's fucking gone!'

There was a moment's hesitation.

'Are you sure you checked the right road?' Saddam asked.

'Yeah, I've even checked the other fucking side roads to make sure.'

'Well, someone must have fucking taken it.'

'He must have come back and driven it off,' Sponge surmised. 'It wasn't blocking a driveway or causing an obstruction.'

'Must have,' said Saddam.

'What do you think he's going to do when he discovers there's nothing in the car?' Sponge asked.

'Well, the man is obviously an amateur,' said Saddam, 'or he wouldn't have been so nervous behind the wheel, let alone do a light with us behind him. Secondly, he wouldn't have been on his own, and he'd be armed. Thirdly, he wouldn't run away.'

'You're right. See you at the nick. I need to go and pay off my overdraft,' replied Sponge, his panic suddenly allayed.

CHAPTER 4

On Monday afternoon Slippery took parade. As was typical of a quick changeover, few words were spoken and there was an atmosphere of lassitude. This was further exacerbated by the events that had occurred that morning.

Slippery assigned them to their vehicles and they made their way to the canteen.

'Hello, Angie,' Slippery greeted the African canteen lady as they walked in. 'Bloody hell, your hair's grown. It was really short last week, now it's down to your shoulders. How come Afro hair grows so fast?'

'It's a wig, you foolish man. Don't you white people notice anything?' replied Angie, her accent harsh.

'These are two new officers starting on our team,' Slippery said.

'Hello.' Angie nodded at them.

'Rigsby's going to buy the coffees,' Slippery said.

'Hello, Angie,' Sponge said as he entered the canteen. 'Is that a wig you've got on or is your head wedged up a ferret's arse?'

'At least you can tell the difference,' Angie replied.

'Yeah, and it's a bloody awful syrup,' said Sponge.

They left Rigsby at the counter to pay for the coffees. They didn't stay in the canteen long before dispersing to their respective vehicles.

Bubba, not in a talkative mood, hardly spoke to the new probationer in the van. His mind was full and he needed time to think.

He looked at her as she sat gazing out of the window. She was quite small, five feet four inches tall, with short dark hair, modest looks and a slim figure. She was nineteen, very reserved and spoke only when spoken to. 'What do you want to do in the job?' he asked in an attempt to break the silence.

'Join Special Branch or the Royalty Protection Squad once my two years' probation are up,' replied Sonia.

'Well, you've got a fucking ice cube's hope in hell of getting there with five years' service, much less two,' said Bubba.

'I thought I could join any branch I wanted once I finished probation?' said Sonia.

'According to the glossy brochures the Met hands out to people telling them they can fly the fucking helicopter after two years if they want to. Well, you've got a better chance of buying a cat with three arseholes.'

Bubba began to think once more about his own problems as he drove. He thought about the money and the reasons for taking it. He thought of how pleasant life could be if he emigrated to Ireland, away from the mêlée of police and city life and settled quietly with his family. It could be the only way to save his marriage.

'That's the Prado Village estate, a fucking scum bucket.

You don't go there unless you're with somebody and the control room knows where you are,' said Bubba, pointing out two tower blocks on their right. Two young boys were spraying graffiti on a wall. Bubba pulled up beside them. 'What would your mother do if you got nicked for that?' he asked paternally.

'She'd hug and kiss me,' replied one of the boys.

'That's right, mate. Incest is best,' Bubba exclaimed before putting the van in gear and driving off.

'Is it really this rough?' Sonia asked.

'It's a fucking shit hole. The birds around here fly upside down because there's fuck all around worth shitting on,' Bubba replied. 'The only good thing I can think of to come out of this place is the fucking road out of here!'

They were halfway down the road when a call came across the main set of the area car to attend the DHSS office. Sponge duly accepted.

The sirens and blue lights were put on and Speedy forced down the accelerator, making the car kick as it surged forward. Rigsby sat in the back squirming with excitement as they launched past the pedestrians who stopped to look on with interest.

The DHSS office was ninety yards up the Broadway. They switched off the blue lights and siren once they reached the Broadway, opting for a more silent approach.

A man was wielding a plastic bar in pixilated derangement. Speedy took care to pull up in front of him, half mounting the pavement so that, if the man decided to attack them, he could run him over without any loss of energy or damage to police property.

'Looks like your dad's got out again, Rigsby. Someone forgot to lock the cellar door?' Sponge said jocularly.

They sat in the car and watched the man for a couple of minutes.

'Well, get on with it then,' Speedy suddenly said to Rigsby, nodding at the man.

Rigsby got out, not knowing what to do, while Speedy and Sponge sat in the car and looked on in amusement. He knew he had to do something, but in a professional and adroit manner as his credibility was being tested. As he approached the man, he racked his brains trying to remember the things he had been taught in training school. His memory failed him. He was standing so close to the man that he did the only thing that automatically came to him: he spoke to him.

'What's the matter, mate?'

'Fuck off, rozzer,' the man shouted back, moving in circles and flicking the pipe from side to side.

'I haven't got much time to speak to you,' said Rigsby. 'You hear those sirens in the background, they're coming for you, so let me look after you. You can speak to me. If no one else will listen, I will.'

'Just you then?' the man asked, fishing for assurance.

Without any further display of violence, he put down the pipe and held out his hands. Rigsby took out his handcuffs and handcuffed him. The cavalry had now started to arrive, including armed response vehicles and Territorial Support Group personnel carriers.

Speedy and Sponge got out and helped Rigsby escort the man to the van for transportation. A considerable crowd had convened to witness the spectacle and was beginning to cause congestion.

'Can you all go away, please,' said Speedy in an effort to disperse the onlookers.

Ignoring his entreaties, they remained still.

'There's obviously fuck all on television,' said Sponge as they shut the back of the police van.

Speedy pulled Rigsby to one side. 'What did you do, quote fucking Shakespeare?' he asked. 'Why didn't you just fucking stick him?'

'I wanted to speak to him first,' replied Rigsby.

'Let us know when you've finished with your prisoner,' said Speedy, leaving him under no illusions: he was going to deal with the matter on his own.

The rest of the shift passed with few calls and the team met up in the pub after work for a quick drink. Jazz went straight home, too tired for alcohol. Slippery had left straight away and the probationers had not been invited.

'I'm not fucking sure you realize the decision you made this morning,' Bubba said to Sponge as they walked to the locker room.

'You're talking to *me* about decisions. When was the last time the job treated you like a human being?' Sponge remonstrated. 'These days, if you join the job, you pound the beat for life. You know what they fucking think of us. I took the fucking decision because I realized I have to look after number one.'

'You've abused the fucking loyalty and closed shop of this team. You knew no one was ever going to grass on you,' said Bubba.

'Just remember you have a stack of cash waiting for you if you change your mind over the next six months. Think about it,' said Sponge.

'See you tomorrow,' said Lionel as he came out of the locker room.

'Aren't you coming to the piss tank?' Sponge asked.

'Sorry, mate. I'm too tired.'

They got to the pub just after last orders; the landlady began pouring pints for them straight away. Sponge paid for the round. 'So have you thought whether you're in or staying out?' he asked Bubba.

'I'm still considering it,' Bubba replied.

'Good man, you know it makes sense,' lauded Sponge.

'That's the thing: nothing makes fucking sense. A few days ago we were happy-go-lucky coppers and this week we're jumpy crims,' said Bubba.

'Bollocks,' barracked Saddam. 'Was I fuck? I wasn't fucking happy! I was making the best of a bad situation. Extracting what little fucking humour there was from our dismal existence.'

'Look, let me think about it,' said Bubba. 'You blokes have already fucking changed even in this short time.'

'Rubbish! We're still the fucking same, just a bit richer,' said Speedy.

'Crime doesn't fucking pay,' said Bubba.

'Not unless you're a policeman,' retorted Sponge.

Downing his pint, Speedy turned to Saddam. 'Come on, lad. We've got business to do. I need to get my dosh into a bank account,' he said earnestly. They said goodbye and left.

'Why was Jazz left out of this?' Bubba asked Sponge.

'Because the less fucking people that know the better,' replied Sponge, sipping from his pint.

'That is utter dog shite! We're a fucking unit. You know that. Everything we've done, we've always done together. Why are you leaving him out?'

'Listen, shit for brains! What would happen if Jazz went to CIB? You know how hung up he is about police politics. He's got fucking ambitions; he's halfway to becoming a skipper, for fuck sake. How many times has he kept crapping on about "the black community"? Black coppers being in the middle and all that fucking bollocks? Quite frankly, I find his loyalty questionable.'

'That's a bit fucking unfair,' objected Bubba.

'No disrespect to the bloke, but he is a fucking spade,' said Sponge. 'What's that organization he belongs to? You know, that black copper thing.'

'The BPA, Black Police Association.'

'Yeah, that fucking shite. We've already got a federation, so what does he want to join them for? They've created a them and us, and he's obviously not going to stick with us and, like I said, too many cooks spoil the broth.'

'I think you're a fucking hypocrite,' accused Bubba. 'He's supposed to be a mate.'

'Whatever you fucking think I am,' said Sponge, getting up, 'I'm going home.'

*

The team assembled for parade as usual on Tuesday afternoon and were all assigned to the same vehicles as the day before. Straight after parade, they left for the canteen. Slippery was already in there watching the cricket and Sonia was delegated to buy the coffees. 'Would you like one, sarge?' she asked.

'Yes please, and a coffee as well,' Slippery answered, trying not to break his concentration on the game.

Sponge began to bang on the Coke machine beside the television in annoyance.

'What's the matter?' asked Jazz. 'Is it playing up again?'

'It won't give me my fucking money or a fucking can,' replied Sponge angrily. 'When will they sort this fucking machine out?'

'Stick an out-of-order sign on it,' suggested Jazz.

Sponge pulled out his pen and pocket book and began to write a note.

Suddenly Slippery got up in annoyance as another England wicket fell. 'We are absolutely fucking shite,' he exclaimed.

'Don't worry about it, sarge,' said Speedy. 'You English will win a game one day.'

'I've got to go over to the custody suite again; I've got a prisoner in. Tell Doris to bring my coffee over, will you?' Slippery said.

The shift was quiet and at 7 p.m. they were back in the canteen for their refreshment break.

They placed their orders and Andy, the canteen assistant, disappeared into the kitchen to prepare the food. They watched television while Sponge played on the game machine. 'Anyone coming to the Emporium tonight?' he shouted across the canteen.

'What's on tonight, then?' Speedy asked.

'It's over-twenty-fives night. Easy pickings, wall-to-wall fanny,' replied Sponge.

'I'm game,' answered Speedy.

'I'll come along,' said Jazz.

'I'm in,' said Lionel.

'I suppose I might as well,' said Saddam.

'The missus ain't gonna fucking like it, but I'll come too,' said Bubba.

They ignored the probationers, who sat there pretending not to hear the conversation.

Andy came out of the kitchen and called out the shoulder numbers on the slips for the orders he had prepared. Fifteen minutes later, he came out again to collect the empty plates and used cutlery and to clear the tables.

'Some soup,' Speedy complimented Andy sarcastically.

'Nice?'

'Nice? Did you have a fucking bath in it?' replied Speedy. 'You deserve a tip for that meal, you know. The tip of my fucking police boot!'

Offended, Andy ignored him and continued to clear away the plates. After refreshments, Speedy drove to the Northwick Road to find Rigsby some work.

The area car waited at the traffic lights, its occupants idly looking at traffic as it passed in front of them.

Speedy was picking his nose enthusiastically as he watched the cars whiz by. Sponge winced in disgust as Speedy extracted a bogy and rolled it in his fingers. 'You can fucking walk,' he uttered as he flicked it out the window.

The lights were just about to change when a red BMW drove past, drum base music emanating from it.

'That looks tasty! We'll give it a tug,' said Speedy. He leaned forward, clutched down and put the vehicle in gear.

They turned right into the Broadway, caught up with the car and nestled behind it, allowing a generous stopping distance.

'It's about four up,' said Sponge, referring to the number of occupants in the vehicle.

'They look like wogs to me! We'll get more units before we stop them. Four of them in a car is a riot waiting to happen on four wheels,' Speedy said.

'The car looks in good nick,' said Sponge.

'We'll find something.'

'I'll do a car check on it, you never know.' Sponge did a vehicle check.

'November 1, you should be looking at a red BMW 318i, no reports, not known to CAD. Owner since the 139th day of 1996 a Mr Charles Oko . . . Oko . . . Okon . . . Okon . . .'

'What's that, some kind of fucking voodo curse?' asked Speedy.

'Some African name,' said the controller, giving up on the pronunciation. *'It's registered to 15 Caledonian Road, Kingsbury, NW9.'*

'Yes, received,' replied Sponge. *'Can we have a few units to assist us in stopping it? It's got four IC3s in it, northbound, the Broadway.'*

The van and the Irv volunteered. The area car continued to follow the vehicle down the northbound lane along the Broadway until the driver, realizing he was being followed, pulled into a petrol station, parking a little distance from the pumps but still under the cover and luminosity of the forecourt canopy.

'Vehicle stopped, Total petrol garage,' said Sponge, transmitting an update.

Speedy pulled up behind the vehicle and switched on the blue lights so that the approaching units would spot him and to impress upon the driver a more conspicuous police presence. 'Well, fucking get out then,' he shouted at Rigsby.

'I don't know how to go about this,' said Rigsby candidly.

'This is like teaching a fucking turtle to jump through a burning hoop!' Speedy turned to Sponge. 'Give him a hand, will you?'

Sponge and Rigsby got out. Sponge walked to the driver's side of the BMW while Rigsby stood beside him as an observer. The driver made no attempt to get out of his car but instead lowered the music to an inaudible murmur. Sponge motioned to the driver to get out of the vehicle. The driver said something to his passengers, leant over towards the glove compartment, retrieved his vehicle documents and stepped out to meet Sponge. Speedy got out of the area car and walked over to the front passenger's side of the BMW while Sponge took the driver back towards the police car, followed by Rigsby. One of the passengers, keen to lend his support, tried to open the car door.

Speedy gently pressed his thigh against it. 'Stay inside, mate, you can come out in a minute,' he said aggressively.

Shortly afterwards, the Irv with Jazz and Lionel and the van with Bubba and Sonia arrived. Lionel and Jazz walked over to Speedy, while Bubba joined Sponge and Rigsby with the driver.

'What have you got?' Bubba asked Sponge.

'Just a stop. His documents are OK, so we'll just turn over the car and do name checks,' Sponge replied. He then turned to the driver. 'Have you got anything on you you shouldn't have, mate?'

'No,' the driver replied in a Nigerian accent.

'Have you got your passport, mate?' Sponge asked.

'No,' the man answered, 'I haven't got it with me. Besides, I'm British.'

'I'm just going to search you, mate, make sure you haven't got any credit cards, passports, travellers' cheques or documents that you shouldn't have,' said Sponge. He moved forward and ushered the man to the side of the police vehicle.

'I'm not a fraudster! I'm a final-year economics student,' muttered the driver irascibly.

'How could you afford a car like that then?' Sponge retorted.

The driver ignored him.

'Empty your pockets on top of the car, mate,' Sponge instructed.

The driver put his hands in his pockets and pulled out a set of keys, several rumpled items of correspondence and his wallet. Bubba reached over and took the wallet. He selected the various cards and compared the names on each. Watched keenly by the driver, he unzipped the money compartment and flicked through the notes which were tucked inside.

'How come you're a student and you've got so much money?' Bubba asked, without looking up.

Again the driver did not answer.

'You Nigerians are always at it, it's just a matter of catching you at it, isn't it?' said Sponge, moving forward. 'Spread your hands out, mate, I'm just going to pat you down.' The driver complied. Sponge ran his hands over the man and, finding nothing, took out his pocket book. 'I'm just going to take your details and do a quick name check on you. If it comes back OK, you'll be on your way. Have you been in trouble with the police before?'

'No,' the driver replied, 'I've never had anything to do with the police, apart from getting stopped every day driving this bloody car.'

'If you don't like getting stopped, buy yourself a less flashy car,' Bubba interjected.

'I think I will,' the driver confided. 'This is the third time I've been stopped by your lot today.'

Speedy and Sponge decided to go over to the pub and wait for the others. They had all agreed to go to Watford in Sponge's car and left shortly after the end of the shift, Sponge's raddled Escort being pushed to its maximum capacity. They had barely driven quarter of a mile when Sponge began to complain.

They arrived at the Emporium car park at 12.20 a.m.

'Do you think we can brief it in?' Sponge asked the others.

'I don't know how the bouncers will react when they see our warrant cards,' replied Lionel.

'How much is it to get in, anyway?' asked Jazz.

'A fiver, I'd guess,' answered Sponge.

'Well, let's get to the door first. If they look dodgy then we won't bother,' suggested Bubba.

They joined the small queue that meandered its way to the entrance of the club.

'I'll go and check it out,' said Sponge, leaving the queue and heading for the entrance.

Two bouncers stood in tuxedos by the reception. 'There's a queue, mate,' one of them said to Sponge.

'I know, I just wanted to know whether you let coppers in free,' Sponge said.

'You Met or Hertfordshire?' the bouncer asked.

'Met.'

'Sorry, mate. Met have to pay like everybody else. You lads cause quite a bit of trouble each time you come,' he replied.

Not wishing to haggle, Sponge walked to his car, opened the glove box, pulled out a bunch of fifty-pound notes and returned to the queue. It had moved quite rapidly and his colleagues were almost at the front.

'Where did you go?' Jazz asked Sponge.

'Just went to the car to get something.'

They got to the reception and their turn came to pay.

'Six pounds each,' the receptionist said, looking vacuously at them.

Sponge made a mental count of heads and handed her a fifty-pound note.

She raised her eyebrows enquiringly. 'Is this just for you or for all six of you?' she asked, accepting the note.

'All six of us,' replied Sponge. He looked on intently as the receptionist held the note up to the light, scrutinizing it.

'You coppers get paid a fucking packet,' one of the bouncers said aloud.

'No, we don't,' answered Speedy jocularly. 'Fucking overworked and underpaid, that's what we are.'

The receptionist looked down and, after inspecting something on the underside of the counter, picked up her telephone.

Sponge was suddenly overtaken by anxiety. This was his first tentative experiment to see whether or not the notes were indeed authentic. All the others except Jazz realized where the note had come from and waited anxiously too. The receptionist looked up at them and smiled as she waited for the person at the end of the line to answer.

'Hi, Sophie,' she said. 'Is Gordon there? Can you ask him to come to reception, I've got a problem. Thanks.' She put down the phone and waited.

After what seemed an eternity, the manager appeared. 'What's the matter, Debbie?' he asked as he sauntered towards the reception, a huge bunch of keys jingling in his left hand and a walkie-talkie in his right.

'Hi, Gordon,' she said, holding up the fifty-pound note. 'I can't find the mercury light switch.'

The manager shook his head, leant over the counter and flicked a switch. Suddenly the underside of the desk was illuminated with a bright ultra-violet light. Together they examined the note.

'It's OK,' the manager agreed with the receptionist.

She rang up the till and gave Sponge the tickets and his change.

'Cheers, Sponge,' said Jazz with unveiled glee. 'Has that uncle of yours finally pegged it?' he asked unwittingly.

'No, I just feel good,' answered Sponge, avoiding the expressions on his colleagues' faces as they walked into the dance hall. 'I'll get the beers in,' he shouted, working his way through the crowd towards the bar.

'I'll come with you,' said Speedy, braving his way behind him. 'Where are you lot going to be?'

'We'll be waiting in the corner over there,' said Lionel, pointing towards a set of illuminated cubicles.

Speedy caught up with Sponge just as he made it to the bar. Pulling him by the shirt, he said, 'You're bang out of fucking order!'

'Doing what?' asked Sponge innocently. Pushing several less aggressive punters aside, he caught the barmaid's eye. 'Six pints of your strongest lager, please,' he requested.

'We only serve Carling here. Will that do?' she asked.

'Will it do? I'd drink piss if it could get me pissed!'

'What the fuck are you playing at?' Speedy ranted. 'You want to have us all picking up the soap in the showers in a couple of months' time? What's the idea telling somebody you're a copper then handing them a moody fifty-quid note?'

'I had to test the waters. It wasn't as though I handed her a mint-fresh fifty either. Besides, we're rich. Why can't we chill and spend some of that lovely dosh?'

'Listen, you fuckwit. Even if that fifty was as worn out as a rent-boy's ass, you could still have got us into trouble,' Speedy reproached him. 'Just slow down. Remember the agreement? "Nobody spends any money or leaves the job for the next six months."'

'Bollocks to our agreement. You seriously think I'm going to sit on all this money for six months and live like an eagle in a rabbit nest? I could be fucking dead tomorrow! Fuck the job! I'm only staying in it for as long as I think it's bloody necessary, not for as long as you say. We're even, Speedy. We're both very rich men.'

'OK, then, do what you like. But just remember you're part of a team, part of a culture. The team's welfare has always been first, so don't just think about yourself, think of us as well,' said Speedy.

Sponge leaned over to Speedy and said, 'You know, you're part of a dying breed, Speedy. I've never had the guts to say this to you, but you're a dinosaur, a square peg in a round hole. You're so old-fashioned, you'd parade in a cape and top hat it they let you. I'm from a different fucking generation where the only crime you can commit in this society today is to be poor. It's not about them and us any more, it's about rich and poor. You're rich now and every other fucker is poor, so enjoy it!'

'Listen, mate –' Speedy began before being cut short by the arrival of the drinks.

They picked up the glasses and made their way towards the others.

Sponge brought the car round to pick them up from the front of the club. The five others piled in and they began the journey back to London. Sponge still had a pint of beer in his hand and had problems changing gear, balancing his pint and driving at the same time. As they came into North London, the petrol tank gauge plunged into red and Sponge drove into the next petrol station.

'Where are you going?' Lionel asked sleepily.

'I've got no petrol in the tank,' Sponge said, stopping by a pump.

He got out and waited for the pump to be released, sipping from his pint. Nothing happened. Not sure whether the petrol station was open, he traipsed across the forecourt with his pint and peered into the shop. It was fully illuminated and at the counter before him sat a Bangladeshi assistant, fast asleep in his seat. Sponge tapped on the window with his key but got no response.

'Excuse me,' he shouted, knocking harder. 'Sorry to fucking disturb you, but I thought, since you were at work, you wouldn't mind me waking you up. Could you release the pump?'

The assistant stretched back in his seat, taking his time, then looked at Sponge with a blank expression, as though he had only just figured out the human form in front of him was a customer. He nodded at Sponge enquiringly. 'The fucking pump, please?' Sponge asked again, pointing at his car.

The assistant nodded in comprehension.

Sponge put three pounds' worth of petrol in the car, then went across to pay. The assistant was already asleep again. Sponge knocked on the glass partition, again waking him, and put a fifty-pound note through the wick. The assistant opened his till, then tossed the fifty-pound note back. 'No change,' he said.

Sponge walked across the forecourt to his car. He realized how difficult it was going to be to spend the money. He would have to get a different form of ID and open a bank account tomorrow. 'Has anybody got three quid?' he asked his colleagues. 'I've only got a fifty-pound note.'

'Why don't you put thirty quids' worth of petrol in the car? You always fucking do this,' said Speedy, dipping his hand into his pocket. He counted out four pounds and handed the money to Sponge. 'I'll have a Coke and a packet of salt and vinegar crisps as well.'

Sponge went back to the counter. This time the assistant was sitting up half-awake as Sponge tossed the coins into the wick. 'Packet of crisps and a Coke, please,' Sponge requested.

Peeved at having to get up, the assistant went to the cooling unit and picked up a large bottle of Coke.

'A can of fucking Coke,' Sponge shouted as loud as he could.

Unable to hear him, the assistant walked over to the crisps section and looked at him enquiringly. Sponge attempted to mime 'salt and vinegar', then, giving up, pointed out the packet he assumed would be the right one. The assistant returned and tossed the items on the counter.

'A can of Coke, I said, not a bottle,' Sponge said loudly.

The assistant walked back to the cooling unit, selected a can of Coke and returned.

'Are those salt and vinegar crisps?' Sponge asked.

'Cheese and onion,' the man replied.

'Well, I asked for a packet of salt and vinegar,' said Sponge as a look of exasperation broke over the assistant's face. He returned with a packet of salt and vinegar crisps and threw everything into the wick. Sponge took a final swig from his pint and tossed the glass away. Oblivious to the sound of it disintegrating on the concrete forecourt, he staggered back to his car with his purchases and off they went.

CHAPTER 5

After parade on Saturday morning, they assembled in the canteen. Slippery had left the duties as they had been on the last tour of duty, the same officers driving the same vehicles.

No calls had come over the radio so far and there was a languid atmosphere in the canteen. They had been out again the previous night and come straight to work from a nightclub in the West End.

Sponge got up and changed the television channel after a fruitless search for the remote control.

'What happened to those slags we nicked on nights?' Speedy asked Lionel.

'Charged them to attend Northwick magistrates' court,' Lionel replied. 'They're thieving fucking bastards, had it coming for ages. The only problem was catching them at it.'

'I know those two quite well,' said Saddam. 'The younger Evett brother is one of the best car thieves about. He can hot-wire a car wearing boxing gloves and shades.'

'Are we going for a drink tonight?' asked Jazz, changing the subject.

'I fucking hope so. Not at the Mason's Arms again; I can't afford another punch-up before the shift,' said Speedy.

'It was a bit manic,' agreed Jazz.

'The last time I was fucking hit like that was in Trafalgar Square during the poll-tax riots,' said Speedy.

'I saw it on telly; it was just before I joined,' said Sponge. 'It was like a fucking war zone.'

'Bloody war zone?' echoed Speedy. 'It was like fucking Father's Day in Brixton. Utter fucking chaos!'

'I was there,' said Lionel.

'I didn't know you had kids,' Bubba joked.

'No, you fuckwit, at the poll-tax riots,' said Lionel.

'We hadn't joined by then,' Jazz pointed out.

'I just turned up to chuck rocks at the Old Bill,' said Lionel. 'Before I joined, I couldn't stand the police.'

'Not much has changed,' said Speedy. He looked at his watch; they had been sitting in the canteen now for an hour and a half. 'We might as well go for a spin,' he said to Sponge, getting up.

'We might as well go ourselves,' Jazz said to Lionel.

'Do me a favour, I'm absolutely fucked,' said Lionel. 'Besides, I've got case papers to do.'

'If you stay in that canteen any longer, you'll have to change your postcode,' said Jazz.

'Piss off. I'm the only one on this team who ever nicks anyone. You all belong in the CID,' said Lionel.

'We all do our bit,' said Jazz remonstrating.

By 8 a.m. the whole team was in the canteen watching television. Slippery had come over to take back a cup of tea to the custody suite. It wasn't long before their personal radios started transmitting.

'Any unit available to deal? A noisy party, 26 Gresham Road,

NW12. Informant states his Nigerian neighbours are having a party; apparently it's been going on all night. He's asked them to turn it down once and does not wish to be known.'

Jazz took the call. 'We'll be off as soon as we finish our coffee,' he said to Lionel, putting his feet on the table.

'You get your kids on Friday, don't you, sarge? Did you do anything interesting yesterday?' Lionel asked, turning to Slippery.

'I went to pick up my eleven-year-old from school and he was stood outside snogging our next-door neighbour's daughter,' said Slippery.

'What did you say?' asked Jazz.

'Go on, son!'

'What would you have done if it was some boy snogging your daughter?'

'I'd kill the little bastard,' said Slippery with feeling. 'It's different when it's your daughter, isn't it? You don't want some boy's paws over your little girl.'

'How did you get on with that bird from the Mason's Arms the other night?' Bubba asked Jazz.

'OK. I'll be seeing her when we come off nights next week, as it goes,' Jazz replied.

'Must be a fucking relief to get picked out from a group of blokes by a white lass and not be standing behind tinted glass in an ID parade for an IC3, eh?' said Speedy jocularly.

'I fancy getting a few hours' sleep in today,' said Bubba, changing the subject. 'My kids wouldn't let me sleep this morning.'

'We might as well go out,' said Jazz.

None of them had moved, however, when the inspector walked into the canteen. 'Are you blokes going to do any work?' he asked. 'Get them to do some work, sergeant.'

Slippery automatically shifted into supervisor mode. 'Right, lads, let's have you out!'

'See you at the lock-ups,' Speedy muttered to Bubba as they left.

No. 26 Gresham Road, NW12, was a small semi-detached house in the northern section of the division, an affluent pocket that interfaced abruptly with the Prado Village estate.

As the Irv pulled into Gresham Road, the sound of music drifted towards them. The road was choked with double-parked vehicles, making it difficult to manoeuvre. Outside the house, groups of people chatted loudly as music blasted from the open door and out into the street.

'It's been going on all night and they're still enjoying themselves,' said Lionel jealously.

Jazz double-parked. As they got out of the car, the conversing groups stopped momentarily then continued as Jazz and Lionel walked past.

'What are they saying?' Lionel asked Jazz.

'How the fuck should I know? They're speaking Nigerian, I'm Jamaican.'

'Same thing, isn't it?'

They entered the house without bothering to wait and ask for the host at the door. The music was louder now; Lionel and Jazz nodded rhythmically to the beat as they made their way to the kitchen. Suddenly, a well-dressed black woman appeared in the passageway. 'Anything I can do for you officers?' she enquired.

'Are you the owner of the house?' Jazz asked.

'Yes I am. Is there a problem, officer?'

'We were called by your neighbours complaining about the noise, so we thought we'd join in,' said Jazz.

'We just came in to ask you to keep the noise down a bit,' Lionel said.

'Well, this is the only party I've ever had here, and I told all my neighbours. I even bought them chocolates,' she protested.

'I understand. Well, our intention isn't to break up other people's fun,' responded Jazz.

'Well, seeing as you're here now, officers, do you fancy a drink?' she said.

They hesitated momentarily before accepting the offer. 'I suppose so,' said Lionel. 'I'll have a can of lager, if you don't mind.'

'I'll have the same,' said Jazz.

The host returned with two cans of lager, handed one to each of them, ushered them into the kitchen and invited them to help themselves to food. 'So what are your names?' she asked them.

'I'm called Lionel and he's called Jazz. Don't ask why,' said Lionel.

They chatted in the kitchen until the woman's sister came in. 'Annie, wetin you de do?' she asked. She looked bewildered at seeing her sister chatting and laughing with two uniformed police officers.

'Come over here,' Annie beckoned her sister. 'This is my sister Shola,' she said. 'This is Lionel and this is Jazz.'

Lionel stared at her, bewitched by her beauty and shape. He looked up and down her body as she nodded acknowledgement at them. They were still chatting to Annie and Shola when the controller called up, curious to know whether they were encountering any difficulties.

'Excuse me,' said Lionel, in mid flow to Shola. '*Go ahead, over.*'

'*Is everything all right over there?*' the controller enquired.

'*Yes, yes, sarge. Just giving advice to the celebrant. We should be finishing shortly.*'

They rounded off their conversation and left with four cans of lager, which they put into the back of the car. Jazz belched. 'So did you get her telephone number?' he asked, fumbling about trying to put the key in the ignition.

'I gave her my home number and asked her to call me. She's a cracker! Absolutely gorgeous!' Lionel exclaimed.

'Exactly! What would she do with you?' replied Jazz.

'I'm the one with the charm. I know all there is to know about birds,' said Lionel boastfully.

'Says the bloke who thinks cunnilingus is an Irish airline,' replied Jazz as he started up the car.

'Are you sure you're OK to drive?' Lionel asked.

'I only had three,' said Jazz, pulling off.

Speedy was asleep at the wheel of the area car parked at the bottom of a group of secluded lock-up garages. Next to the area car were the van and the Irv. Sponge, the operator, could not sleep and Rigsby sat quietly in the back of the car, not daring to ask why they were spending the greater part of the shift there. He and Sponge listened to the main set as Scotland Yard issued calls to units on other divisions.

'All these calls going out on Stoke Newington's and Holloway's ground and there's fuck all happening here,' said Sponge. 'It's far too quiet on this division; I might transfer one of these days.'

'Shut the fuck up, will you? And turn down that main set, it's too fucking loud. I'm trying to get some sleep,' muttered Speedy.

Sponge sat there, idly poking at the controls of the main set. He picked up the mouthpiece and pressed the transmission button. '*I'm bored!*' he announced.

There was no answer. The sombre voice of the Scotland Yard controller continued to issue calls to the response vehicles of the various divisions.

'A bit of trivia,' Sponge said lethargically.

'What?' asked Speedy.

'What's got sixteen balls and fucks rabbits?'

'No idea.'

'A shotgun.'

'Very funny. Now shut up, will you?' said Speedy.

Sponge sat there for a while looking into the sky. Still restless, he squirmed about in his seat to get into the most comfortable position. 'Can I ask you a personal question?' he asked suddenly.

'What?' said Speedy petulantly.

'I mean a real personal question.'

'Fucking what?' said Speedy, exasperated.

'Have you ever had sex with a pig?'

'No, I haven't,' said Speedy, heaving a great sigh.

'You should try it. It's a right squeal,' said Sponge, shifting around in his seat again.

'Gordon Bennett,' exclaimed Speedy. 'Fucking sit still, will you?'

Sponge remained still for a while, then began to fiddle with the vehicle controls.

'I'm bored,' he transmitted a few minutes later on the main set.

'I hope no one recognizes your voice,' said Speedy with his eyes closed.

'All cars channel two, all cars channel 2. Would all units please stick to correct radio procedure? MP out,' the Yard controller transmitted.

Two minutes later Sponge picked up the mouthpiece. *'I'm bored!'* he transmitted again.

'Would the unit that made that transmission give his call sign, please?' the Yard controller asked in vexation.

Sponge picked up the mouthpiece again. *'I said I was bored, not fucking stupid,'* he transmitted.

Bubba and Sonia sat in the van behind the lock-up garages, parked beside the area car and the Irv.

'Why are we parked here?' Sonia asked.

'This is where we come for a kip when we're on nights or we haven't had any sleep the night before early turn. We were on the razz last night,' said Bubba, adjusting his position. 'Earlies are normally quiet anyway.'

Sponge's voice came over the main set. *'I'm bored!'*

'That's Sponge,' said Bubba, recognizing his voice.

'I find him really immature,' exclaimed Sonia.

'Well, even a black sheep has warm wool,' replied Bubba. 'When you get to know him well, you realize he's harmless.'

Sonia said no more and looked out of the van window, realizing she might have said too much.

'So, are you married?' he asked her.

'No,' she replied.

'Got a bloke?'

'No,' she said. 'I went out with a copper when I was at training school and it turned out to be utter grief. I think I'm better off on my own for the meantime.'

'You must fancy one of us,' said Bubba.

'No, I don't, actually.'

'What, eight blokes and you don't fancy even one?' asked Bubba in disbelief.

'Do I have to?'

Bubba thought about it and decided not to answer.

'Are you married?' Sonia asked.

'Got two boys and a wife who's doing my fucking box in at the moment.'

CHAPTER 6

'We'll leave the duties as they've been,' said Slippery as they sat in the team office early on Sunday morning. 'Same vehicles as yesterday.'

'Can't we change it around a bit, sarge? I'm fucking sick of driving that coffin,' Bubba protested.

'In that case, you and Doris in the Irv,' Slippery said, nodding at Sonia. 'Lionel and Jazz, take out the van.'

'Sounds fair,' Bubba agreed.

'Jump in the area car with Speedy,' Slippery said to Rigsby. He concluded parade and made for the canteen.

The area car zoomed into the yard in time to catch Bubba entering the canteen with the biscuits. They settled in front of the television to watch an early-morning film on Sky.

'Which one of us is driving the van?' Jazz asked Lionel.

'Pass us a breathalyser,' said Lionel. 'The least pissed of us will drive.'

They both took turns to blow. 'Two seconds longer for a red light. You lose,' Lionel said, handing the alcoholometer back to Jazz.

Their radios crackled into life moments later. '*All units November X-ray, in front of the G-Spot Nightclub, seven to eight males fighting, one male unconscious.*'

The canteen was suddenly filled with the sound of chairs

scratching the linoleum floor. All the officers hustled to gather their things while trying to assign themselves to the call on their personal radios. The entire run to Watford took eight minutes, the sirens left on until the last moment in the hope of dispersing any fighting before they appeared. They arrived to meet a crowd loitering on both sides of the road. There was no broil, no disorder and no argument, just people hovering about.

One man, bleeding from the head, was being propped up by his confederates outside a fish and chip shop. Speedy accosted the man, whose shirt was blood-soaked, bereft of buttons and torn around the collar. He had swollen lips and a bruised eye but, as he saw Speedy, he slipped into the middle of the group.

'Cunt,' one of the youths called out to Speedy as he followed the apparent victim. Speedy stopped and looked at him, not believing what he had just heard. 'Stable,' the man added, as if as an afterthought.

'What did you just call me?' Speedy asked.

'Cunt . . . stable. That's your rank, isn't it?' the man repeated, drawing out the syllables.

'Any of you overstep your bounds and I'll have some drama for you,' Speedy warned. 'What's happened to you then, mate?' he asked the bleeding man.

'I fell over on the pavement,' the man replied in a slurred voice.

'It looks to me like somebody hit you with a fucking pavement,' replied Speedy.

'He's told you the truth. Why don't you fuck off and leave us alone?' said one of his friends.

'Shouldn't you be in bed? Do your fucking parents know you're out this late?' Speedy asked, turning to him.

'I should be, but your wife said she couldn't make it round to mine tonight,' he replied. His companions joined him in a chorus of laughter.

'A fucking comedian! Mind you, to go through life looking as ugly as you do, no wonder you've got such a good sense of humour,' Speedy mocked. 'If my dog had a face like yours, I'd cover it, shave its arse and make it walk backwards.'

Other officers from the next division arrived and joined the group. Bubba turned to explain the situation. 'Thanks for coming, lads, but this is one load of bollocks!'

The Broadway was alive with spectators and pedestrians.

'Come on, we'd better get out of here before something happens or someone says something,' urged Bubba.

He spoke into his personal radio. '*This call is sosno, over.*'

'*Yeah, received, I'll mark it up as no trace of a disturbance, over,*' replied the controller.

'What does sosno mean?' Sonia asked Bubba.

'Scum on scum no offence,' he replied.

They sat in the canteen. Bubba had made the coffees and teas and they settled in to watch an afternoon film. Lionel remembered he had to make a phone call to the girl he had met at the noisy party the day before. He took out his pocket book, flipped through the pages and, having found her number, walked over to the CID office carrying his cup of coffee, settled at a desk close to the wall and clipped his personal radio to its lowest volume. Putting his feet up on the desk, he settled the telephone on his lap and picked up the receiver to dial the number.

Suddenly he remembered he had left his pocket book on the canteen table. Realizing how costly his mistake could be, he rushed back to the canteen and went straight over to where he had left it. It still sat there but the last two pages were no longer empty. A sketch of a large penis, two testicles and pubic hair had been drawn in black ink across them. 'Cheers, lads! I just hope I don't have to produce this in court,' he said.

'You shouldn't leave it lying around,' replied Sponge.

Lionel put the book back into his pocket and returned to the CID office.

Without warning, their personal radios were activated. *'All units, November X-ray! Believed involved in a robbery within the last ten minutes is an IC3 half-caste male, five foot ten, wearing a black bomber jacket and dark jeans, last seen heading along the Northwick Road towards the crossroads,'* the controller said.

It took one hundred and twenty seconds to get to the crossroads. As they turned down Northwick Road, they stopped beside the area car, which was parked on the opposite side of the road.

Speedy wound down his window and, dragging from his cigarette, looked insouciantly at Lionel. Sponge sat next to Speedy looking bored.

'Have you done the Road?' Lionel asked Speedy.

Speedy nodded. 'No trace,' he said. 'We'll try the bus stop, you try the tube station.'

Lionel put on his blue lights, turned round and drove to

the tube station. He turned into the forecourt and drove slowly past the people going in and out of the station. 'What's the description again?' he asked Jazz.

'IC3, half-caste male, five foot ten, wearing a dark bomber jacket and trousers,' Jazz answered.

'That's fucking helpful, you all look alike to me,' Lionel said sarcastically. He crawled towards the station lobby, drew level with the entrance, switched off the engine and watched.

A short while later, a black man, about five feet six inches tall, wearing a baseball cap, a green bomber jacket and black jeans, emerged on to the walkway, looked around and then turned back into the lobby.

'He looks a likely candidate,' said Lionel.

'He's a bit too short for the description,' replied Jazz. 'And he's not fucking half-caste.'

'What's the matter with you? You act as though every black guy we come across is your fucking brother. How accurate do you want the description to be? Do you need his fucking shoe size as well?'

'No! Sometimes I just think that you guys are a bit fucking arbitrary in the way you stop blacks.'

'You trying to say I'm racist?' asked Lionel. 'Bearing in mind I only go out with black women, which is more than I can say for you.'

'Did I say that?' replied Jazz. 'Besides, just because you go out with black women doesn't mean you can't be fucking racist.'

'So now I'm a fucking racist?'

'I'm just fucking saying that I don't think he matches the

description, and you can't tell the bloody difference,' Jazz argued.

'And that's my fault, is it?' asked Lionel.

'It's just sometimes I get caught in the middle. Black people look for me to speak up for them, and you guys look for me to take your side,' Jazz remonstrated.

'And whose side are you on?'

'I have to rely on you blokes. I don't have much fucking choice, do I?'

'Look at him,' said Lionel as the man appeared again. 'Why is he acting so furtively? Right now he's looking about as shifty as a boy scout buggering a guide dog!'

'He might be waiting for someone,' suggested Jazz.

'How many people here fit the fucking description? This bloke wants his collar felt!'

Jazz ignored Lionel and leant back in his seat.

'Can units meet me at the tube station? There's one here that fits the description,' said Lionel on his personal radio.

'247, are you saying you have the suspect in sight?' the controller asked.

'Someone who fits the description,' Lionel answered.

'Can units make their way to the tube station? Lionel's just spotted the suspect,' the controller concluded.

Lionel opened the door of the van. 'I think we'd better go and have a word, don't you?' he said.

Reluctantly, Jazz followed. They walked slowly over to the lobby but there was no sign of the man.

'He must be on the platform,' deduced Lionel. He started for the closest platform, mounted the steps and reached the top. It was an open-air station, so they could see all the platforms.

The man was standing with his back to them on the middle platform. Feeling he was being watched, he suddenly turned round. He looked uneasy and made towards the steps, disappearing down the stairwell. They started in pursuit.

The passages were linked; this meant he would have to pass them in order to leave the station. He was fifteen yards from them by the time they descended the stairs into the passage. He stared intently at them for a short while, then looked away and continued walking towards them. Beneath the bomber jacket he was wearing a black string vest; he moved with a rhythmic gait, leaning back slightly. They waited for him to approach, made cautious by his confident air.

When he was within arm's reach, Lionel spoke. 'I want a word with you, sunshine.'

The man ignored Lionel, walked past and then turned round.

'Well, I ain't got nothing to say to you.'

Before he could take many more paces, Bubba, Sponge and Speedy appeared by the ticket office, trapping him between themselves and Jazz and Lionel. The two probationers had been ordered by Speedy to stand aside and watch the team in action. Realizing he was outnumbered, the man slowed his pace, then resignedly approached the ticket office. He stopped in front of them and raised his arms. 'What?' he shouted.

The three stood silently, waiting for Jazz and Lionel to

arrive. The man was shepherded to the entrance where Lionel proceeded to question him. 'Where have you come from, mate?' Lionel asked.

'Fuck you! Me no answer no Babylon-man questions,' the man exclaimed in a West Indian accent.

'Don't raise your voice at me,' replied Lionel.

'White boys think you can stop us black people for nothing and distress us anyhow, innit?' the man said loudly.

A crowd was starting to gather, drawn by curiosity and amusement. Seeing that a racial dimension had developed and feeling compelled to intervene and neutralize the situation, Jazz stepped forward. 'Calm down,' he said soothingly.

'Wat's your facking problem? Facking Judas! You follow them, man, harass up black men on the street! You facking bounty! Tink you'se white ... char?' the man shouted angrily before kissing his teeth in an expression of supreme defiance and disgust.

'He doesn't like you, does he?' said Sponge.

'Just answer our questions, mate, and you'll be on your way,' enjoined Lionel.

'What do you want then?' asked the man curiously.

'Where have you come from and where are you going?' Lionel asked.

'Free facking country, innit? Besides, you feel you've got enough, facking nick me!'

'Are you going to be civil or not?' Lionel asked, getting impatient.

The controller called up. '*Can I have a sit-rep?*' he asked.

'*Yeah. It's all under control at the moment. We've got one stopped and sufficient on scene. If you've got any further information, we'd be obliged; if not, it looks like he's going to be coming in anyway. He's failed the attitude test,'* Lionel said.

'Yeah, received nothing, still trying to contact the informant. No luck at the moment, over,' the controller replied.

The situation was becoming rather heated.

'Listen, star! You lot better just facking nick me and stop wasting my time, you get me?'

'That's a bit of a contradiction in terms,' said Sponge. 'Stop wasting my time and nick me?'

'I don't business! I'm always getting facking stopped by you lot, know what I mean? I ain't taking this shit no more!' he protested loudly, addressing the crowd rather than the officers beside him.

'I don't think we're going to get anywhere with him. Lift him! We'll sort it out when we get back to the factory,' Speedy muttered to Lionel.

Conceding the point, Lionel moved forward to touch the man's elbow. 'Come over here, mate,' he coaxed.

In vexation, the man flung his elbow away. 'Don't touch me,' he screamed.

Lionel and the others closed in. Sensing he was about to be grabbed, the man stepped back quickly.

Lionel followed. He increased his pace until he was within reach of the man, then extended his arm and grabbed the seam of the man's bomber jacket to prevent him from moving back again. The man took a step forward, then, his left hand clenched in a fist, threw a punch. Lionel skipped back in a belated attempt to parry the blow. The man's fist connected with his temple.

The others sallied forward. The man turned and ran, sidestepping right and then left in order to throw off his pursuers. He took a sharp turn to the left towards the main road.

Anticipating this, Lionel ran transversely away from the pursuing officers and their quarry. As he ran, he tried to extricate his baton. All of a sudden, he was between the man and his best route of escape on to the High Road. His baton was in his hand and the man was within striking distance. Lionel needed more time and space to think! He never got it. He took three skips back and swung his baton. With no time to dodge the blow, the man received the full force of the baton on his cranium.

The man staggered back, then charged forward again. The distance was so short Lionel had no time to strike a second time. He grabbed hold of the man and wrestled him to the ground.

'Get the fuck off me! Get the fuck off me!' the man screamed. The others had caught up with them and piled on top. He tucked his arms underneath his torso, abandoning his escape attempt for active resistance and disobligation.

'Grab hold of his arms,' instructed Speedy from within the mêlée.

'I can't get at them,' shouted Sponge.

'Give us your quick-cuffs,' Speedy said.

Beneath the confusion of bodies came a weak voice. 'I ain't done nothing! I ain't done nothing! Get the fuck off me!'

Bubba grabbed hold of one of the man's legs and knelt on it while Jazz grabbed the other. Sponge pinioned his left shoulder while Speedy took the right. In doing so, they leant so far inwards that their shoulders almost touched. The man moaned under the pressure of the bodies on top of him as Sponge and Speedy wrenched at his arms, which he'd linked underneath himself. Suddenly succumbing to the strain, he released them. They pushed his hands together in an attempt to manacle his wrists.

'Cuff him!' Lionel shouted from within the scrum.

Bubba let go of the man's leg and stepped over them all.

'What the fuck do you think we're trying to do? Bugger him?' said Speedy.

Bubba guided his quick-cuffs on to the nearest available wrist.

'You've put the bloody cuffs on me, you fuckwit!' exclaimed Lionel.

'Someone else use theirs,' Speedy suggested.

The man started to hurl rabid insults.

'Calm down, mate,' Sponge coaxed.

Jazz handed his handcuffs to Speedy. It did not take long to place the handcuffs on the exhausted man and secure his wrists.

The radio buzzed as the controller tried frantically to get in contact with the officers. '*Units down there, is everything OK?*' he asked.

'*Yes, yes,*' Lionel answered. '*We've got one detained, can you inform custody we've got one coming in?*'

'*We haven't been able to trace the informant who we think is the victim. Apparently a male phoned through to the Yard on a mobile phone. We've tried to phone him back but his phone is switched off. We'll keep trying. At the moment, that's all the information we have.*'

'Fucking great,' Lionel muttered to himself.

A formidable number of spectators were watching.

'We'll take him in anyway. After this spectacle, we can't just uncuff him and tell him he can go home. He can come in for assault on police and public disorder,' Speedy calculated.

'Excuse me,' somebody said, tapping Speedy on the shoulder.

'Yes, mate,' Speedy answered.

'I know you're busy, officer, but can you tell me which line I could take to get to Tottenham Court Road?' the man asked.

'You fucking what?' Speedy asked in disbelief.

'How to get –'

'I fucking heard you the first time. If you don't piss off, I'll nick you! Do I look like I work for the fucking tourist board?' threatened Speedy. 'Let's get the fuck out of here,' he said to the others.

They grabbed hold of one limb each and carried the suspect to the van.

CHAPTER 7

The prisoner was still hurling abuse as he was escorted into the custody suite. Slippery, the custody sergeant, was playing solitaire on the computer as they entered. He did not bother looking up as they came in.

'Sit down,' Lionel said, pushing the prisoner on to the long bench in front of the desk.

'Can you take these cuffs off, mate? They hurt!' the man asked.

'In a minute, mate, when the custody sergeant says we can,' answered Lionel.

'I'll just go and move the van, it's blocking the yard,' Jazz said to Lionel.

'I'll go out and speak to the CAD room, see if they've got more information,' said Speedy.

Everybody remained stationary, waiting for Slippery to finish his game.

'Can somebody take these cuffs off me, please?' the man asked again.

Without looking up, Slippery pointed at him. 'Take the cuffs off him,' he ordered.

Lionel took the cuffs off.

'I've got a splitting headache. Can I have some aspirin or something?' the prisoner asked, holding his head.

'We'll sort that out in a minute, one thing at a time,' Lionel promised.

'Right!' said Slippery, switching off his game. 'What have you got here?'

'He's been nicked, sarge,' answered Lionel.

'Obviously,' said Slippery. 'What for?'

'I'll speak to you about that in a minute,' Lionel replied.

Slippery let out a sigh and turned to the prisoner. 'Cell number two,' he said to Lionel.

'I've got a headache. Hit my head pretty hard, you know,' the man said.

'Had a smoke? You IC3s smoke cannabis more than you breathe in,' said Slippery. 'Bin him. Number two. I want to get on with my game.'

'Come on, mate,' Lionel said.

Sponge and Bubba moved in to help shepherd the man towards the cells.

'Can I have a doctor or something for my headache?'

'I'll see what I can do for you, mate,' said Lionel.

As Lionel came back, the phone rang. Slippery ignored it, leaving Lionel to deal with the call. It was Speedy. 'Have you done a name check?' Lionel asked.

'Yeah. He's quite an active slag, your bloke. He isn't wanted but he's got plenty of form,' Speedy said. 'It looks like we're going to charge him with affray and assault on police and bail him on suspicion of robbery until we can speak to the informant.'

'I'll tell the skipper that,' replied Lionel.

*

They were sitting in the canteen writing up their notes. 'Right, where are you?' Lionel asked Jazz.

'I'm at the point where you asked him where he was coming from,' replied Jazz.

'Right, we'll put in the old lady in the red dress who was walking past at that point,' said Lionel. 'I asked him, "What's your name, sir?"' he continued at dictating speed while the others wrote. 'He replied, "Fuck off, you white wanker!" The old lady looked visibly shocked and shaken by his use of such language!'

He waited for them to stop writing. 'I said, "Now, there is no need to use such language, you could get arrested and appear before the magistrates for it." He replied, "Fuck you, and the magistrates couldn't pass wind let alone pass a sentence."'

'Hang on, slow down, will you? We've got to catch up with you,' complained Sponge.

'Where are you now?' asked Lionel.

'How do you spell magistrate?' asked Saddam.

Sponge held out his notebook for Saddam to copy.

'Right, is everybody up to where I just stopped?' asked Lionel. From the silence he inferred the affirmative.

Suddenly the canteen intercom blared out. '*Lionel!*' It was Slippery.

'Yes, sarge,' he called across the canteen.

'*Get over here, will you? And somebody call an ambulance, I can't rouse your prisoner.*'

Within seconds, they were all in the custody office. 'What's the matter?' Lionel shouted as they piled in.

There was nobody there to answer his question. He

looked up the passage to the cells. The door of cell two was open and the custody sergeant was slouched over the prisoner as he lay in an ungainly heap on the concrete slab, apparently unconscious.

'Call an ambulance,' Lionel said to Sponge. 'Is he breathing?' he asked Slippery, peering over his shoulder.

'I don't think so. Who's been on a first-aid course among you lot? One of you is going to have to give him mouth to mouth,' Slippery said.

'He is breathing,' Lionel observed.

'Keep an eye on him. I'm going to have to get hold of the duty officer,' Slippery said.

'He's really going to know what to fucking do,' Jazz said sarcastically. 'He couldn't pull a greasy stick out of a dead dog's arse!'

'I've got a bad feeling about this,' said Speedy.

They placed the man in the recovery position and stood silently looking at him.

'I'll go outside and wait for the LAS. An ambulance should be here soon,' said Lionel.

The ambulance pulled up in front of the police station five minutes later. Lionel ran over. 'We've got a prisoner who's lost consciousness in the cells,' he gabbled.

'How long ago?' the operator asked.

'About ten minutes.'

'What happened before he lost consciousness? Does he have a medical condition?'

'Nothing . . . Hang on,' Lionel mused, 'he did complain of a headache.'

'Why did he complain?' asked the operator.

'I hit him on the head with a baton.' Lionel ushered them into the custody suite. 'The LAS are here, sarge,' he called out.

The medical staff of Newpark General Hospital stood in the bay area and awaited their arrival. The ambulance crew carried the patient out of the ambulance and wheeled him into casualty before apprising the casualty officer of the man's medical condition.

As the casualty crew entered the examination area, the doctor turned to Lionel and the others. 'I'm afraid I'm going to have to ask you to wait here; you can't come any further,' she said.

'But he's still under arrest,' complained Speedy.

'He's hardly going to run away in his condition,' she snapped.

They obeyed her and watched in silent contemplation as he was carted round the corner out of sight. A nurse came up to them. 'You can stay in the staff room if you want,' she said, a warm expression on her face.

'Thanks,' replied Sponge. 'We're going to have to wait around here a while until we find out what's happening.'

The nurse nodded and walked away.

'Think she fancies me? Reckon I could get in there?' asked Sponge, looking after her.

'Sponge, mate, there are two certainties in life: death and shagging a nurse,' replied Speedy.

'We might as well finish our IRBs. Did anybody finish theirs?' Lionel asked.

There was a silence.

*

It took them twenty minutes to complete their Incident Report Books. The controller had phoned to inform them that the duty officer had been found asleep in his office and was on his way to the hospital. He had instructed that they should return to the station, leaving two officers behind to look after the prisoner. Unsurprisingly, that duty fell to the two probationers.

It was while they were back at the police station making themselves a cup of tea that the phone rang and the controller gave them the news. The man was in a coma and had been transferred to intensive care, his chances of survival slim.

This was looking ominously like a death in custody: a young black male arrested by police and dying while in their care. The negative publicity was the last thing needed in a racially diverse division such as theirs.

Lionel called Slippery straight away.

'I'll have to get hold of night duty CID. We're going to have to cover ourselves from now on,' said Slippery.

'I don't know, Jazz. Information is scant. Apparently he's in intensive care, something to do with a suspected blood clot in the brain,' said Lionel as he meandered the streets in the van for the last hour of the shift.

'Has the duty officer turned up yet?' Jazz asked.

'He turned up, spent five minutes trying to chat up some nurse, got blown out and fucked off. At the moment the probbies are on their own.'

'Well, if what you're looking for is sympathy, I did warn you before you stopped the bloke,' Jazz said.

'We had the grounds, didn't we?' asked Lionel.

'Not really. The bloke we were looking for was half-caste,' replied Jazz.

'What's the bloody difference? Still fucking black, isn't it?' said Lionel.

'A half-caste is creamy-skinned; the bloke we stopped was so fucking dark he'd leave fingerprints on charcoal,' replied Jazz.

'Don't fucking start, Jazz. Sometimes I wonder whose side you're on,' said Lionel.

CHAPTER 8

After what had happened at the nightclub, Sponge had become a concern. Because the entire team had been around for the past few days, everybody had continued as normal. Monday was a rest day, so Speedy took the opportunity to make a few phone calls to arrange a meeting at the Mason's Arms at 3.30 p.m. He left Bubba and Jazz out of his earlier considerations but later phoned to invite them there at 5 p.m.

Sponge had woken up early to go to the West End for some shopping and spent much of the day in expensive designer shops, from Bond Street to Mayfair. By the time he'd finished, he'd made so many purchases that he had to hail a black cab to get home. He had a shower, changed, then left for the pub. When he arrived, much later than the others, they could not contain the shock of seeing him clad in designer clothing still fresh out of its wrappings. He ordered some drinks and the moment he sat down Speedy began to chastise him.

'What the hell are you doing?' he fumed.

'You know, you should mind the way you talk to me, Speedy. You're not in charge any more. This ship runs itself now,' Sponge replied.

'You look like a fucking pimp, not a policeman.' Speedy glanced around for support.

'He's right, you know,' said Saddam quietly.

Speedy looked at Sponge, happy at the backing he believed he had just received.

'We're not at work now, Speedy,' Saddam continued. 'You can't tell him what to do with his money. As long as he doesn't do anything stupid, he's quite entitled to do a bit of shopping.'

Speedy regarded Saddam in surprise and shock at the mutiny being threatened. 'How can you fucking say that when he can sink the whole fucking lot of us at the same time? Coppers can't afford the type of luxuries and clothes Sponge has got on.'

'So I'm supposed to wear the type of clothes you've got?' Sponge asked.

'What's that supposed to mean?'

'You wouldn't be allowed on a fucking building site wearing half the fucking clothes you go out in,' said Sponge.

'You fucking watch your mouth, pal,' said Speedy, getting up.

'I just think you should relax,' said Saddam. 'He's a single bloke who's come across a bit of money and wants to spend some of it on clothes and a few other things. After all, you've been drinking the beer he's bought without complaining.'

Speedy sat back down again.

Lionel sat quietly and ignored them until Jazz arrived. 'How long have you lot been here then?' Jazz asked, surprised to see that they were already drunk.

'Not long,' answered Speedy. 'What you having?'

'Fosters, please,' replied Jazz.

*

Bubba had decided not to go to the pub after all. He was confused and bewildered by the temptation that was overcoming him. It would pay him to take the money. Make one clean break away from the job and the team. He could barely sleep at night with the torment whirling around in his head. Needing to be alone with his thoughts, he went to the nearest underground station and sat on a train. When he wanted to think, the tube was the best place to do it. He would travel up and down the Jubilee line lost in thought until the rattling of the train sent him to sleep.

He woke up at Green Park and looked around the carriage at the other passengers. During this fleeting moment of consciousness, he glanced down at a commuter's dog. The dog stared back sympathetically as though it could read Bubba's thoughts. If only he could speak to somebody and find out what they would do if they were in his shoes. He would have to make this decision on his own, he thought, as he drifted back to sleep and the train juddered towards Charing Cross.

Tuesday was another rest day. Lionel had a date with Shola, the Nigerian girl he had met at the noisy party. She worked as assistant manager of a bank in Golders Green. They arranged to meet outside the McDonald's nearby at 5 p.m. and he planned to take her for a meal in one of the restaurants that lined Golders Green Road.

Sponge was worrying him. Just like the fool he was, he was starting to spend money impetuously. The team was inevitably going to fall apart now they had exercised the option to take the money. They were sailing uncharted waters and the composition of his crew frightened him. It was only a question of time. If he was ever going to participate in this scam, he had better do so now rather than later.

He arrived at Golders Green early and spent ten minutes looking for a parking space. He walked into a newsagent's and, in order to look intelligent, broke with his normal tradition of the *Sun* and bought a copy of *The Times*. He hung around, idly window-shopping, then ambled towards their rendezvous. He was pleasantly surprised to see she was already there. Dressed in a formal but trendy black skirt with a white blouse underneath a black jacket, she looked very pretty. He was still undecided as to whether he was going to kiss her on the lips or on the cheek.

She turned, saw him and smiled nervously. 'Hello,' she said warmly, extending her arms for an embrace.

He moved towards her and kissed her on the cheek as she offered her face sideways. He looked down at her. She was every bit as beautiful as when he had first seen her. He might only have kissed her on the cheek, but it was a start. He grabbed her by the hand. 'Where shall we go?' he asked excitedly.

'I don't know. You're the one who asked me out on a date. What did you have in mind?'

'I just wanted to get you on your own and spend some time with you. Let me know how long I've got you for and then I'll decide.'

'That sounds ominous. My sister told me to be very wary of policemen,' she replied.

'If you can't trust us, you can't trust anybody,' he said.

'Well, where are we going then?'

'There's a nice Italian restaurant up Golders Green Road. Let's go for a meal and then we can take in a movie afterwards.'

'That sounds good.'

At the very same time that Lionel was enjoying the company of his recent acquaintance and the sumptuousness of a three-course meal, Saddam and Sponge were sitting in Saddam's living room in front of the television, deep in conversation. Empty six-pack cans of beer lay on the centre table.

Saddam flipped through the channels with the remote control.

'Put it back on one, I'm watching something,' his wife said, putting her head round the door from the kitchen.

'How can you be watching the fucking television from another room?' Sponge shouted back. He grabbed the remote control and switched the television back to BBC 1 again. 'I reckon there's got to be at least ten kilos, whatever it is,' he said, resuming their conversation.

'Yeah, that's the point. We don't know what it is,' replied Saddam.

'It's either coke or heroin. Whichever it is, we'll be able to flog it for a decent enough amount and fuck off out of the job. Speedy's beginning to do my fucking box,' said Sponge.

'The biggest problem is who we flog the gear to. We don't know anybody. I don't even know how to start putting feelers out without attracting suspicion,' complained Saddam.

'In that case, let's sit tight on the gear. I'm sure in the next few weeks something's going to come up,' said Sponge. 'In the meantime, I can't resist the fucking urge to get myself a few more things.'

'Yeah,' said Saddam, 'I've been thinking of buying my missus a few presents.'

'What you thinking of getting her?' Sponge asked.

'I don't know. She's a bit fussy, you know how women are?'

'You must have something in mind,' said Sponge. 'What about a watch?'

'She doesn't need a fucking watch, there's a clock on the fucking cooker,' replied Saddam. 'Besides, as I said, she can be really fucking choosy.'

'Then buy her a watch and a vibrator and if she doesn't like the watch she can go fuck herself,' said Sponge.

'You know Speedy's going to throw his toys out of the fucking cot if he finds out?' said Saddam.

'Fuck Speedy,' shouted Sponge. 'That arsewipe is beginning to get on my fucking tits. Who is he to tell us fucking what to do? I do what I like! And once we flog this gear, I hope I don't see his bollocks again. I've been working with the bloke for the past few years and I'm only just beginning to realize how fucking sad he is.'

'He says he only wants what's best for the team,' reasoned Saddam.

'He only wants what is best to secure his pension, so he can go back to Scotland, wear a kilt and sit around with other E. coli-infected, whisky-drinking Jocks. Well, I'm going to get paid,' said Sponge cynically. 'Where are my fucking fags?' he asked, routing through magazines beside him.

'You haven't got any,' said Saddam.

Sponge stopped and looked at Saddam enquiringly.

'You don't smoke,' Saddam explained. 'Well, not cigarettes.'

Sponge hesitated for a minute, thinking about it. 'Oh yeah, I forgot,' he said. 'I've had a few to drink.'

'You've been having a bit too much to drink over the last few days and started forgetting things.'

'Spare me the fucking lecture,' said Sponge. 'I think I'm going to take up smoking after all. Pass me your fags.'

Lionel dropped Shola outside her flat in Hampstead; he had thought she lived at the house where they had attended the call.

I'm going to have to act the perfect gentleman and not try to get into her knickers tonight, he'd thought to himself as they sat there talking. It had therefore come as something of a surprise when she invited him in for a coffee. He had pretended to waver, not sure whether it was appropriate, but she had seen straight through him and told him there was no need for that. That was what he liked about her: she was so perspicacious. She saw through all his blusterings and exaggerations and she fell for nothing. Eventually he gave up and just stuck to telling her the bare truth.

He sat on the couch politely waiting and listening to the all-familiar sound of the kettle bubbling as she rummaged around in the kitchen. He was inspecting her CD collection when she returned with the coffees. He sat himself back on the sofa beside her and she nestled herself comfortably into his arms. They sat talking until they finished their drinks. Once Lionel had set down his empty cup, he did what he had been dying to do all evening: he gently pushed her back and kissed her. They kissed and cuddled until, feeling the urge to use the loo, Lionel got up and excused himself, asking directions to the lavatory.

He locked himself in and eased his bladder. Behind the door was a full-length mirror of which he decided to take full advantage. He removed his shirt and inspected his physique. Unsatisfied, he sank to the floor and did fifty press-ups as quietly as he could, before collapsing in an exhausted heap on the bathroom floor. Raising himself to his feet, he posed in front of the mirror again. Satisfied his muscles were sufficiently taut, he wiped the sweat off himself with her towel.

'Are you OK?' she asked as he sat down and put his arm round her.

'Yeah, why?' replied Lionel nonchalantly.

'You're sweating and breathing heavily,' she said, looking intently at him.

'Forget that,' said Lionel, leaning over to kiss her.

After a few minutes of passionate kissing, keen for her to appreciate his muscles before they returned to normal, he whipped off his shirt. The passion was quickly resumed as she ran her hands over his body. Feeling his chest, arms and abdomen, she exclaimed, 'Gosh, you've got a good body. Do you work out?'

'No, not really,' Lionel lied, trying to sound modest.

'You lying shit! I heard you grunting and groaning, doing press-ups in the bathroom.'

'Well, count yourself lucky. Normally when women see my muscles they're all over me like a cheap shoe.'

'Cheap women,' she replied.

Once again she had seen through him. He liked that.

The members of the team, including the probationers, were in the office by 6.45 on Friday morning.

'Apparently the superintendent wants us to take the probationers out walking so they can get properly acquainted with the division,' said Slippery.

'Well, why can't they go out walking by themselves?' objected Saddam. 'That's what I had to do on the first day I came out. I got given an *A–Z* and was told not to come back to the nick until the end of the shift. I don't know what the job is coming to today, having to chaperone probbies.'

'The super says we're to leave the vehicles in the yard; he's got some officers doing a nine-to-five shift to take the cars out,' Slippery continued.

As he finished speaking, Sponge and Speedy walked in. 'We've been thrown off the car,' announced Sponge resentfully. 'We've been told we have to take these probbies out.' He looked at the probationers with disdain. 'They can bloody well walk out on their own, I'm not fucking going out with any probby. Does the super want us to hold their hands while they're having a shit as well?'

'Well, if he did I'd volunteer to hold Doris's hand,' joked Lionel.

The phone rang and Slippery took the call. 'Doris,' he said to Sonia. 'You're needed to search a female prisoner at West Hampstead nick. They've got no plonks on duty and neither have any of the other surrounding divisions. Someone will run you over there once we've finished parade.

'My name's Sonia, sarge, in case you're confusing me with someone else.'

'All plonks on this team are called Doris,' said Slippery. 'And if you're going to answer back, you can fucking walk to West Hampstead; I'm sure it'll do you some good.'

Another officer opened the door of the office. 'WPC 411,' he called out.

Sonia looked up at him. 'Yes,' she replied.

'Come on, I've got to take you to West Hampstead nick,' the officer said in a friendly tone.

Relieved to escape the present wave of intimidation, Sonia got up and left the room.

'Right,' said Slippery after she had shut the door behind her. 'To get on with the order of the day. When Doris gets back, the two probbies can go out walking together. Keep an eye on them, Speedy.'

'Keeping an eye on those two working together would be like watching Ray Charles and Stevie Wonder playing fucking table tennis,' said Speedy.

'Jazz, you can go out with Speedy, Sponge with Saddam, and Lionel with Bubba.

'I'll try and get us a lift in the van to the Underground Café. We can't use the canteen; the governor's keeping an eye out today,' Slippery added at the end of parade.

The six officers got into the van and left for the café. Sophia gave them a frosty reception when she saw Lionel was among the fold.

The place was already full of the builders, roadworkers

and dustbinmen who frequented it on weekdays. They spotted the only spare table in a corner and made their way through the morass of furniture. There were only four chairs at the table, so Saddam pulled up one from the table behind. Lionel looked around for another seat as Sophia came over to take their orders.

'There are no seats,' complained Lionel.

'Try the toilet seat,' she replied.

'Listen, just get us some coffees,' said Lionel, spotting a chair that had just been vacated. He weaved his way round, picked the chair up and, carrying it above his head, brought it over.

They ordered their food and sat eating in silence. Just as they finished, a call came out to report a burglary that had occurred overnight. Speedy and Jazz accepted it and got up to leave.

'I'll get the bill,' offered Lionel.

'Cheers,' said Speedy and Jazz.

'What's come over this team? Everybody's offering to pay for things,' exclaimed Jazz.

Speedy gave Lionel a sharp, knowing look before they left.

'So, have you lads changed your minds yet?' Sponge asked. 'All you need to say is yes, and you've got one hundred and eighty grand in your pocket.'

'I need time,' Bubba answered.

'Well, that's a start,' replied Sponge. 'How about you, Lionel?'

Lionel looked at Bubba and realized he was not on his own. 'You can carry on without me.'

Sponge nodded. 'Just remember, you've got money waiting for you if you want it. Anyway, we'll leave you with the bill. Thanks, I'll repay the compliment soon.'

He and Saddam got up and left. Bubba waited for them to leave before turning to Lionel. 'Are you tempted?'

'Of course, I've thought about it,' Lionel replied.

'And what do you reckon?'

'I reckon no. Even if it was yes, Sponge is too much of an idiot to be in with,' answered Lionel.

'I know this sounds ridiculous, but I've got a marriage to save and two kids to look after; the money would come in handy.'

'You might think that, but have you thought about what would happen if we were caught and you went to prison? What would happen to your marriage then?'

'Do you know, all I've been considering is the money. I never really thought about getting caught. You've put me right off now,' continued Bubba pensively. 'I might as well be playing leapfrog with a unicorn!'

They sat in silence until Lionel got up to pay the bill and go to the loo. He couldn't quite decide which to do first. He had to walk past the counter to get to the lavatory, so he decided to pay the bill. He got to the counter and fumbled for his wallet as Sophia waited.

'My zip's stuck,' said Lionel, trying to get his Gore-Tex jacket open.

'Pity it's not your parachute,' replied Sophia.

'Listen, we don't have to be at each other's throats,' he said, finally able to release his zip.

'I've never been close enough to have the pleasure and I hope I don't forget the bread knife if ever I do.'

'Just give me another two coffees and keep the change. I'll collect them when I come back from the bog. And sort out your tables and chairs: people have got to weave more than a fucking dog in traffic to move about in here!'

'Try not to flush yourself down the pan as well,' she shouted at him as he pushed open the door.

Bubba and Lionel ambled along the pavement of Northwick Road, hands behind their backs and chins up, in imperious and majestic gait.

'Let's go back to the nick, I need a shit,' Bubba said, looking at his watch. 'It won't be long before refs, anyway.'

'I've never fucking worked with a bloke who could shit over six times his own fucking body-weight five times a day,' replied Lionel sarcastically.

They turned round and began to walk towards the crossroads. They had not got within twenty yards of it when they heard a sudden screech and a bang: the dreaded sound of a car-versus-car collision. They looked at each other, then changed direction again, doubling back the way they had come to find another route to the police station. They hastened their pace, crossed the road and headed for the nearest side road to disappear down. Just before they reached it, a driver on the opposite side of the road tooted his horn.

'Whatever you do, don't fucking look,' muttered Lionel.

'Excuse me, officer,' the driver shouted.

They ignored him and carried on walking.

Thinking they had not heard him, the driver called out again, but, as before, they ignored him. He drove further up the road, double-parked and ran over to them. 'Excuse me, officer,' he panted.

'You can't double-park on the road, sir. If you don't move your car, I'll have to give you a ticket,' Bubba interrupted.

'There's been an accident up the road.'

'Any excuse to double-park,' replied Lionel.

'No, seriously, there has been.'

'If there has been, then someone will call the police. In the meantime, I'm going to ask you one more time to move your car,' said Bubba impatiently.

'OK! I was just trying to be helpful,' replied the driver. He turned and hurried back to his car.

'Phew! That was close,' said Lionel, watching him drive off. 'We'll have to take off our helmets until we get at least a hundred yards away from the main road, so no one else can recognize us.'

Sponge and Saddam took a bus up to the Broadway to pay a leisurely visit to the various car showrooms. They drifted into a Range Rover showroom and took their time looking over the cars.

Within a short while, a salesman came over to greet them. 'Hello, officers, can I help you?' he enquired.

'Oh no! We're fine, just looking around, thanks,' replied Saddam.

'Car enthusiasts, are you?' the man asked.

'No,' replied Sponge. 'Customers.'

The salesman raised his eyebrows. 'Not being funny, officers, but I don't think you can afford these cars,' he said.

'I'll be the judge of that. Can I see your brochures and price list?' Sponge asked.

With a look of bemusement, the man walked back to his office to get them.

By 11 a.m. they were all back in the canteen for refreshments.

'How did you get on with that Nigerian? You had a date with her, didn't you?' asked Speedy, his mouth full as he munched heartily away at his second breakfast that morning.

'We got on very well, as it goes,' replied Lionel.

'And?' quizzed Sponge.

'And what?'

'Did you shag her?' asked Sponge.

'So well she was walking around like John Wayne,' boasted Lionel.

'I've told you for the millionth time, don't exaggerate,' said Speedy.

A detective sergeant came in and approached them. 'Jazz, that CRIS report you put in,' he said.

'What about it?' replied Jazz. 'Someone forced a window from the outside, didn't find anything and left.'

'Nothing was taken. It's not a burglary, it's a criminal damage, so you classify it as a criminal damage, a beat crime,' said the detective sergeant.

'But you and I know it was a burglary. You don't wrench a window and go into a flat for the sake of it,' said Jazz.

'It's divisional policy, not my decision. The senior officers want to keep the divisional statistics down. There'd be uproar if we recorded all the attempted burglaries properly; our statistics would go through the fucking roof,' said the detective sergeant.

'The job thinks it can deceive the public, tinkering with statistics by reclassifying crimes. This division has a ninety per cent clear-up rate for burglaries instead of five per cent. I'm surprised we don't classify a murder as a fatal common assault,' said Jazz.

'It would be in my household,' said Bubba.

'You're never going to get into the CID, son,' replied the detective sergeant. 'As a matter of fact, I'm surprised how you ever got into the job at all. Just reclassify the crime, will you?'

'Fucking CID. Why would anyone want to join you?' said Speedy. 'CID couldn't find their arseholes with both hands and a shaving mirror.'

Taking offence at the earlier comment, Jazz got up to follow the detective sergeant out when Speedy grabbed hold of his arm. 'Leave it,' he said. 'He's a DS. He can make life very difficult for you. It's not worth it.'

Shaking Speedy's arm off, Jazz sat back down. One of the other CID officers on the table next to them lit up a cigarette and the smoke wafted in their direction.

Sponge sniffed the air and grimaced; tobacco smoke irritated him. 'For fuck sake! People are trying to eat. Not everybody smokes, you know. Unlike you pissheads in the CID, we have to go out and do some work,' he said, putting down his knife and fork.

The CID officer ignored him and continued to smoke his cigarette. 'You fucking woodentops just don't know a thing about respect,' he finally said. 'I'll finish this one now I've started it.'

'Fucking respect? You think because you wear a fucking suit you're above us?' Sponge challenged him.

'Has he got a Duracell battery rammed up his arse?' the CID officer asked Saddam.

'No, why?' Saddam replied.

'Because he goes on six fucking times longer than everybody else.'

'I can't be bothered with these wankers,' said Sponge, beginning to eat again.

In an attempt to defuse the situation, Speedy got up from his chair. 'I think we should go back out now,' he said to Jazz.

'Where do you think we should go?' Jazz said. 'We've got about two hours to kill.'

'Tit-watch, on the Broadway! Good weather for it,' replied Speedy.

'Sounds like a good idea,' said Jazz. 'How do we get up there?'

'Bus it. Finish your coffee.'

Jazz gulped down his remaining coffee and picked up his helmet. They walked out and crossed the road to the bus stop. A young black mother stood with a child of about eight months cradled upright in her arms almost halfway over her shoulder. The baby was looking around curiously at the people and uniformed officers standing behind his mother.

The bus arrived and the queue moved forward to bring

them more compactly together. Standing behind the young mother was an elderly woman with a bag over her right shoulder. Seeing something within reach and naturally curious, the child reached out and took hold of the strap of the bag. The elderly lady, suddenly aware of what was happening, smiled and gently wrested it from the baby's grasp. Feeling her child stretched further over her shoulder, the mother looked round and, with an embarrassed laugh, apologized to the elderly woman. They smiled at what had happened.

Speedy and Jazz watched in amusement. 'Your lot start young, don't they?' Speedy said to Jazz.

'Very funny,' replied Jazz as they boarded the bus.

After the shift, Sponge went over to the newsagent's and collected single copies of all the car and pornographic magazines on the shelves for their special assignment downtown the next day. He needed something to ease the boredom involved in sitting in the personnel carrier. He wanted to go back to that Range Rover showroom after the march and wipe the smile off the salesman's face. He was fed up with people assuming he was an impecunious nonentity.

CHAPTER 9

On Saturday, they paraded at 7.30 a.m. Lynda Wallace, the female sergeant, ticked off their shoulder numbers as they trooped into the canteen. 'Right, ladies and gentlemen, good morning,' she greeted them once they were all in. 'You know why we're here. In case you have any doubts, we're a designated serial, policing the Gay and Lesbian Pride March. Our serial number is two one two; I'll distribute this information sheet in a minute. We'll be stationed at the south part of Trafalgar Square. Any questions?'

'Yes, what time are we expected to be back at the nick?' asked Sponge.

'Hopefully we'll be stood down by three, and should be back here by four at the latest.'

'What time do we get to eat at?' Bubba asked.

'We should be leaving for operational feeding at Wembley the minute we finish parade,' she answered. 'Any more questions?'

As there was no reply, she concluded the briefing and they all climbed on to the police carrier. Speedy was driving, Lynda Wallace sat in front, while the others were in the back. Sponge picked up some of his police equipment and put it into his rucksack to make more room on the seat. He picked out a pair of extra-padded leather police-issue gloves and stuffed one into each pocket.

'Where did you get those gloves from, Sponge?' asked Bubba. 'They look like mine.'

'Are you calling me a thief?' replied Sponge.

'I'm calling you a bloody good thief,' said Bubba.

'They're not your fucking gloves. Just be careful with the kind of language you use.'

Bubba realized Sponge's character was beginning to change. He was becoming more boorish and mercurial.

'So how did you end up being the skipper today for our team?' Speedy asked the sergeant curiously. 'Isn't your team on long weekend this Saturday?'

'I just got called up at home and asked if I wanted any compulsory overtime. I had to cancel a hospital appointment to be here,' complained the sergeant.

'What were you going to hospital to have? A strap-a-dick-to-me,' Speedy joked.

'Is she the lesbian sergeant?' Rigsby whispered, hearing Speedy's comment.

'Yes,' said Bubba quietly, 'and she picked the wrong team to come out with.'

'Rigsby, put down the windscreen wipers, will you?' Speedy casually requested before they set off. Obligingly, Rigsby got out of the vehicle and went round to the front windscreen to put down the wipers, thus placing him within range of the water jet. Speedy pressed the switch, suddenly letting out a stream of water that narrowly missed Rigsby. Realizing he'd nearly been the victim of another prank, Rigsby darted back into the van, embarrassed but relieved.

'What a fucking waste of acid,' hissed Speedy as he leant forward to start the van.

They parked among the myriad of police vehicles around the feeding hall and, leaving their gear in the van, walked over to the hall in a group. An officer at the entrance checked in the serials as they arrived.

'Serial two one two,' Speedy said, introducing the group as they walked through the door.

The officer looked at his list and ticked them off, then waved them in. They joined the queue of other divisional officers who were also waiting for food. Selecting their plates and cutlery, they surveyed the hall. There were about three hundred officers eating there.

'Ever felt like the odd one out?' Jazz asked Sponge.

Sponge looked at him. 'What are you going on about now?'

'All these coppers are giving me a look like "Oh, we've got one of you, have we?"' said Jazz, meeting some of the glances being thrown his way.

'You've got to admit there aren't many black coppers in here,' said Sponge.

'I just hate being looked at like I'm an outsider.'

'You know a lot of these blokes have never been south of fucking Sheffield before they joined. They've never been around IC3s, and the only time they come across them now is when they stop them in the street. It's fucking hard for them to accept one entering their domain, much less see you as their equal,' said Sponge.

'I have this feeling I'll never be fully accepted into the

Met – no matter how fucking far I progress or how fucking hard I try,' lamented Jazz. 'I just want to be seen as a copper who happens to be black rather than a black copper.'

'Well, you know that's never going to fucking happen. Policemen aren't used to working with IC3s. Besides, the job's got no choice; they can't find enough recruits in London. It's going to get even worse now that they've abolished rent allowance: they're paying new probationers money I wouldn't even get out of bed for,' said Sponge.

Their turn came at last. Speedy was the first to get his food and he looked around for a free table. Spotting one, he walked over to it.

Sonia sat next to him, Sponge opposite and the rest filled the table gradually. Lynda Wallace was the last to be served and by the time she came over there was no space for her at the table.

'Pull up a chair and we'll make some room for you,' Jazz suggested to her.

'That's a good idea,' she replied, looking for the most convenient place. 'Can you make some space?' she asked Sonia.

'Look out! She sits on our side of the church,' Speedy whispered to Sonia.

'Is she gay?' she asked, not quite sure what he meant.

'Bent as a fucking boomerang,' he replied, shifting over.

'I know I'm not your team sergeant, and you lads aren't used to being supervised by a woman. But I hope we'll get on with each other today and make the best of the situation,' she said, knowing they'd left her out deliberately and had expected her to sit on another table.

'We've got something more in common with you than most other plonks,' said Speedy, not attempting to disguise his disdain for her superiority.

'Why is that?' she asked suspiciously.

'We're all fucking lesbians!' retorted Speedy.

'Very funny,' she replied, unsure how to respond. It was becoming obvious to her that this team resented having a woman in charge, especially a gay woman.

'Leave her alone, will you? She's a good bloke,' Sponge joked.

'Who's going to get our lunchbox?' Lionel asked.

'Rigsby can do that, he's the probby,' said Bubba. 'You're not going to get very far on this team if you wait to be volunteered for things, mate.'

'I don't know what to do,' protested Rigsby.

'Rigsby, you worry me sometimes. I've got a feeling if you had dynamite for brains you wouldn't be able to blow your fucking nose,' Speedy said. 'You'll have to work some things out on your own; you're getting our grub, not projecting the fucking rate of inflation.'

'I've got this joke,' said Sponge. 'This bloke has three sons and a daughter. His eldest son comes over to him and says, "Dad, I've got something to tell you." "What is it, son?" his father asks. "I'm gay," his son says. "Fair enough, I can handle that. Live and let live. I've got three other kids, I can still have grandchildren, carry on the family name." His second son comes over to him. "Dad, I've got something to tell you." "What is it, son?" his father asks. "I'm gay," his son says. "Fair enough, I can handle that. Live and let live. I've got two other kids, I can still have grandchildren, carry on the family name," he repeats. His third son comes over to him. "Dad, I've got something to tell you." "What is it, son?" he asks. "I'm gay," his son says. "Fucking hell!" he shouts. "Isn't there anyone in this house who likes a bit of pussy?" And his daughter shouts, "I do!"'

'I'm going for a cigarette,' said Saddam, smiling at Sponge's joke.

'I'll come with you,' said Sponge, getting up.

They walked out into the open air and Saddam took out his cigarette packet. 'Fag?' said Saddam, offering him a cigarette.

'No, I'm straight, actually,' Sponge joked. 'Any luck with your feelers?'

'Not at the moment.'

'Having that gear in my shed is making me nervous. The sooner we can get rid of it the better.'

'We're talking about flogging over ten kilos of Class A, not selling a secondhand wardrobe. You're going to have to hang on to it a little longer. If you can't, then you'll just have to destroy it.'

'Piss a million quid against the wall? No fucking way!' exclaimed Sponge.

Amid chants of 'Two, four, six, eight, is that copper really straight? Three, five, seven, nine, does he take it from behind?' serial two one two stood and watched the rumbustious parade pass by. There were thousands of people, blowing whistles in open proclamation of their sexuality, creating a milieu of happiness and festivity along the entire course of the route. They looked a happy, proud and exuberant community, a sight that would impress even the most ardent homophobe.

Speedy, Sponge and Rigsby stood in a doorway and watched with cynical amusement.

'Look at that, Rigsby. The highlight of our fucking career! Policing a bunch of limp-wristed fairies poncing about the West End in pink!' said Speedy.

'It's quite comforting to know there are as many gay people as this in England,' Sponge commented.

Rigsby looked at him, befuddled.

'The more of them there are, the less competition for us straight blokes,' Sponge explained.

One of the revellers broke out of the procession and came up to Speedy as the rest of his coterie looked on. He took hold of Speedy's hand. 'Excuse me, officer! Can you tell me what time the 189 bus is coming by?' he asked, looking mischievously into Speedy's eyes.

'If you don't let go of my hand, you'll be underneath it,' Speedy retorted waspishly. 'Haven't you got any shame?'

'No. But you could tell me where I could get some,' the man said.

'It must be your upbringing,' surmised Speedy.

'I know! Strict Methodist.'

'Well, I think men should be men,' said Speedy.

'Listen, sweetie,' the man replied, 'I've got more frocks than Monica Lewinsky and more trousers than Sylvester Stallone. I don't know what gives you the impression you're more of a man than I am.' Blowing his whistle loudly, he ran back to join his friends.

*

It had not been a bad day. They watched the last of the revellers dawdle past before returning to the vehicle to be deassigned. They sat waiting on the forecourt of Charing Cross station. Sponge got changed on the carrier and jumped on a train to North London without giving his colleagues a proper explanation. The real reason was to buy a new car. Everyone else was dozing off or watching curious commuters watching them. It did not take long for the call deassigning them to come through.

Then Bubba upset the whole carrier. 'Oops! Better out than in, boys,' he said, suddenly breaking wind. 'Oops! You almost got left behind,' he exclaimed again, letting out a shorter second one.

Jazz flung open the carrier doors and Speedy wound down his window.

'Don't wind down the windows or open the doors, lads, it's cold in here,' said Bubba, amused at the palaver he'd caused.

Grabbing hold of him, they threw him out of the carrier, shutting the doors as Speedy sped off and shouting at him, 'You can bloody well take the tube back!'

The area car crew, Speedy and Jazz, arrived for work at 5.30 a.m. on Sunday, got changed and took their paraphernalia into the canteen to await the arrival of the car and its night-duty crew. They wandered into the utility room.

'I saw some biscuits on the table when I came into the canteen; see what you can nick from the other team's tea cupboard,' said Speedy.

'They left the tea cupboard open,' announced Jazz, looking into the cupboard. 'Bad mistake.'

They made a cup of tea and sat down. The area car arrived shortly after, so they booked on and drove out of the yard.

'I wonder what'll happen to that bloke who's in hospital,' Jazz said as they drove along the High Road.

'Fuck knows,' replied Speedy, sipping his coffee.

'That nurse wasn't bad looking, though; Sponge quite fancied her.'

'Remember the job saying: "Coppers who shag nurses and plonks are too lazy to wank,"' Speedy replied caustically.

'You always say shit like that. I'm sure you've shagged a plonk before,' Jazz said.

'I've got nothing against women in the police. I don't mind them as admin officers and typists, but I do have a thing about women as coppers. This is a man's job; a woman can't clear a bare-arsed builders' pub on a Saturday night,' said Speedy. 'Besides,' he continued, 'I don't want to have to worry about the plonk beside me in a brawl.'

'I'm not talking about the semantics of working with them; I'm talking about shagging them,' Jazz retorted.

'Ninety-five per cent of them are so ugly Satan wouldn't want them in hell, let alone me wanting to shag them,' replied Speedy. 'The other five per cent only joined to find themselves husbands and they jack the job in once they get married and pregnant.'

'So what about working with a bearded lesbian plonk

with a tool belt round her waist and a black belt in karate?' asked Jazz.

'Same fucking shit!' Speedy replied. 'We'd still end up with a hormonal woman who'd shag her way through the team. The job's already dropped standards to let blacks, women and faggots in. It's those do-gooders who won't let us get on with things as best we know how. The only reason we don't carry guns is because we can keep the lid on things; anybody who needs it gets tucked away.'

'Is there anybody you fucking like?' asked Jazz.

'I hate fucking everybody! Especially my ex-wife! What I hate most is the thought of having to clear a pub one day with a team of overweight black, lesbian and queer coppers because it looks politically correct.'

'No wonder your wife fucking left you,' said Jazz. 'All you've got left in your life is the job.'

'The only difference between being in the job and having a wife is that after ten years the job still sucks.'

'So what would be your ideal woman?' Jazz asked.

'A deaf and dumb nymphomaniac who owns her own fucking pub,' replied Speedy. 'Anyway, I've had enough of your opinions, I'm going in for a shit.'

He swung the vehicle round and headed back, leaving Jazz as frustrated as ever.

A brand-new black Range Rover hurtled into the yard, forcing Lionel to jump out of its path. 'Bloody idiot!' he muttered to himself as he walked into the locker room.

The Range Rover reversed into a space and its driver stepped out to inspect the paintwork. Satisfied no loose chippings had scarred it, he activated the alarm. Pleased with his new buy, Sponge walked across the yard and into the locker room. He strutted over to his locker and started to get changed.

Shortly afterwards, Bubba came in. 'Can somebody tell that Force medical examiner he can't fucking park in the back yard? It's reserved for us officers on weekends. I've had to park in the fucking street,' he shouted. 'The prick's not even going to be here for that long!'

'Which car's that?' Sponge asked, putting on his boots.

'The black Range Rover parked by the Portakabin.'

'It's not the FME's,' answered Sponge. 'How do you like my new machine?'

'Fucking what?' asked Bubba.

'Picked it up yesterday,' replied Sponge.

Bubba was prevented from saying anything further by the arrival of Rigsby. Lionel, who had been standing by his locker and listening to the conversation, shook his head.

Sponge locked his locker and walked to the toilets, the keys to his new car giving him a feeling of pride as they jingled in his pocket. Lionel followed him in, checked the cubicles were empty, then grabbed Sponge by the arm. 'What the fuck are you trying to do? Get us all fucking sunk?' he whispered.

'I just bought a fucking car,' replied Sponge, 'not a fucking yacht!'

'It's almost fifty grand's worth of machine,' said Lionel. 'No copper can afford that.'

'Stop nagging me! You're beginning to sound like a

short-changed King's Cross whore,' rebuffed Sponge. 'Now, I came in to have a fucking piss. Care to join me?'

'Piss off,' said Lionel before leaving the lavatory.

Slippery phoned to say that he wouldn't be able to take parade. He asked Lionel to speak to him in the custody office before the end of the shift.

Saddam took parade, sending the probationers out walking, assigning himself to the Irv with Sponge as his operator, Bubba to the van and Lionel to the Panda. Speedy and Jazz were the area car crew.

The team assembled in the canteen to have their usual cup of coffee and biscuits. Speedy remembered something. 'I've got to change this radio. It's working like a plonk at the moment – only when it fucking feels like it,' he said.

Bubba entered the canteen with the biscuits and threw the bag on to the table. The team pounced on it. Bubba disappeared into the utility room to make them their coffees.

A call came across their personal radios. '*Units November X-ray. 7-Eleven Northwick Road, a disturbance, two drunken males refusing to leave, information from the shop manager*,' said the controller.

They got to the 7-Eleven to discover the culprits had already left. Speedy spoke to the manager briefly before driving off. As they approached the crossroads, a man stepped out into the road waving them down.

'I suppose we can't pretend we didn't see him,' said Sponge.

They pulled up by the traffic lights, leaving the man to walk towards the police car, in the hope that having to walk the extra distance would make him give up. The tactic failed and he ran up to the car. Jazz wound down his window.

'Excuse me, officer,' the man said to Jazz. He was soused and they could barely comprehend his Irish accent, compounded as it was by the effects of the drink. 'Could you tell me the closest hospital?' he enquired.

'Newpark General, mate,' answered Jazz.

'How far is it?'

'Three miles up the road.'

'How long will it take me to get there?'

'You walking?' Speedy asked, leaning forward.

'Yeah.'

'Why you going to hospital,' quizzed Speedy.

'Nothing really. Just lost my finger, that's all,' the man replied, holding up his right hand. The index finger was missing and his hand was covered with congealed blood.

'What the fuck happened?' asked Jazz.

'I got into a fight with my flatmate and he bit it off. My fault really: he got into an argument with his girlfriend and I stepped in. I should have minded my own business.'

'Where did this happen?' asked Speedy.

'My flat.'

'How long ago?' said Speedy.

'About two hours.'

Jazz had got out to retrieve the first-aid box from the boot.

'So why the fuck's it taken you so long to go to hospital?' Speedy asked.

''Cos I've only just fucking realized I ain't got it,' he replied. 'I'm pissed out of my box and didn't fucking notice. It was only a few minutes ago when I wanted to pick my nose that I realized my finger wasn't there!'

'Where's your flatmate?' asked Jazz.

'He went out with his girlfriend.'

'Do you want to press charges against him?' enquired Jazz.

'No, it's my fault. Besides, no disrespect, I'm not a fucking grass.'

'Did he spit it out?' asked Speedy.

'Don't know.'

'Where's your flat?'

'620 High Road,' the man answered.

Jazz began to administer first aid, while Speedy called up the control room to explain the development. *'You're not going to believe this, but we need an ambulance for a bloke who's had his finger bitten off by his flatmate. The address is 620 the High Road.'*

'Yes, received. Does he want the assailant nicked, over?'

'No. Apparently he doesn't want to point the finger,' joked Speedy.

'Well, if he's not got a finger, I suppose he's got nothing to press charges with,' retorted the controller.

'Can we have other units come along? We might need to search for the finger,' Speedy said.

They bandaged the hand, put the man in the car and drove to the High Road.

*

They walked up the stairs into the flat. The front door opened straight into the living room. The walls were smeared with blood and the contents disarranged.

'Where did you fight?' asked Jazz.

'All over the fucking place,' the man answered.

Jazz and Speedy searched for the finger in the sitting room. A few minutes later, Bubba, Sponge, Saddam and Lionel arrived and joined in.

'Well, that's your sex life down the pan,' Sponge said unsympathetically to the man.

'Let's call a dog van; a dog could probably find it,' Speedy suggested.

Sponge radioed the control room and they adjourned the search until the dog van came.

'Have you got any ice in the fridge?' Saddam asked.

'I don't know. Sorry, I'm too pissed to think at the moment,' the man replied.

The paramedics arrived and escorted the man to the ambulance for first aid.

Saddam drifted into the kitchen and searched for ice cubes in the fridge. When the dog van turned up, they went down the steps to speak to the dog handler. Speedy explained the situation.

'Well, you blokes will have to stay outside while we search the flat,' said the dog handler, returning to the van to retrieve his dog. They waited outside the flat while he went in with the dog to search for the finger. The dog capered about the sitting room, for several minutes sniffing items in excitement. Suddenly the dog handler called out, 'I think he's found it!'

They piled back into the room and went over to where he was pointing.

'Good boy!' The proud handler cosseted his highly excited dog as it swanned in between his legs. 'It's just behind the cabinet. I don't think we can get to it, though. You blokes are going to have to help me move it to one side until there's enough room for the dog to fit in.' They gathered around the wall unit, heaved it up with immense effort and were only just able to shift it to the side. 'Come on, boy,' the dog handler commanded.

The dog leapt into the cleft, but was unable to reach the finger. The handler beckoned them over to move the cabinet further to the side. They heaved at it again. The dog crept in, grabbed hold of the finger and dropped it. 'Go on, boy,' the dog handler goaded.

The dog went for the finger again and this time grabbed hold of it tentatively. Then it bounded back over the sofa and darted about the living room, playfully parrying its handler in what it thought was a highly amusing game. The handler excited the animal even further by giving chase around the living room before, in a pure frenzy of excitement, it finally gulped down the finger. They all stood there, mortified.

The dog handler grabbed hold of the dog and futilely prised open its mouth. 'You stupid fucking dog,' he cursed.

'I don't fucking believe you! Didn't it occur to you your stupid dog would do that?' said Speedy.

'It's never fucking happened before,' replied the handler defensively. 'Besides, you're not the one going to have to sit around his arsehole for the next three weeks waiting for him to shit it out.'

'Then what are you going to do, blow off the speck and hand it back to him?' Lionel asked.

'Well, there's only one thing for it: we never found the finger,' Speedy concluded.

'It's not that bad. He's still going to be able to have a wank with the four fingers he's got left,' joked Sponge.

'He'll just have to use his dick to count to ten,' said Lionel.

'I don't think it's funny,' said the handler.

'Let's just switch off the lights and get the hell out of this place! I want a cup of coffee,' said Bubba.

They left the flat in darkness and handed the keys to the man before he was taken to hospital.

They went straight from the High Road to the canteen.

'I know this is the wrong time to bring this up, but is anyone still on for a curry?' Bubba asked.

'You eat so fucking much you'll end up getting a tan from the fridge light,' said Speedy. 'Just make the coffees, will you?'

'I'll ask you all in a few hours, and if no one gives me an answer I'll take it you're not interested,' Bubba replied before going into the utility room.

Lionel went to the custody suite to see the custody sergeant. Slippery was asleep in the chair, his feet up on the desk.

'Sarge,' Lionel said quietly to wake him.

Slippery opened his eyes and looked up at Lionel. 'What do you want? I hardly had any sleep last night; if it's not important, come back later.'

'You asked me to come and see you,' Lionel reminded him.

'Oh yeah,' Slippery said, remembering. 'Sit yourself down, I'd like to speak to you.'

Lionel sat himself on the bench opposite Slippery.

'Remember that IC3 you nicked the other night?'

'Yes,' replied Lionel.

'I heard through the grapevine he's pegged it, and apparently his family are up in arms. I don't know what's going to happen, but the senior management have been so busy running about disappearing up their own arses I'm pretty sure something's going on. It's more than likely, if anything does occur, the job will make a scapegoat of you.'

'Cheers, skipper,' replied Lionel. 'What could happen?'

'Well, CIB are obviously going to get involved. The one thing I will say is, however the job decide to deal with you, they won't afford you an ounce of fucking dignity, and all the years' service and sacrifice you've given will amount to nothing. I'm just telling you now so you aren't taken by surprise, because I've seen it time and time before: officers thinking the job will give them consideration.'

'I was only doing my fucking job,' Lionel remonstrated.

'That's what every copper says, Lionel. Believe me, it accounts for sweet fuck all. The only way to avoid complete bitterness is to realize that.'

'Thanks, sarge,' said Lionel, getting up.

'Just be prepared, because if you're not, you'll be grabbing your ankles in B Wing before you know what's hit you.'

Lionel didn't bother going to the canteen; he booked out the Panda and went for a drive. He spent the time thinking about his position, until suddenly all he wanted to do was go home. He never put on his uniform at the beginning of a shift to go out and harm people. Accidents happen and this was one. He turned the car round and headed back to the police station, having decided what to do.

Lionel caught Sponge just as he was going into the canteen for refreshments. 'Have a word, mate?' he asked.

Sponge hesitated. 'Yeah, mate, what do you want?'

'Upstairs in the Burglary Squad office?'

'It's locked on weekends,' replied Sponge.

'The scene of crime officer's office next to it, then,' Lionel suggested.

'OK,' said Sponge.

They went upstairs and Lionel shut the door behind him. 'The black bloke we nicked a week ago?' he started.

'The one in a coma?' Sponge asked.

'Apparently he died.'

'Dead?' Sponge said in disbelief. 'Well, don't worry about it; nothing's going to happen to you. Criminal charges are only for coppers who don't know how to cover their backs.'

'Well, it's only a rumour, but you know we're only told things at the last moment,' said Lionel.

'So why have you called me in to say this?'

'My portion of the money,' said Lionel. 'Apparently his family are up in arms and, if this goes public, the job will probably use me as a scapegoat. My career's probably fucking over. So, I need an insurance policy in case the job turns on me, which is ninety-nine per cent guaranteed.'

Sponge considered. He was secretly hoping Lionel and

Bubba would not take part in the scam. He had just spent fifty-five thousand pounds on a brand-new Range Rover and he planned to pay off his mortgage to buy a new house. He had spent all that money in the belief they wouldn't want any. If he paid Lionel and Bubba, he'd be left with less than fifteen thousand pounds. He'd never be able to leave!

Without even blinking, Sponge said, 'I can't give you all of it.'

'Why the fuck not?' Lionel asked him.

'I've blown some of it.'

'You've fucking what?' Lionel stood speechless for a few seconds, red with anger. He grabbed Sponge by the shirt and shook him violently. 'Listen, you stupid prick. You mean to tell me that, in less than a week, you've blown over two hundred grand? Not just your fucking cash, but everybody else's? Now fucking listen! I'm going to go back with you to your place after the fucking shift and, if you haven't got my full share, I'm going to knock the shit out of you.'

Realizing Lionel was serious, Sponge decided to recant. 'I was only fucking joking,' he said, smiling nervously.

'I know what you were trying to fucking do, you double-crossing shite! Trying to squeeze me for thirty or forty grand,' Lionel retorted. 'As far as this ship is concerned, everybody gets their share; nobody gets fucking conned. I'll see you at the end of the shift.'

With that, Lionel left the office.

'What a machine! Lionel, you're sitting in the ultimate fucking pussy wagon! There's no bird that wouldn't drop her knickers once they got into this baby,' Sponge boasted as they drove home. 'I'll have more fucking trouble getting the legs apart on an ironing board. Just driving it makes my dick hard –'

'Sponge,' Lionel said, cutting him short. 'Shut the fuck up!'

They got to Sponge's flat. Lionel stood in the living room and waited for Sponge to come back with his money. He had become so paranoid he hadn't wanted to come in his own car and he'd brought a large sports bag. He was going to ask Sponge to drop him off somewhere and then he'd take a circuitous route to his parents' house. There were several places he had discovered while playing as a child where he could conceal it. Before long, Sponge came back and they counted the money.

One hundred and eighty thousand pounds! Cash! Lionel packed it all into the bag. 'Can you drop me off at a mini-cab office?'

'Yeah, sure,' answered Sponge.

Sponge drove Lionel to the cab office and said goodbye. 'I'll see you at the Mason's Arms tomorrow?' he asked.

'Maybe,' Lionel replied.

Sponge nodded and drove off. Lionel realized he was now well involved. Whether he was suspended or not, it was only a matter of time before he would be out of the police service.

CHAPTER 10

'Hello, Bubba,' greeted Joe as Bubba walked up to the bar at 11 a.m. on Monday. He was the first of the team to arrive. 'How's your missus and my kids?'

'You're not her type, mate.'

'You're right there; I'm bloody wasted on her.'

'Right,' said Bubba.

'Just tell her Joe says he's coming round to slap the monkey, and see how excited she gets.'

'Somehow I don't think she'd understand.'

'No, I don't think she would, come to think of it; she's about as thick as a cube is square,' replied Joe.

Bubba bought a pint for himself and one for Joe, then excused himself to go to the loo. His mind was occupied as he walked to the lavatory. He thought about what Lionel had said on Friday. Had he known that since then Lionel had taken his share of the money from Sponge, he might have been more sure what to do. Still overwhelmed by temptation, earlier that morning he had phoned his cousin Vinny in the Republic of Ireland and asked him about any restaurants up for sale in Dublin. Vinny, an astute businessman, said he would keep an eye out for him but stated the obvious quite emphatically: he would need at least ninety thousand pounds.

'You don't have that sort of money, do you? I mean, working in the police over there,' he'd asked Bubba.

'Just keep an eye out and an ear to the ground for me. I'll be interested to hear what's available,' Bubba instructed him.

'Leave it to me, big fellow. There'll be a small commission, me having to use my contacts and all that, I think you know?'

'Anything for a squeeze,' Bubba replied.

'I take it you've come across some money, asking these sort of questions?'

'Very clever,' answered Bubba. 'I'm trying to do a bit of research for a friend.'

'If that was true, you wouldn't complain about my commission,' replied Vinny.

'Just do as I've told you and don't ask too many questions.'

'How's your missus and the boys, by the way?'

'They're OK. Things just aren't too good at the moment. With me working shifts and that, it isn't easy trying to keep a marriage together.'

'Tell them to give you time off to sort things out,' suggested Vinny.

'I wish it were that easy, but the last thing they care about is family life. All they want is for you to be at work when you're supposed to be, and that's that.'

'Well, I hope you sort it out.'

Sponge picked Saddam up at home and drove to the pub. 'How far have you got with making your contacts? Lionel's taken his share and I need a bit more money to get out of this fucking job,' he said.

'I've got a contact at my local,' replied Saddam, shutting the car door.

'Which local?'

'The Three Queens, the scummy pub down the bottom of my road. Went in yesterday and asked about; I've got a mobile-phone number for a dealer. We could give him a ring later from the pub. It's an Irish set-up.'

'Is he safe?' Sponge asked.

'We'll find that out when we speak to him, won't we?'

Tuesday was another rest day. At 11 a.m. Lionel had a knock on his door. 'Who is it?' he shouted, not bothering to get out of bed.

'Terry!' said the section-house warden.

'What the fuck do you want? I'm asleep!'

'I've got some blokes from Scotland Yard who want to speak to you downstairs.'

'What do they want?' asked Lionel, jumping out of bed.

'I don't know, but it's something big, Lionel. They've come in three cars. One's a superintendent, two are inspectors and the rest are in plain clothes,' Terry whispered excitedly. 'I think you're in trouble!'

Lionel's mind went straight to the money, hidden in the attic of his parents' house. There had to be a leak somewhere. It had all gone wrong. But at least he had money stashed away. This was the end of the road. But, strangely, he had no regrets.

'OK, I'm coming,' he said.

'I think you'll need to put on some clothes,' Terry said.

'I'll just put on a shirt and see what they want,' said Lionel, going to his wardrobe.

The minute they pushed open the swing doors of reception, the look on their faces told him he was not being seconded for a special assignment. Some of the officers were in uniform; the others, in plain clothes, wore the cheap, tawdry and ill-fitting suits and ties characteristic of police detectives.

'PC Matthew Flett?' the most senior uniformed officer addressed him. 'I'm Superintendent O'Flynn, and this is Chief Inspector Andrews and Chief Inspector Stevenson,' he continued. 'I'm afraid I'm going to have to ask you to come with me.'

'Why, what's wrong?' asked Lionel, playing ignorant.

'Where is your room, PC Flett?' the superintendent asked, ignoring Lionel's question.

'Number one eleven.'

'PC Flett, I'm going to take you back to your room. You're going to put on some clothes, then I'm going to ask these officers to search your room,' said the superintendent.

'Listen, my nickname's Lionel and my first name's Matthew; can we skip the protocol, sir? Call me Lionel or Matthew.'

They followed Lionel back to his room, watched him dress and then took him to the television room while the other officers carried out the search. Two hours later, they came back.

'Right, PC Flett, from now onwards you'll not be allowed to remain on police premises without being under the supervision of Chief Inspector Stevenson; this order includes this section house. I'm now going to ask you to come with us,' said the superintendent.

'Well, I'd rather go with my Police Federation representative, if you'll let me contact one before I go with you,' said Lionel.

'That won't be necessary,' replied the superintendent. 'Have you got your room keys?'

'They're still in the door.'

'Well, we'll have the warden lock your door and, when you return, instruct you further. Do you understand?' asked the superintendent.

'I would if you explained to me what you're doing and what I'm supposed to have done,' remonstrated Lionel.

'Where's your warrant card?' asked the superintendent.

'It's in my pocket.'

'Right then, I'm going to ask you to follow me.'

They arrived at Colindale, the Metropolitan Police and 2 Area headquarters, and took Lionel up to one of the interview rooms where he was held for an hour and a half. He guessed that they had kept the team under some sort of surveillance. He could pretty well imagine that, when they searched Sponge's house, they would not only find the money, but the drugs as well. The only person who was unaware of everything and would be wrongly implicated was Jazz. All the while he expected the rest of his team to appear, but nothing happened.

Finally the door opened and Lionel was taken to a

small office. Sitting on one of the seats was Chief Inspector Andrews.

'PC Flett?' the chief inspector said, with an affected air.

'Yes,' answered Lionel, irritated at such persistent and pointless adherence to formality.

'Take a seat.'

Lionel sat down.

The chief inspector procrastinated and fidgeted in his seat deliberately, using the silence to keep Lionel in suspense and thus allow himself to remain in complete control. Eventually he spoke. 'PC Flett . . . Matthew. I'm afraid I have to inform you that the decision has been made to suspend you from your duties.'

'Why?' Lionel queried.

'Your arrest the Sunday before last of a black man, Trevor James, on suspicion of robbery resulted in his being taken to hospital. He died last week from what has been alleged were injuries inflicted by you with your baton.'

Relief and surprise swept through Lionel. They hadn't brought him here over the money; in fact, they didn't have a clue! As he sank back in his chair, a wave of anger came over him. Was this any way to treat an officer? After the sacrifices he had made and the insults he'd received? His mind never once went to the deceased man and the bereaved family. 'So why have you allowed me to keep working? Why didn't you suspend me straight away?' Lionel demanded.

'I can't answer that,' the chief inspector replied, claiming ignorance. 'Once you've seen the deputy assistant commissioner, I'll take you to the nick, where we'll collect all your property, then to the section house where you can pack your things under my supervision and be escorted off the premises.'

'But I have nowhere to go! You can't just throw me out with less than two hours' notice,' Lionel remonstrated.

'While an officer is suspended, he can't go anywhere near police premises. You'll have to find somewhere else to go.'

One of the plain-clothes officers came into the room. 'The DAC's ready to see him now, sir,' he said.

'Listen,' said Lionel, stopping the chief inspector in his tracks. 'Why do I have to go through the pointless rigmarole of having to hand over my warrant card to him?' He wanted to deny the DAC the luxury of indulging in his own self-importance. 'I just don't want to sit there while he goes through the ridiculous formality of asking for it,' he persisted.

'Just come with me,' said the chief inspector.

They entered the secretary's office, which adjoined the DAC's room. 'He'll see you now,' said the secretary to Chief Inspector Andrews.

Lionel followed him into a large austerely furnished office. Behind the only desk sat Deputy Assistant Commissioner Westerman. As was the case with all senior management, the capaciousness of the office served the DAC's ego rather than his function.

'PC Flett, sit down,' he requested.

Lionel complied.

'As you know, you're now officially suspended, but you'll still be on full pay. A decision will be made by the CPS whether to prosecute you or not when the papers go up. I understand that all items of police equipment issued to you have been seized. The chief inspector will escort you to the police station where your uniform will be taken for forensic examination. We'll seal up your locker so that, if and when you're reinstated, everything will be there for you. Can I have your warrant card?'

Lionel handed over his warrant card, knowing that it was the last time he would ever see it. Then he realized that this was his chance: with one hundred and eighty thousand pounds behind him, he could pack it all in. After this morning's events, he wanted to have the last word.

'I could have handed it to the chief inspector upstairs; there's no real need for this ceremony,' he said. 'This is how you treat beat officers! I don't think I want to be a part of this shite any more. As a matter of fact, you can stick that brief up what you speak through.' He got up. 'If you'll escort me back to the nick and section house, I'll collect my belongings.'

'Very well. You'll have to give us a forwarding address, though; we will still need to get in contact with you,' the DAC replied with some apprehension.

'One thing,' said Lionel as he walked out of the room. 'I'll be appointing a solicitor. Any future correspondence between me and the Met will be through him.'

Lionel knocked on Shola's front door that evening.

'Hi, is everything OK? I wasn't expecting a visit from you,' Shola asked, surprised to see him.

'I've just resigned,' he blurted out.

'Why?'

'It's a long story.'

There was an awkward silence. 'Well, don't just stand there, come in,' invited Shola, helping him with some of his bags.

An hour later they were sitting in her kitchen drinking coffee.

'How are you going to live?' Shola asked him.

'I've taken care of that. I've decided I'm going to university in September. Can I stay with you until I sort myself out?' Lionel replied.

Shola thought for a moment. 'Yeah, of course,' she said.

Saddam phoned Sponge at 11 a.m. that morning, arranging to meet him at Archway tube station.

'Shall I bring all the gear down?' Sponge asked.

'Don't be fucking stupid! Stick a few packets in your sports bag and use the tube in case you're followed. I'll meet you outside the station. Leave your brief at home,' instructed Saddam.

Sponge went to the shed and selected ten bags of drugs from the suitcase. Saddam was waiting for him impatiently at Archway when he got there just after 11 o'clock. He was pacing up and down in front of a busker who was playing the violin. 'Here, get yourself some fucking violin lessons,' he said as Sponge joined him, throwing her a few coins. 'Have you got the gear?' he asked Sponge, not bothering to greet him.

'Yeah. Ten in the bag. We don't know what the stuff is, though, do we?'

'Well, it's either coke or heroin. Did you make sure you weren't followed?' asked Saddam, looking around furtively.

'Yeah.'

As they walked west down Junction Road, Saddam told Sponge how they were going to conduct the transaction. 'I hope you don't have your warrant card on you?' he asked.

Sponge paused momentarily, then dipped his hand into his pocket. 'Shit! I forgot! It's in my pocket,' he exclaimed.

'Well, it's too fucking late now. Just make sure you don't show it, whatever you do,' said Saddam. 'And another thing.'

'What?' asked Sponge.

'No jargon. Don't use any job slang. From now on, it's street language,' said Saddam as they walked into the pub.

The Three Queens was a quiet local with a few punters present, yet the atmosphere was forbidding. In the far corner an old man playing on the fruit machines threw them only a cursory glance as they reached the bar.

'Well, where is he?' Sponge asked Saddam.

'I don't fucking know; all I know is he's Irish. He told me to come in, get a drink and he'll come to us.'

'They obviously know each other in here well enough to tell who the strangers are,' said Sponge, looking around nervously.

The barman came up and Saddam ordered the drinks. When they arrived, Saddam seized the initiative and paid, fearful Sponge would either produce a fifty-pound note or drop his warrant card while getting out his money. They went over to the far corner of the pub and settled down to watch Gaelic football on the big screen in front of them.

'Get the fucking bag over here, you fish,' Saddam said sharply.

'Oh yeah, sorry,' apologized Sponge, getting up to retrieve the bag, which he had left on a stool by the bar. He sat down again with the bag on his lap. 'Just think,' he said, giving it a pat, 'this bag I've been carrying has at least three hundred and fifty grand's worth of gear in it: that's one hundred and seventy-five grand each. Once we've flogged the gear, I don't care what Speedy fucking says, I'm chucking the job in.'

'One step at a time,' said Saddam. 'Let's not count our chickens.'

The old man finished playing his game and walked over to Sponge and Saddam. 'Have you got any change for the machine?' he said.

Sponge moved to get up but was stopped by Saddam. 'How much do you want?' Saddam asked, standing and dipping his hand into his pocket.

'Just a quid's worth, to make a call,' said the old man.

Saddam fished out some coins. 'I thought you said you wanted change for the machine?' he asked suspiciously.

'No, I said the phone.'

'No. You said the machine first,' said Saddam. 'He said the machine first, didn't he, Sponge?'

'Just give him the change,' said Sponge.

Saddam handed the old man the change and sat back down again.

'You fellas want to see Mickey?' the old man asked.

Saddam looked up at him in surprise.

'You got the money?' said the old man.

'Yes,' answered Saddam.

'Then I'll give him a ring,' the man said, walking towards the pay-phone by the entrance to the bar.

'OK,' replied Sponge.

'Wait one second,' said Saddam, standing up. 'How do we know you even know Mickey or that he sent you?' he asked.

'I'm an Irishman, son; we don't fuck about in this business,' the old man answered.

He went over to the phone while they sat anxiously at the table.

'This is making me nervous,' said Sponge, shifting around in his seat.

'Of course you're going to feel fucking nervous. We're trying to fucking flog a third of a million's worth of Class A drugs,' said Saddam.

The old man finished the call and came back to them. 'Finish your drinks, lads, we've got business to do,' he said.

No longer having an appetite for his drink, Saddam looked at his glass, then at Sponge, then at the old man. 'I don't think we should waste time. Let's do business,' he said, getting up.

With some uncertainty, Sponge followed suit.

'Where are we going?' asked Saddam.

'I take it you've got enough money on you, fellas?' the old man asked Sponge, looking at the bag he was carrying and ignoring Saddam.

Sponge looked at Saddam for an answer.

'Well, we've got something that'll interest him,' replied Saddam.

'What?' asked the old man suspiciously. 'Have you got cash on you or not?'

'Why speak with the monkey when I can speak with the organ grinder?' replied Saddam impatiently. 'I didn't call Mickey, or whatever his name is, to do business with you.'

Nodding, the old man hesitated, then said, 'Just go to the cab office and I'll be over the road to speak to you shortly.' With that, he walked out of the pub.

Saddam and Sponge hesitated, not sure whether to follow him or not, then Saddam started for the door. Sponge grabbed Saddam by the arm, an uneasy expression on his face. 'Are you sure this is OK?' he asked earnestly.

'How the fuck should I know?' snapped Saddam. 'Just don't act frightened or they'll pick up on it. We get as much money as we can, and then we fuck off. If he hasn't got enough, then we'll flog what we can and go back with the rest, OK?'

'This whole deal doesn't make sense,' Sponge remonstrated. 'You should have just told him you had some gear to sell and it would have been more fucking straightforward.'

'You don't do stuff like that because you don't know who you're fucking talking to. Besides, I'm the one that had to take the fucking risks to make the contact. If he doesn't have the fucking money, he'll put us on to someone who does.'

Saddam's logic imbued Sponge with fresh confidence and he made for the door. They walked over to the cab office. Sparsely and slovenly arranged, it occupied half a shop. Outside loitered men of languid appearance, engaging in snatched conversation before disappearing into their cars.

With the constant movement, it was difficult to tell who was a cab driver and who wasn't. All in all, the whole place smacked of trouble. With some apprehension, Sponge and Saddam entered. The stench of cannabis smoke mingled with the odour from the damp carpet and wafted up their nostrils.

There was barely any room inside. In front of them was a cubicle with a reception window behind which sat a bedraggled middle-aged woman, insouciantly dragging on a cigarette. Before her was a microphone, into which she spoke from time to time. She barely looked at them as they walked in; instead, she got up and opened the door of the cubicle. 'Four one!' she shouted in a shrill Cockney accent, without bothering to take the cigarette out of her mouth.

There was no answer and two drivers who stood by the door paid her no attention.

'Four one!' she shouted again even more loudly. 'Where the fuck is he? I saw him a minute ago?' she asked the drivers in the doorway.

A shout came from outside and an elderly Nigerian man came into the office.

'Four one, pick up! Seventy St John's Way, and fucking listen to your radio!' she yelled, slamming the door. She turned to Sponge and Saddam. 'The red Volvo estate outside,' she said.

'What?' Sponge asked, not sure whether she was speaking to them.

'The red Volvo estate outside is waiting for you,' she said with such finality it was obvious she was not going to repeat herself. 'Black fella with a bald head wearing a turtle neck. Looks like a burst condom!'

'Charming woman,' Sponge said to one of the drivers in the doorway. 'Don't you feed her in that box?'

'Come on,' Saddam said to Sponge.

'But that old bloke told us to wait for him,' said Sponge.

'I've told you, you have to be a bit more on the ball and read between the lines if you're going to deal with these people. If you act like a novice, they'll pick up on it straight away.'

They walked out of the office, glad to be out in the open again. Parked in front of the building was an old Volvo estate; standing beside it was the old man in mid-conversation with a young black man who was leaning up against the car with his arms folded. He nodded towards Saddam and Sponge and said something to the old man.

The old man turned and came up to them. 'Well, I'll leave you to deal with Mickey. I'm off,' he said.

Left alone, both parties looked at each other suspiciously.

'All right, mate?' Saddam said, making the first move.

'Just call me Mickey,' the man replied in a strong Dublin accent. 'You the fella I spoke to on the phone?'

'Yes.'

'In that case, what can I be doing for you?'

'Can we speak somewhere more private?' replied Saddam, glancing round.

'What do you want me to do for you?' asked Mickey again, ignoring Saddam's request.

'I've got something that might interest you,' said Saddam.

'Like what?' asked Mickey.

'Some Class A,' replied Saddam quietly.

Mickey was suddenly animated. 'In that case, step into my office, gentlemen,' he said, opening one of the car's rear doors.

They got in, Sponge clutching the bag close to his chest as he settled into the back seat. Behind the wheel was a dreadlocked mulatto man, who did not even glance behind at them but started the engine and waited for Mickey to get in. As they drove, Mickey remained silent, lighting a cigarette for himself and then for the driver.

It was when they stopped at a pelican crossing half-way down the Holloway Road that Mickey started to speak. 'I thought you told me you were buying not selling?' he asked casually, looking out of the window. The weather was becoming hot for a turtleneck; his bald head was beginning to exude beads of perspiration.

'I've got some gear here which you might be interested in,' said Saddam, keen to get on with the deal. Sponge began to unzip the bag.

'What kind of gear have you got there, fella?' Mickey asked languidly.

Saddam put his hand into the unzipped bag, took out a single packet and handed it over.

Mickey, being no amateur, sensed Saddam's inexperience and once again probed. 'So what have you got here?' he asked.

'Open it and see,' replied Saddam evasively.

Mickey leant to one side, pulled a penknife from his pocket and, with a single thrust, punctured the bag. He examined the sample on the blade of his penknife. 'It's a bit difficult to tell,' he said, looking even closer.

'Why don't you taste it and see?' suggested Sponge.

'I don't touch the stuff,' answered Mickey aggressively. Finally he concluded, 'It's coke.'

'So, are you interested?' asked Saddam, pleased at the progress that had been made.

'Yes, I'm interested,' replied Mickey. 'What sort of price were you looking at?'

'You know the score,' blurted out Saddam, not having a clue what to suggest.

Sensing a deal was imminent, Sponge intervened. 'We can get you more gear if you buy this stuff from us at a decent price,' he said.

The driver continued along the Holloway Road. Suddenly reaching underneath his seat, Mickey produced a handgun, turning round and pointed it at Sponge. He looked threateningly at both of them as he leant further back against the dashboard to keep both of them in his sights. They sat silently, not quite believing what was going on.

'Right, fellas. I'm going to have to ask you to get out and leave the bag behind,' Mickey said calmly. The driver pulled up ten yards away from Holloway tube station. 'Will you throw the bag over the seat into the back?' Mickey commanded Sponge.

Sponge did as he was asked, too frightened to speak.

'Right, fellas. Being the complete Irish gentleman, I'm setting you down outside a tube station with a bus stop so you can get home quickly. Have you got Travelcards?' Mickey asked.

They both nodded.

'Nice doing business with you fellas. You'll understand

that when you're new in this business you're bound to be ripped off. It happened to me and me mate Magic here,' Mickey said, nodding at the driver. 'Now will you open the door,' he instructed Sponge. Then he turned to Saddam. 'Just get out the same side.'

Sponge opened the door and they got out. The car sped off up Holloway Road, tyres screeching.

Saddam stood there watching it recede out of sight. 'I think we've just been done,' he said to Sponge.

'If there's one thing you're master of, it's stating the fucking obvious,' replied Sponge.

'Shut the fuck up,' retorted Saddam. 'Black Paddy bastard!' he cursed under his breath.

'Do me a favour,' said Sponge. 'Let me make the arrangements from now on. We've just lost over three hundred and fifty grand, thanks to you.'

CHAPTER 11

At 2.45 p.m. on Wednesday afternoon the team, except for Saddam, who'd not yet arrived, assembled for parade. Instead of straight away assigning them to their vehicles, Slippery surprised them all by announcing, 'I've got some bad news for you lot.'

They stood in silent anticipation.

'Yesterday morning Lionel was suspended from duty.' He waited for the shock of the revelation to subside.

The minds of three of the team members went to the money and the drugs.

'The IC3 you nicked last night duty has died,' explained Slippery, unwittingly allaying their fears.

'So what 's going to happen to him then?' asked Speedy.

'I don't know. But they certainly can't sack him, that's for sure; he's fucking resigned,' answered Slippery.

It took a while for the further shock to subside.

'Now, I know you'll all be feeling the injustice of the whole incident, but you lads know as well as I do that when you're a beat copper, you're nothing but a doormat for everyone else to step on. That's why you should use the job to get whatever you can from it, because it doesn't give a flying fuck about you.' Sponge smiled meaningfully at him. 'CIB are going to be speaking to you lads at some point; they've seized custody records and other bits of paperwork. They might want to seize bits of clothing and stuff. I don't know what's fucking going on because, as per fucking usual, nobody's telling me anything,' continued Slippery.

'This is a load of fucking crap! Lionel only fucking hit him once! Anyway, he was completely conscious when we brought him in,' protested Sponge. 'Besides, why did they wait till he died and leave Lionel to work the streets? They should have suspended him that night.'

'You know the answer to that,' replied Slippery. 'The bloke's family are up in arms and the job wants to be seen to be doing something.'

'This job is fucking shit,' exclaimed Bubba.

'It's what I told you when you started,' Slippery said to the two probationers. 'Just remember the four fucking Ps: prisoners, property, prostitutes and plonks.'

They stood in silence.

'Anyway, they expect us to be professional and get on with the job as though nothing has happened,' said Slippery. 'I'll have to redo the postings, as Lionel's gone and Saddam's not come into work yet.'

'Where is he?' Jazz asked.

'I don't fucking know,' said Slippery. 'He hasn't phoned up sick or to say he's coming in late.' He hesitated. 'Right, Jazz, you'll have to come off the area car. Rigsby, you'll take over as operator.'

'Probationers shouldn't be allowed on the area car; they're still arse-wipers,' objected Speedy. 'I was never allowed on the area car by my team; I had to fucking walk everywhere.'

'I know,' sympathized Slippery, 'but we're going to have to break with tradition today. There's not enough of us on.' He assigned the others to their duties and ended parade.

They went straight into the canteen after parade; a melancholic air hung about them.

'Why aren't you in the area car maintaining a listening watch on the main-set radio?' Slippery asked Rigsby sharply.

'I didn't know I was supposed to,' replied Rigsby.

'So that's your excuse?' Slippery asked.

'I was just about to get a cup of tea before going out,' Rigsby said.

'That sounds much better,' complimented Sponge.

Slippery began to sniff the air around him and examine the soles of his boots. 'Can you smell it?' he asked.

'Smell what, sarge?' Rigsby asked.

'Bullshit, son! It's called bullshit! You'll go a long way in this job. Keep bullshitting like that and you'll probably get to commissioner in less than twelve years.'

Rigsby turned to leave. The canteen phone started ringing.

'Answer the phone, Rigsby,' Slippery shouted. 'When I was a probby, if I was in a room with other coppers and the phone rang more than twice, I got a bollocking.'

Rigsby went to the phone and picked it up. 'It's Saddam, sarge. He wants to speak to you.'

Slippery got up and took the receiver. 'Where the hell are you?' he asked. 'I see, round the corner,' he echoed. 'In that case, I'll assign you to the van. Take it out as soon as you come in.'

Sponge got into the driving seat of the Irv with Jazz. Feeling uncomfortable, he reached into his Gore-Tex jacket, produced a Nokia 9000 mobile phone and placed it on the dashboard.

'Got yourself a mobile phone?' Jazz asked.

'Yeah, I just had to get myself one; the carrier pigeons were getting too fucking messy,' said Sponge.

Jazz picked it up and looked at it. 'It's one of those flash ones, isn't it?' he asked.

'It's linked to the Internet. It's got a fax, a personal organizer, spreadsheet, the works,' said Sponge, showing him the different functions.

'How can you afford all this stuff? A Range Rover, new clothes, now a mobile phone! Where's all this money come from? Speedy said it was something to do with your uncle dying?'

'Yeah. He left me quite a bit,' said Sponge.

'How much did he leave you, then?' asked Jazz.

'Can't say,' answered Sponge, starting up the engine.

Speedy took Rigsby to the Prado village estate to introduce him to one of the most hostile patches on their ground.

'This is it,' said Speedy, pulling up in front of one of the towerblocks. 'Fucking Shellsuit City! This is the dustbin of Northwick Borough, where the council dump their PPFA lasses,' he said, half turning to look at Rigsby. 'If you dropped a bomb here and it destroyed everything within a mile radius, there would be about two hundred quid's worth of damage.'

'What's PPFA?' Rigsby asked.

'Prams present, father absent! It's just fucking shellsuits and prams around here, and the only fucking reason I can think of is it's because Adidas and Nike don't make condoms,' Speedy lectured Rigsby. 'The kids round here would fucking rob you if you were naked.'

'It sounds really sepulchral,' Rigsby said.

Speedy looked hard at Rigsby as though he could no longer recognize him. 'Yeah, fucking sepulchral,' he finally exclaimed. He turned round and huffed under his breath. 'Very sepulchral. Very fucking poetic word that. Sepulchral! Did you learn it at university?'

Rigsby stayed silent.

'You can nick anybody you fucking like around here.'

'What for?' asked Rigsby.

'Listen, anybody on this estate not within fifteen yards of the dole office and not fucking heading towards it is out fucking thieving,' answered Speedy. 'It's called pre-emptive policing. That's a word for you: pre-emptive.' They got out of the car and he turned to Rigsby. 'Come on then, let's introduce you to some of the plant life here!'

It was 3.45 p.m. when Saddam walked into the locker room. He had spent the whole morning with his wife, organizing a money transfer into an account in an offshore Mexican bank. In order to avoid suspicion, his wife would complete the process in two further transactions. He had been so absorbed that he had forgotten he should have left for work.

Now his money was beyond the reach of any investigation, he had an overwhelming desire to phone up the station and tell them he wanted to resign. Something stopped him; somehow he knew this was not quite the moment. He needed a bit more money behind him.

They sat in the canteen on their refreshment break as the cook prepared the last meals before shutting down for the day.

The news that Lionel had resigned after being suspended had spread rapidly. As was typical in these situations, distortions had developed, and by 5 p.m. the rumour had been embroidered further by stories that the CPS was prosecuting him for murder. Most distortions and rumours, particularly those concerning uniformed officers, were fabricated in the CID office. Some of the CID officers were now sitting at a table at the other end of the canteen.

Andy, the canteen assistant, began to call out the names on the food-order slips. 'Richard!'

There was no answer.

'Anybody know Richard?' Andy asked.

'There are two Richards, both in CID. Which one?' asked Slippery.

'He's tall with a moustache,' Andy said.

'Oh, Richard Head,' said Sponge. 'He's a detective. We call him Dick so we don't confuse him with the other Richard. Ask the CID at that table.'

'Have you seen Dick Head? His food is ready,' Andy asked them.

'Excuse me?' said one of the CID officers angrily.

'Dick . . .' Andy began, stopping as he realized he had been taken in. 'The tall one with a moustache,' he explained.

'Dick Tillotson, you mean? Who told you his surname was Head?' the CID officer asked.

'He did,' Andy said, pointing at Sponge, who sat chortling with his colleagues.

'You lads having a whipround to buy Lionel a pink nightie and dressing gown in case he gets banged up?' asked one of the CID officers in retaliation.

'Ignore them,' Slippery said.

Jazz woke up on Thursday to the sound of his television; he had left it on throughout the night. His mother was clattering about the kitchen as usual when he walked in at 9.30 a.m.

'Morning, Mum,' he greeted her.

'Hmm,' she grunted. 'Why do you always leave your plates unwashed?'

'Mum, not again! I got back late, I was going to wash them this morning.'

'That's what you always say. I'm fed up of cleaning up after you; what do you take me for – a slave?'

Jazz opened one of the cupboards, took out a box of cornflakes and went over to the fridge to retrieve a bottle of milk.

'Make sure you cover the milk properly,' his mother continued.

'Mum, I always cover the milk properly,' Jazz retorted.

'Well, somebody left the top off,' she complained, leaving the kitchen and walking upstairs.

Jazz remembered he needed to collect his police uniform from the dry-cleaner's. Suddenly he heard his mother shouting. 'Why don't you ever put the toilet seat up when you use it? There are women in this house who have to use it too.'

'This isn't going to be a good morning,' Jazz muttered to himself. He rushed upstairs, put on his shoes, grabbed a jacket, put his warrant card into his pocket and ran to the front door. 'I'm just popping out for a while,' he shouted.

'Have you washed your plate?' his mother shouted back.

'It was a bowl, Mum, and I'll wash it when I come back,' he replied, opening the door.

'That plate . . . bowl, whatever it is, is going to be left for me to wash.'

'When I come back, Mum,' shouted Jazz, shutting the door.

He walked down to the dry-cleaner's on Watling Avenue. As he passed the tube station, he felt a tap on his shoulder. He turned round to face the broad smile of a man dandily dressed in a red designer suit and sunglasses.

'All right, Samuel?' the man asked Jazz.

Jazz winced slightly, in an effort to remember the face. 'Dylan Jarvis?' he asked, a recollection coming to him.

'Yeah. I haven't seen you since school, doing our O levels,' said Dylan.

'What happened to you? You didn't turn up to take your exams and never stayed in contact,' Jazz said.

'I know, I had a few business opportunities,' Dylan explained.

'Well, you wouldn't have passed them anyway; you were

about as bright as a lump of wet charcoal. Your parents had to burn down your nursery to get you out of kindergarten.'

'Nice to see you've still got your sense of humour,' Dylan replied.

'And looking at that suit you've got on, you've still got yours.' Jazz paused. 'We were best mates for ages,' he remembered. 'I suppose people drift apart at some point in their lives.'

'It's fucking good to see you, mate,' said Dylan.

'It must be . . . what . . . eleven years now?' Jazz said.

'About that.'

'You haven't really changed,' said Jazz. 'Still the same flash fuck you used to be. Look at the way you're dressed! Are you still a bit of a shyster?'

'You don't look too bad yourself. Where are you off to?'

'Pick up my dry-cleaning.'

'Well, listen, if you've got time I live in Watling Avenue, just above one of those shops. Come round and we'll catch up on old times,' invited Dylan. His mobile phone rang just as he finished speaking.

'I'll pop to the shop and see you back here in a few seconds,' Jazz said, not wanting to interrupt him.

'This is quite a plush place you've got here,' complimented Jazz as he eased himself into the leather couch in Dylan's living room.

Dylan came out of the kitchen with a large bottle of Coke and two generous glasses of whisky. He handed one to Jazz and sat down.

'So tell me, D,' said Jazz, remembering Dylan's nickname,

'what do you do for a living to afford all this gear? It can't involve hard work because you always were a lazy sod.'

'I'm a baron.'

'Sorry?' asked Jazz.

'A drugs baron.'

'Right! You haven't changed, have you? You're still the same bullshitter you were then, always trying to impress,' said Jazz dismissively.

'No, seriously,' said Dylan. 'I'm in the big time.'

'That was something I should have remembered: you couldn't be legal. You always were a dodgy fucker.'

Dylan produced a packet of cannabis and some Rizlas and began to roll a joint. 'It's a huge fucking industry, drugs. I found a hole in the market and took the opportunity. You'd be fucking surprised; you can make a fortune fucking selling. I've got contacts in Northern Ireland. All I do is go over to Belfast, pick up a kilo for two grand, bring it over to the mainland and flog it for sixty grand. It's fucking brilliant! In three years' time, I could fucking retire!' Finally he asked, 'So what do you do at the moment?' Leaning back, he lit up the joint and took a long drag, then handed it over to Jazz.

'I haven't had one of these in ages,' Jazz said, examining the joint as he exhaled.

'Just like old times, eh?' Dylan said, rolling another one for himself.

'Yeah,' replied Jazz.

'So tell me what you're doing with yourself. What do you do for a living?' Dylan asked Jazz again.

'I'll tell you when we've finished these spliffs.'

'Why?' Dylan asked.

'Because you won't finish that spliff.'

'Let me tell you, man, nothing will stop me from finishing this.' He drew in more smoke, held his breath and examined the remainder of the joint with a smile. Still holding his breath, he asked in a strangled tone, 'Go on, tell me what you do for a living.'

'Seriously, finish your spliff first,' said Jazz.

'Fucking tell me, will you?'

'I joined the Old Bill a few years ago,' Jazz explained.

'What? You? A policeman?' Dylan said, bursting into laughter.

'Fucking yeah,' Jazz replied, producing his warrant card and handing it over to Dylan.

Dylan's laughter ceased abruptly as he scrutinized the evidence. 'This isn't fucking real, is it?' he asked. 'You're just fucking with me, right?'

'I've got my uniform here as well,' said Jazz, reaching over for his dry-cleaning.

'Fuck! Fuck! This isn't really fucking happening,' Dylan exclaimed in disbelief. 'Just tell me I'm having a really bad fucking trip!'

'Chill, man! If I wasn't on a level, I wouldn't be smoking a spliff with you,' said Jazz.

Dylan relaxed. 'Yeah, I suppose you're right. You wouldn't have a smoke with me if you weren't safe. Besides, old mates, hey?'

'The one mistake I made when I joined was losing my friends. It's piss easy to do. You learn after a few years that, being a black copper, you don't have many friends in the police. Anyway, you and me go back a long fucking way; we did everything together. We were like brothers! I'm not going to sacrifice my fucking youth and my past any more because I joined the fucking Met.'

'Why the fuck did you join the Old Bill?' asked Dylan, leaning forward to roll another joint.

'Long story,' said Jazz, taking a drag.

Saddam had come in late again and Slippery was not too happy about it. Jazz was sitting in the canteen telling the team about his meeting with Dylan that morning. 'I could get some decent information from him about the scroats on our ground,' he said. 'He'd make a fantastic snout.'

Sponge listened with intent; he could not believe such serendipity. 'Here he is,' he said as Saddam walked into the canteen.

'Where the fuck have you been? Slippery's doing his nut. You didn't even phone to say you weren't coming in,' Speedy said.

'Well, I'm fucking here now, aren't I?' Saddam growled back.

'What's the matter with this team? No one seems the same any more. Fucking spooky,' said Jazz.

CHAPTER 12

On Friday night they met up in the Mason's Arms and, after a few drinks, took a bus to Northwick tube station to get a train into the West End. The pub they had arranged to meet in was not far from Charing Cross.

Dodgy was already there with some of his colleagues when they arrived. 'It's my old buddies from November X-ray,' he shouted drunkenly. It was his stag night.

They exchanged greetings and Sponge volunteered to get in the drinks, asking Jazz to come and help. 'What time are you going to the reception tomorrow?' he asked Jazz on the way to the bar.

'About seven thirty,' replied Jazz.

'Listen, Jazz, about that bloke – you know, your mate? The one who deals,' Sponge began.

'Yeah, what about him?'

'What are you going to do? Cultivate him as an informer or keep an ear to the ground and get intelligence info from him?' enquired Sponge.

'He's a close mate and I go back a long way with him. In the meantime, we're catching up on old times.'

'Are you sure you can trust him, though?' Sponge asked.

'He used to be a best mate. Why all the questions?' said Jazz suspiciously.

'Nothing,' Sponge answered. 'Can we get some service

here, please?' he shouted down the bar. 'If you were any slower, you'd all be going backwards.'

They rejoined the group as Bubba advised Dodgy, 'It's not easy staying with only one woman for the rest of your life.'

'That's going to be really difficult,' Dodgy said.

'Being married is like batting in a cricket game: you can stick your balls anywhere you want as long as you don't get caught,' said Bubba.

'I'll tell you the real secret to a marriage – it's for a woman to love her husband a little and try to understand a lot, and for a man to love her a lot and try not to understand her at all,' said Saddam.

'You can never really satisfy them, you know,' said Bubba.

Dodgy listened to them in a state of bewilderment.

'Still, for whatever fucking it's worth, I wish you a long happy marriage,' said Bubba. 'Personally, I can't fucking picture it, but I wish you the best all the same.'

Sponge phoned Saddam the next day to discuss his new idea. 'Remember Jazz told us about that old mate of his?' he said.

'Yeah, don't tell me you want to try and set up a deal,' said Saddam.

'Well, there's no fucking way we're going to be able to shift that gear. We don't have any contacts. I've been thinking about it all day and it's just fucking perfect. It's fortune knocking at our door.'

'You've forgotten one essential thing,' pointed out Saddam.

'What's that?'

'We won't be able to get hold of him or do business with him without Jazz.'

'We could try and get in contact with him by getting Jazz to take me there or something,' suggested Sponge.

'What if Jazz finds out?'

'We just have to fix it so he doesn't,' answered Sponge.

'Have you seen my socks?' Bubba shouted to his wife from the bathroom.

'You never spend any time with this family,' she accused him, ignoring his question as she walked into the room. 'You went out last night and you want to go out again tonight.'

'I work with these guys; I have to socialize with them,' he remonstrated.

'I don't want you to go out tonight. This is the only long weekend you've had for four weeks and I want you to spend it with me and the children.'

'I'm sorry, babes, I can't,' replied Bubba.

'I see. So you're going to leave me on my own again?'

'I'm not leaving you on your own; I'll be back soon.'

'The only thing you're going to be when you get back is completely pissed! I'm not taking it any more,' she shouted.

'Listen, I don't want to argue. We've got tomorrow and a bit of Monday before I go back to work. Besides, what about my sanity? The job I do isn't exactly easy!'

'There you go again. It's all about you! What you and that fucking stupid job of yours wants. How do you think I feel when you leave each day for work, not knowing whether you're going to come back alive?'

'You don't understand,' said Bubba, looking for his jacket. 'I work hard and I have to play hard. Sponge and the others go through what I do every day.'

'But Sponge and the others aren't married to you,' she retorted, almost in tears.

'They understand me,' replied Bubba.

'Most of those blokes, Sponge and the rest of them, are single. They don't have a wife and two kids.'

'Maybe they're single because they can't find a woman who'll understand them or the work they do,' said Bubba, beginning to get annoyed.

'Tell me then?' shouted his wife, tears beginning to flow. 'Why did you marry me then?'

'That's a question I sometimes ask myself,' answered Bubba.

'As long as you're in this job, this marriage won't work out,' she said in a wavering voice.

'Well, I can't get another job, if that's what you want. We won't be able to afford the mortgage, I'm not trained to do anything, I'm too old . . .' remonstrated Bubba.

'Well, it's time for you to decide which is more important: our marriage and your sons or your bloody job,' she shouted.

'Not again,' said Bubba.

'Yes, and this is the last time. You go out tonight and this marriage is over!'

'That's what you say all the time,' said Bubba, adjusting his tie in the mirror.

A car horn sounded twice outside the house.

'That's Sponge,' said Bubba resolutely.

'I'm warning you! If you leave tonight –' she said as he slammed the door behind him.

'Are you wearing that suit for a bet or something?' Sponge asked as Bubba clambered into the car.

'Leave it out, will you?' Bubba replied. 'I've just had GBH of the fucking earhole from the missus.'

'She fucking moaning again? Don't worry about it. They're born to moan, it's in their genes. That's why they've got two sets of lips, so they can piss and moan at the same time.'

'Shut the fuck up and drive,' commanded Bubba.

CHAPTER 13

Sponge had bought an airline ticket on Saturday; he was intending to travel to New York for some shopping. He woke up at 6 a.m. on Sunday morning, called a cab and left for the airport, even though he was rostered to work the following night. By 9 a.m. he was on board a Virgin Atlantic 747, making a nuisance of himself and demanding a parachute after being refused alcohol.

For the first time in his life, he was doing something he had always dreamed of – doing something on a whim and being able to afford it. If all went according to plan, he would be back in time for night duty the next day. Next week, Paris!

Bubba woke up on Sponge's sofa and remembered the argument he'd had with his wife the night before. He'd been dropped off by Sponge only to discover he'd been locked out of the house, a bag and a note left for him on the doorstep. Not wanting to wake the neighbours, he'd walked to a public telephone and phoned Sponge's mobile.

'Can't you sleep in your car or something?' Sponge had asked, music blaring from his car stereo.

'Just come back and fucking pick me up, will you?' said Bubba.

Now he got up from the sofa and went into the kitchen for

something to eat. The fridge was empty, save for cans of beer. He opened the cupboards to find them filled with bottles of beer and spirits.

Bubba picked up the phone and dialled his home number. After a few rings, one of his sons answered. 'Hello,' he said.

'Hello, Mark, is Mummy there? It's Daddy.'

'Daddy, Mummy said you didn't love us any more and you weren't going to leave your job. She says she doesn't want to stay married to you any more.'

'Well, put your mother on the line for me, will you?' requested Bubba.

After a short while his wife came to the phone. 'What do you want?' she asked abruptly.

'Listen,' said Bubba angrily. 'We might not be getting on very well at the moment but, whatever happens between you and me, don't you ever try to turn my kids against me.'

'I'm not turning them against you. I'm telling them what they need to know and that our marriage is over.'

'What do you mean, our marriage is over?'

'I warned you, didn't I?' she replied. 'Tomorrow I'm going to see a solicitor. In the meantime, I suggest you do the honourable thing and stay away. I put all you need for your week of night duty in your sports bag.'

'I didn't think you were this serious,' exclaimed Bubba. 'Can't we talk this over?' he implored.

'I warned you, it's over! I've been trying to tell you this for ages: I've been having an affair.'

It hit him like a sledgehammer. 'What?' shouted Bubba, almost dropping the receiver.

'I told you, I've been having an affair,' she repeated.

'With who?'

'Someone I work with.'

'Who?'

'No one you know,' she replied. 'Just someone I work with.'

'How long has this been going on for?' Bubba asked.

'About six months.'

'When do you two shag – I mean, meet up?'

'While you are either getting pissed or are on nights,' she replied.

Bubba was too dazed to ask any further questions.

'Everyone tells me you obviously don't care about me and the kids,' she continued. 'This person is different. She takes an interest in me and how I'm feeling, doesn't take me for granted, I'm not the obedient little wife.'

'I can't believe you could do this to me,' stammered Bubba.

'You had it coming, and do you know the best thing?' she said. 'I don't feel a bit guilty.'

'Does, does . . . ?' he faltered. 'Does this mean you're leaving me?'

'No, I just want to know if you mind me going out and shagging while you're on night duty,' she said. 'Of course it's bloody over. I'm leaving you.'

'Hang on, did you say "she" a second ago?'

'Yes, I've met a woman.'

'What, you? A fucking carpet-muncher? You've been sleeping with another woman?'

'Would it have been different if I'd been sleeping with a man?'

'No . . . no,' said Bubba, after a moment's hesitation. He'd received more information than his mind cared to process. 'I've got to go,' he mumbled, putting down the receiver.

The clock had once again turned full cycle: on Monday the team began another week of nights. As a result of Lionel's unexpected departure, Sponge and Speedy were back in the area car. Jazz was out with Sonia in the Irv and Bubba and Saddam were assigned to the van. Rigsby stayed behind in the canteen to do some paperwork.

It did not take long before night duty kicked off.

'*Any unit available to deal with a drunk causing a disturbance on the Broadway, over?*' asked the controller.

'*November X-ray 21*,' transmitted Speedy, taking the call.

'*Yeah, received, I'll show you, assigned*,' concluded the controller.

Speedy pulled up at the Broadway and spotted the drunk facing a wall rocking backwards and forwards, barely able to stay upright. He had a Bible in his left hand and a can of extra-strong lager in his right. It was Martin Summers again.

'For fuck sake, Martin,' said Speedy. 'What's the longest you've been without a drink over the last four weeks?'

'About ten fucking feet,' replied Martin.

'You're making a bit of a habit of this, aren't you?'

'What do you expect? I'm an alcoholic,' said Martin. 'Of course I'm going to make a fucking habit of getting drunk.'

'Why don't you just go home?' said Sponge.

''Cos I've got one leg shorter than the other, you see,' said

Martin. 'And I've got such a bad limp I end up walking round in circles.'

'Do you know you're one of our worst fucking drunks?' Speedy asked him.

'I'm an alcoholic, not a drunk,' said Martin obstinately. 'There's a big fucking difference!'

'What's the fucking difference?'

'I've got a fucking job to go to in the morning.'

'What's with the Bible?' asked Sponge.

'Well, this is my last day getting pissed. I'm going to become a Christian,' he announced. 'I'm going to church tomorrow. I'm going to become a changed man.'

'I've got a cure for your limp to get you home, Martin,' said Sponge.

'Yeah, what's that?' asked Martin suspiciously.

'Try walking with one leg in the gutter and your short leg on the pavement; when you walk that way, it'll cancel out.'

'Get fucked!' he retorted.

'Well, if you're going to be like that, you can bloody well come in,' said Speedy. *'November X-ray, from November X-ray, can we have the van up here?'* he asked the controller. *'We've got one coming in for drunk and dis.'*

'Yeah, November X-ray 2, ETA five minutes,' replied Bubba over the radio.

Bubba was deep in thought as he drove the van to the Broadway to pick up the drunk. He felt out of shape and ugly; no wonder his wife had gone off him. He had spent the whole of Sunday and Monday wallowing in self-pity and misery. But he needed to ask certain questions. He had decided to put aside his feelings of pride and phone her, using the children as an excuse.

Bubba stopped the van in front of the custody-suite ramp and waited for Speedy to park the area car.

'There's a body for you in the van,' Speedy said to Rigsby. 'A drunk from the Broadway.'

'What do you want me to do with him?' asked Rigsby.

'Don't ask stupid questions,' replied Speedy. 'Well, fucking get on with it!'

Rigsby walked out slowly towards the van, followed by Speedy. Bubba opened the van door.

'Off the Broadway at 23.41, unsteady on his feet, eyes glazed, clothes dishevelled, and swearing,' said Speedy.

'I can't do it!' blurted out Rigsby.

'You fucking what?' asked Speedy.

'I can't accept a prisoner just handed over to me in the back yard, then make up the evidence,' replied Rigsby.

'You fucking speak to him; I've been punished enough over the last month,' Speedy said to Saddam, turning away in disgust.

'You can't turn down a fucking body,' explained Saddam.

'He's already been arrested,' said Rigsby.

'You're getting a bit too technical,' replied Saddam. 'Now the best tip I can give you is just to do as you're told.'

Rigsby hesitated only briefly before accepting his advice.

Speedy and Sponge picked Rigsby up two hours later and resumed their patrol. It wasn't long before he began to say what he thought. 'If you think I'm going to drive you about while you spend the whole night scratching your arse and rubbing your balls, you've got another think coming,' he said caustically. 'You're sure as fucking hell not going to get through a whole week of nights without doing your fair share of work.'

'I don't expect to,' Rigsby said quietly.

'You graduates are all the fucking same,' said Speedy. 'You join the job and think you're better than everybody else and that you don't need to be told what to do.'

'Like a box of fucking Tampax,' added Sponge. 'Stuck up cunts!'

'I just don't agree with certain things,' said Rigsby placidly. 'Maybe if you took time to hear what I'm saying, we'd be able to work together better.'

They drove on silently until Speedy suddenly broke wind.

'Did you have to do that with three people in the car?' Sponge asked him.

'I'm just giving another arsehole in this car a chance to be heard,' Speedy replied.

Bubba knew his wife would be about to go to bed at the time he phoned. After a few rings, she answered.

'Hello, it's me,' he said.

'How are you?' she replied, sounding concerned.

'I'm staying with Sponge at the moment. It's not easy.'

'I know, I'm not finding it easy either,' she said.

'Listen, I've been thinking,' started Bubba. 'I don't care about your affair; I'm willing to forgive you.'

There was a hesitation on the other end of the phone. 'Well, that's really generous of you,' she said.

'I'm just saying I want to come back,' said Bubba. 'I'll do anything to get you back.'

There was another hesitation. 'No, I warned you. If that's why you called me, I suggest you put the phone down.'

'No, no,' stammered Bubba. 'It's not the reason why I called you. I just wanted to know if you wanted me to pick up the kids as usual?'

'No, Gina's doing that,' she answered.

'Who's Gina?' Bubba asked.

'The person I've been seeing.'

'You mean she's already fucking taken my place?' exploded Bubba. 'I should have fucking known. What is this? Some sort of Tampax conspiracy going on behind my back? She must have put you up to this. I don't want her near my fucking children.'

'If you're going to be stupid, I don't want to speak to you,' she replied.

He put the phone down and went downstairs to the canteen, meeting Slippery in the yard. 'What's the matter with you?' Slippery asked.

'My wife's left me . . . She says she can't handle me being so devoted to the job,' said Bubba, careful to leave out the details.

'What's fucking new?' retorted Slippery unsympathetically. 'Four out of every five police marriages fail. What made you feel yours would be any different?'

'What was it like when you were married?' asked Bubba.

'I can't remember, I was pissed most of the time.'

'Slippery, you've been through this before. Will she come back?'

'A boomerang that doesn't come back is just a stick,' replied Slippery. 'The first time, my marriage was on the rocks because I was working such long hours on the flying squad as a detective constable. I told my DI and he said to me, "Son, you only get one chance in the flying squad but you can always get yourself another wife."'

'Cheers, Slippery, that's just what I wanted to hear,' said Bubba.

'Look on the bright side: at least your wife is faithful to you. I might as well have married the Whore of Babylon,' lamented Slippery.

'She isn't; she told me she's having an affair,' Bubba said.

'Women, typical, you just can't trust them,' said Slippery. 'Take my advice: never trust anything that bleeds for five days and doesn't die.'

Bubba comforted himself with a banana, marmalade and chicken sandwich. Competing with a woman for his wife's affections was an area where he felt he had little chance of success. Had it been another man, things might be easier. He felt utterly emasculated and couldn't talk to the rest of the team about his feelings. As he ate, he caught a reflection of himself in the window. He looked fat and ugly. No wonder she had gone off him; how could anybody fancy him? Suddenly he no longer wanted the sandwich. He threw it into the bin and walked out of the canteen.

'What's the matter with you?' Sponge asked Bubba as he met him in the doorway. 'You look pissed off.'

'I'm too old for a paper round, too young for a pension, my kids probably hate me, my wife's just left me. Of course I'm bloody pissed off!'

'You know your money's still waiting for you if you change your mind,' said Sponge.

'This enterprise of yours is going to go bent,' Bubba replied pessimistically.

'I'd put my cock on the block and say to you that nothing can go fucking wrong,' replied Sponge with a confident smile.

Bubba went into the locker room and took off his top to examine his reflection in the mirror. He was disgusted with what he saw. He had completely let himself go.

He came to a snap decision. He was going to alter his image. He was going to change everything about himself. He was going to start dieting, join a gym and start exercising. Then renew his wardrobe.

Twenty minutes later he was jogging to the 7-Eleven on the High Road, where he bought the latest male fitness magazines. The first step to becoming a new him. Maybe then his wife would change her mind.

Bubba woke up on Sponge's sofa at about 2 p.m. on Tuesday afternoon. He got up to ease his bladder, passing Sponge's room on the way. Sponge was on the phone with his back to the door. Bubba got to the loo and unzipped his jeans. 'I don't even have a pair of pyjamas to wear,' he muttered to himself. 'Being single just doesn't suit me.'

He walked back towards the living room and, passing

Sponge's room again, wondered who he could be speaking to so soon after night duty. He stopped and listened, trying to pick up the conversation.

'I tried to speak to him about it the other day, but he got a bit suspicious,' said Sponge down the phone.

Bubba went into the living room and picked up the extension phone. He recognized Saddam's voice. 'I say we keep an ear to the ground. If anything comes up, we'll hear about it. I don't think Jazz would go for it anyway.'

Bubba wondered what they were talking about.

'This bloke is a big fish. From what Jazz says, we could use him to shift the gear once and for all. We could give him half of it first and then the other half after.'

Then it all fell into place. They were trying to sell the drugs! They hadn't got rid of them, after all! It was then that Bubba realized he had to get out – not only out of the job but away from these two maniacs. He got changed and went out for a run.

The first thing Bubba did when he got into work that night was to ring his cousin in Ireland to find out if he had any information. Vinny was out but his wife answered the phone, so Bubba left a message. After parade the team assembled in the canteen for the traditional cup of tea until the first call of the night was issued. The assignments remained the same, except that Sonia and Saddam swapped vehicles.

As Speedy and Sponge pulled up in front of the house, the man was still ranting. He was in the front garden, half dressed and utterly soused. He held a can of lager and was shouting obscenities at someone inside.

'Some village has lost its fucking idiot,' said Speedy as they got out.

'*November 1 on scene, domestic incident*,' said Sponge over the radio.

Bubba and Sonia arrived in the van and a woman with a bruised face emerged from the house to meet them. 'Thank goodness you're here. He gets pissed and loses it,' she said.

'Let's go inside, shall we?' Speedy said soothingly.

Moments later they were in the living room.

'What happened?' Speedy asked.

'He gets pissed and starts hitting me,' the woman explained.

'It's all right, love, tell the copper I love you. And you lot fuck off out of my house,' shouted the man aggressively.

'You keep your ugly mug out of this. Speak to the wall – you're both as plastered as each other,' Bubba said.

'You can fuck off, you prick,' replied the man.

'I've got to be a prick to deal with a cunt like you. I can see you're getting brave! Why don't you hit me or do you just hit women?' Bubba said.

'I thought you had to be in reasonably good shape to be a copper, or can you get away with looking like a hamster – huge body and little legs,' the man said, ridiculing Bubba.

'I'm fat, you're ugly! I can fucking lose weight!' Bubba retorted.

'Take her into the kitchen; make yourself fucking useful for a change. Find out if she wants him nicked,' Speedy said, turning to Sonia.

'You can't nick me, I'm in my own fucking living room,' the man said truculently.

'Not when we write our fucking evidence, you fucking won't be,' Speedy replied.

'You're obviously detached from fucking reality,' Sponge added.

Speedy went into the kitchen to speak to the woman. Sonia comforted her as she wept. Speedy took out a cigarette and lit up, visibly annoyed. This was one of the few types of routine call that upset him. 'It looks like the best part of your husband ran down your mother-in-law's leg,' he finally said.

'He's not bad at all; he just gets like this when he's had a bit to drink,' the woman replied.

'So what does she want done?' Speedy asked Sonia.

'She wants us to take him away until he sobers up.'

'What are you waiting for then? Go out there and bloody nick him,' said Speedy.

They returned to the living room where Sonia set about the task of arresting the husband. 'Right, I'm arresting you. You don't have to say anything but anything you do say may be taken down and used in evidence –' she began nervously. This was her first arrest and she had forgotten the wording of the caution.

'Your knickers and bra,' the man replied facetiously.

'That's the wrong caution, Doris,' said Speedy.

'Don't waste your time with scum like that. Telling him he's nicked is enough,' Bubba said to Sonia.

'You can fuck off, you fat fucker. How the fuck have they let you out on the streets? You've got more fucking chins than a Chinese phone book!' said the man.

'He doesn't like you, does he?' Sponge said to Bubba.

'Let Rigsby have him if he's going to take the piss,' said Speedy.

En route to Northwick police station, Bubba became exasperated by the prisoner in the back of the van. He was still hurling abuse and kicking against the cage as they drove into the yard. 'You get shit stains on your collar and use a mirror to take a piss, you're so fucking fat,' he screamed.

'Brace yourself,' Bubba said quietly to Sonia.

'What?' asked Sonia, not sure what he meant.

'I said brace yourself.'

Bubba accelerated hard towards the canteen. As they drew nearer, Sonia began to panic. Suddenly Bubba slammed on the brakes. The prisoner was flung backwards and forwards by the jolt, bashing his head against the cage a few times.

'That fucking black cat again,' Bubba shouted. He turned to Sonia. 'That's one of the many ways of assaulting a prisoner who's being a dickhead without touching him,' he said.

Bubba got out of the van and brought the prisoner out. He was bleeding profusely from a gash on his forehead and had bruises on the side of his head. The area car arrived and Rigsby got out to receive his prisoner.

'He's all yours,' Bubba said.

'How come he's bleeding?' Rigsby asked Bubba.

'It was his fucking fault,' the man replied, pointing at Bubba.

'What happened to him?' said Rigsby. 'He wasn't bleeding when I put him in the van.'

'Just do as you're told and stop asking stupid questions,' Bubba shouted angrily.

'Well, if he's my prisoner and he's bleeding, I think I should find out why.'

Slippery, on his way back from the canteen, intervened. 'Bubba, take him into the custody suite. Rigsby, I want a word with you,' he said, pulling Rigsby to one side. 'You are bang out of fucking order! What the fuck do you think you're doing? You never fucking criticize another officer in front of a prisoner.'

'Don't you think you should be speaking to him and not me, sarge? He's just broken the law.'

'Fuck sake! A probby telling me how to do my job. I think it's about fucking time I spoke to the governor about you.'

'I got rights!' the man screamed as Slippery sat down at his desk in the custody suite.

'The only rights you've got while you're in here are your right arm and your right leg,' replied Slippery. 'Time of arrest?' he asked Rigsby.

'Wait a minute, he didn't nick me. I want the WPC that nicked me,' the man protested.

'So do most coppers at this nick, but they don't make a fucking song and dance about it,' said Slippery. 'Bin him. I'll deal with him when he fucking sobers up. Cell number two.' He threw Rigsby the keys.

Rigsby escorted the man to his cell and came back. 'He says he's a solicitor and he's entitled to a copy of the Police Evidence Act and police codes of practice, sarge,' he said to Slippery.

'We haven't got any copies at the moment,' replied Slippery, opening his drawer and riffling through it. 'Here's a Mills and Boon instead,' he said, handing Rigsby a book.

On Wednesday night, Saddam and Sponge were the area car crew, with Saddam driving and Sponge operating. Sponge had come in with Bubba, who'd gone over to the pub for a drink before the shift began.

'Why are you driving tonight?' the late-turn area-car driver asked Saddam.

'It's my turn,' replied Saddam. 'I'm an area-car driver as well, you know.'

'How did the shift go?' Sponge asked.

'Nothing apart from a GBH. The bloke you nicked yesterday from a domestic went straight back home and slashed his wife twice with a kitchen knife,' replied the late-turn operator.

'How badly was she hurt?' asked Sponge.

'She was OK, just pretty cut up about it,' joked the operator.

Sponge and Saddam checked the equipment and drove out of the yard.

'Let's go up to the Prado to look for a scroat to stop; I'm out of fucking hash,' said Sponge. They drove up to the Prado village estate and began the hunt. 'I think Bubba knows we've still got the drugs,' he said as they went along.

'No, he doesn't,' dismissed Saddam. 'Unless you've said something to him.'

'No, I haven't.'

'Then how does he know?'

'His attitude has changed,' said Sponge.

'It's probably all this shit with his marriage,' suggested Saddam.

'Maybe,' replied Sponge. 'Anyway, I'll just concentrate on Jazz getting this contact for us.'

'How are you going to do that?' asked Saddam.

'I'll find some strategy.'

'I don't think we can do this without Jazz catching on; he's too smart. Besides, I'm not really comfortable with you sitting on over a million's worth of cocaine in your garden shed.'

'So what are you suggesting?' asked Sponge. 'We take a risk and come clean with Jazz? Tell him why we need his contact even if he doesn't want any part of it? But what if he shops us, just goes straight to the Yard?'

'He won't. Canteen culture, my son; it's far too strong for him to do that. Besides, Jazz is ambitious; he knows if he grasses on us, his career is over. Any nick he ever goes to or branch he ever works for will know him as someone not to be trusted. He has a difficult enough problem being a wog.'

'Smart thinking,' complimented Sponge.

'Isn't that what I always told you: leave the thinking to me,' replied Saddam. 'I'll speak to you about it before we go off. We can pay Jazz a visit tomorrow.'

A call came over their personal radios. '*Attention all units. Currently at large is a mental absconder, last seen walking down Tenterden Lane, a male, wearing a black jacket with half of his head shaved,*' the controller announced.

'*Did you say he was bald?*' Sponge asked over the radio.

'It depends which way he's walking,' replied the controller.

'Yes, received, November 1 will take a look for him,' said Saddam. 'On the left,' he said to Sponge, pointing at a likely suspect.

'You throw some weird fucking shouts. That bloke looks more like a pisshead. He's hardly likely to have any fucking gear on him.'

As Bubba walked into the locker room, he met the late-turn civilian control-room operator. 'Some bloke phoned up to speak to you,' he said to Bubba.

'Did he say who he was?'

'Your cousin, said he was phoning from Ireland. I told him you were on nights,' he answered.

Rigsby knocked on the inspector's door once parade was over.

'Yeah, come in,' shouted the inspector.

Rigsby walked in. 'You asked to see me, sir,' he began.

'Who are you?' the inspector asked.

'Richard Gail, sir, one of the new recruits,' said Rigsby.

'Oh yeah,' said the inspector, remembering. 'Sit down.'

Rigsby obeyed.

'You, son, have got the talent bordering on genius of getting on people's fucking tits,' the inspector said.

'I just don't accept what they're doing and how they go about it, sir,' Rigsby replied, cutting him short.

'That's not what I hear. According to the rest of your team, you've been as irritating as a fly around a camel's arsehole,' said the inspector.

'So, do I say nothing when a prisoner's assaulted, sir?'

'Listen, son,' said the inspector. 'Coppers have been knocking people about and stitching people up from the day the Pope was an altar boy – not just in this country but all over the fucking world. You ain't gonna fucking change it.'

'I'm sorry, sir, I can't accept that.'

'The next time you walk into the canteen, take a look around. You'll see over half a century's worth of police experience and knowledge. You think you can walk in with five months under your belt and change everything? Or do you think because you've got a degree you're better than everybody else?'

'No, I don't, sir,' admitted Rigsby.

'Just remember, son, credibility is like virginity: you can only lose it once,' the inspector explained. 'They're gonna start avoiding you like shit on a stick soon and no fucker is gonna want to work with you. You especially don't want to fuck off your skipper 'cos he can really fucking make life difficult for you.'

'I just want to tell the truth,' said Rigsby.

'I'm surprised you made it through the fucking interview to get into the job,' the inspector said ruefully. 'A little bullshit and a few lies can get you a long way. Telling the fucking truth and being fucking pious is going to get you fucking nowhere. I'm a senior officer who's been in the job for twenty-five years, so I should know. Think about it.'

CHAPTER 14

Bubba was fast asleep on the sofa when Sponge left the house on Thursday afternoon. He drove to Saddam's house, picked him up and headed over to North London. They parked outside Jazz's house and rang the bell.

His mother came to the door. 'Come on in. You're just in time, I'm cooking. He's upstairs,' she said.

The smell of West Indian cooking drifted up their nostrils as they walked down the hall and up the stairs. They opened Jazz's door without knocking. He was lying on the bed reading a pornographic magazine and watching television.

'Mum, I've told you –' His words tailed off as he looked up and saw Saddam and Sponge. 'What the fuck are you doing here? I work with you, I don't want to see you at home as well! You're worse than fucking cancer, I can't fucking get rid of the pair of you.'

'You shouldn't read that stuff,' said Sponge, sitting down on the bed. 'No wonder there's never any soap in your house.'

'Aren't those the porno mags we seized from those schoolkids? I wondered where they'd got to,' Saddam said, looking at the pile of magazines beside Jazz.

'Never mind that. What the fuck are you two doing in my bedroom?' asked Jazz.

Saddam came straight to the point. 'We came to put a business proposal to you,' he said, flicking through one of the magazines.

'That bloke you went to college with, the drug pusher. We've got something that might interest him,' Sponge continued.

'Something like what?'

'Some stock,' replied Saddam.

'Listen, don't fuck me about. Just come straight out with it.'

'We've got over a million quid's worth of cocaine to flog, Jazz. If he can shift it, we'll all be near enough millionaires.'

'Where the fuck did you come across a million quid's worth of gear?'

'Sponge came across it dumped in a van in a suitcase. He took it home,' lied Saddam.

'On or off duty?'

'Off duty,' said Sponge.

'Where was the van?'

'Near some lock-up garages where I used to play when I was a kid. I went for a nostalgic walk and found it there,' said Sponge.

'How do you know you weren't followed or it wasn't being watched?'

'Number one, I'm not stupid; number two, I know that area like the back of my hand. No one could have hidden there. Besides, I checked around first. I'm bloody sure this is watertight,' replied Sponge.

'And you say it's coke?'

'Yeah,' they both answered.

'Let me ask you something. Did you come to me because I'm black?' asked Jazz, sounding irritated.

'You see, I told you he'd act like this,' Sponge said to Saddam.

'Shut the fuck up, will you?' Jazz said angrily. 'What did you think? He's black, unpredictable, corrupt and criminal-minded. That's what they're all like. It's just a matter of time.'

'You're getting it all wrong,' said Sponge.

'I said shut up,' said Jazz. 'Do you think I'm stupid? Secret meetings, whispers, getting jittery! Spending an inexhaustible supply of fifty-pound notes! When someone like you, who's as tight as a nun's pussy, starts flinging money about, you know it's from something dodgy. Just answer me one thing: how many of you are in on this?'

'Just Sponge and me,' answered Saddam.

'So none of the others know about it?'

'No,' lied Sponge.

'And you come to me, the black guy, when you're desperate, because you think not only will I join in but I'll have the connections?'

'More or less,' said Saddam.

'Do you want me to –' started Jazz before being interrupted by Saddam.

'No, listen, Jazz, we're not asking you to join us. All we're asking is for you to put us in contact with that bloke so he can flog the gear.'

'Fuck right off,' said Jazz. 'The only reason I'm not reporting you is because it'd finish my career as well as yours. Then again, you knew that anyway.'

Sponge had lost interest and was looking at a framed photo of a young black couple on top of Jazz's dressing table. 'Who are they?' he asked, holding up the picture.

'It's my mum and dad's wedding photo.'

'Wicked sideburns! Your dad looks as though he's got an Afro with a chinstrap.'

'Come on, Sponge, let's go,' said Saddam.

'But –' protested Sponge.

'No buts, mate, let's go.'

Sponge got up and went to the door.

'Tell your mother we can't stay for the food, and not too much of that, eh?' said Saddam.

'Just piss off,' replied Jazz, lying back down on the bed and opening his magazine up again.

'Why didn't you let me speak to him?' Sponge asked Saddam as they walked down the stairs.

'Because we'll be able to speak to him again. Don't worry, we'll break him in.'

On Thursday night, Sponge came in with Bubba, who went out for a run rather than go to the Mason's Arms. He had a lot to think about, particularly the phone call he'd received from his cousin the day before.

Vinny had found a decent restaurant in the centre of Dublin; it would cost him one hundred and forty thousand pounds. He could raise only one hundred and twenty thousand by asking for his share of the money. His cousin would provide the rest. He now had to make the decision whether to stay or leave. Right now he had nothing left: his marriage was in tatters and his job was leading him nowhere. He no longer felt pangs of guilt about asking for his cut. He would have to get away quickly because he was pretty sure Sponge and Saddam were trying to sell the drugs. It was only a matter of time before things started to go wrong and he wanted to be as far away as possible when the shit hit the fan.

Knowing that Saddam and Sponge would be returning to the station in anticipation of the biscuits being brought down, Bubba waited for them in the yard after parade. It was not long before the area car materialized with its two wayward occupants.

'Have a word with you?' Bubba asked, calling Saddam aside.

'Sure, mate,' said Saddam.

'It's about my money,' started Bubba.

'What money?' asked Saddam, playing ignorant.

'My money,' answered Bubba. 'I've decided I'll take my cut.'

Saddam hesitated, unsure how to respond. 'Good man! You know it makes sense,' he said, patting Bubba on the back.

'Don't patronize me,' said Bubba. 'When can I get it?'

'Don't be such a sanctimonious git, Bubba. There's nothing that sets you apart from the rest of us. We're all in it together, outlaws in the same scam.'

'When can I get it?' Bubba repeated.

'I'll bring it round tomorrow. In the meantime, where are the biscuits?'

'I'm off to get them,' answered Bubba.

'We're just in time,' Saddam shouted to Sponge, who was already halfway across the yard. 'Biscuits up.'

Speedy had driven around with Rigsby in the front seat for an hour and it was very quiet on the streets. He turned and saw Rigsby dozing off. Suddenly, he slammed on the brakes, making the car skid and screech. Rigsby was given such a jolt he yelled in alarm.

'We're here to police the streets of London, not to build castles in the air,' Speedy said to Rigsby. 'I've got to find you a body. We'll stop the next person that comes down the road.'

As he spoke, he spotted a man walking along on their side of the pavement. Speedy pulled up about ten yards ahead. 'Get out and search him,' he commanded, pulling up the handbrake. 'And nick him.'

'What reasonable grounds do I have? What do I say to him?' exclaimed Rigsby in bewilderment.

'It's one o'clock in the fucking morning and he doesn't look like a barrister! Now get into his fucking pockets,' barked Speedy.

Rigsby got out and approached the man. He looked back at Speedy, who sat behind the wheel watching intently. Speedy gave him a nod. The man drew level with Rigsby and, unsure whether the police officer wanted to speak to him, walked on.

'Excuse me, sir,' Rigsby said politely.

The man turned round and looked at Rigsby. 'What?' he asked aggressively.

'Could I have a word, please?'

'No,' said the man, starting to walk off.

'Excuse me,' repeated Rigsby, realizing he had lost the initiative.

'Piss off,' the man said, walking faster.

Speedy sprang out of the car. 'Where the fuck do you think you're going, you disrespectful black bastard?' he shouted. 'Don't you ever fucking walk away when a copper's speaking to you.'

Recognizing Speedy as a different breed, the man stopped.

'Now go back and speak to him,' Speedy shouted.

Obediently, the man did so. At that moment, the area car drove past. Saddam turned the car and parked it ahead of Speedy's. Sponge and Saddam got out and joined Speedy.

Rigsby was lost for words. 'Where are you coming from?' he finally asked.

'The tube station,' the man replied.

There was a brief pause as Rigsby foraged about for further questions before searching the man. 'Do you live around here?'

'Yes, down the road.'

Rigsby could think of nothing else to say or do. His discomfort was further exacerbated by the watchful eyes of his colleagues.

'Well, get into his pockets then,' goaded Speedy.

'Have you got anything on you you shouldn't have?' Rigsby asked. He looked more nervous than his suspect.

'Like what?'

'Drugs, anything like that,' replied Rigsby.

'No, I haven't,' the man said, voluntarily pulling out the side pockets of his black bomber jacket.

'You won't mind if he searches you then?' interjected Speedy, giving Rigsby his cue.

'Can you empty your pockets for me?' Rigsby asked.

'I haven't got much choice, have I?' the man said, holding his hands in the air so that Rigsby could carry out his search.

Rigsby went through the man's pockets. Finding nothing, he straightened up and gave Speedy a satisfied look.

'What did you just search him for, loose change?' Speedy asked.

'No, drugs,' Rigsby replied.

'If you're searching for drugs, that's the last place you're going to find them. You've missed out three of the most important places. Tell him to take off his trainers, one after the other, then check his socks.'

Rigsby searched the man's trainers and socks.

'Now check the inner pocket of his jeans, the finger pocket at the top.'

Rigsby searched the pocket.

'Now the sleeve pocket of his bomber jacket.'

Rigsby went to the side pocket on the left sleeve of the jacket. He found a small packet of wrapped cannabis resin. 'Whose is this?' he asked the man.

'Mine. You're not going to nick me for something that small? It's only a bit of puff.'

Sponge stepped forward. 'You look like you've had a bit to smoke. It's got to your eyes,' he said.

'No, I've just had a bit to drink,' the man replied.

'We'll keep the cannabis, mate,' said Sponge. 'I'll give you a verbal warning for possession and my colleague's going to arrest you for being drunk.'

'Am I?' asked Rigsby.

'You're about as much use as a wheelchair with pedals. Just do it! And don't ask questions,' said Speedy.

'I'll take the gear,' said Sponge, taking the wrap of cannabis. 'Put him in the van,' he commanded Rigsby.

Rigsby escorted the man to the van, put him inside the prisoner's enclosure and shut the door.

Speedy walked into the canteen and slung Rigsby's incident book in front of him. 'What the fuck did they teach you at Hendon?' he asked, pointing at the book. 'You didn't just bubble yourself up but everybody else as well! What do you mean, you were told by me to search then nick the bloke you brought in?'

'It was what happened,' replied Rigsby.

'I know it was what fucking happened, but where's the fucking evidence?' Speedy retorted. 'You've written four fucking pages without a fucking line of evidence in it.'

'What do you want me to do?' asked Rigsby.

'Rewrite it, you fuckwit,' Speedy replied. 'It might be the truth, but there's no fucking evidence.'

Sponge and Saddam sat at the junction between the Broadway and the A61, watching the traffic go by in front of them.

'We need to get rid of that gear as soon as possible: I'm getting a bad vibe. I got this feeling that this bloke can be the connection we're looking for,' said Saddam.

'We just need to work on Jazz a bit. At the moment he's in one of his Malcolm X moods. It's just a matter of fucking timing,' said Sponge.

'Bubba staying at yours makes it even more difficult,' said Saddam.

'I've got a feeling he's going to piss off out of the job,' said Sponge. 'Things aren't looking too good between him and his missus.'

'His wife never really liked him being in the job,' said Saddam. 'A bit like my missus.'

'You blokes shouldn't get married,' said Sponge.

'This stuff's really quite powerful,' said Saddam. 'I'm spaced out already.'

'Don't get too spaced out on that shit. You've still got to drive around the division without getting me fucking killed,' said Sponge, rolling another joint from the packet of cannabis resin they'd seized from Rigsby's prisoner.

'At least it'll keep me awake,' said Saddam.

Sponge finished rolling and lit the spliff.

'Open the bloody window, will you? It's absolutely booming the place out; the windows are starting to steam up,' Saddam said.

'This is fucking great weed,' said Sponge, sucking on the joint. 'All I need now is to listen to some music.'

'What happened to that wog box you used to carry in the back on nights?' asked Saddam.

'Someone put the window in and nicked it out of the back of the area car when we were dealing with a domestic on the Prado estate a few months ago,' replied Sponge, handing the joint over to Saddam.

Just then a black Ford Sierra went roaring past, jumping a red traffic light.

'Fucking hell,' shouted Saddam, slipping the car into gear. 'I'll bloody have you!' He put on the blue lights and accelerated off after the Sierra. The Ford had already covered some distance and Saddam pushed the area car up to 130 m.p.h. 'I can hardly bloody see,' he exclaimed as they hurtled in pursuit.

'The windows aren't as steamed up as they were before,' said Sponge.

'Not because the fucking windows are steamed up,' said Saddam, leaning forward and peering through the windscreen. 'I'm fucking stoned out of my box.'

The Sierra up in front of them had stopped at the traffic lights further up the A61. By the time the lights had changed they were within forty yards of the vehicle. Without letting his foot off the pedal, Saddam flashed the Sierra to stop. Compliantly, the driver pulled into the side of the road.

Sponge got out to meet the driver, who made no attempt to move. He walked round the car and motioned to the front-seat passenger to wind down her window. It was the landlady and landlord of the Mason's Arms.

'Congratulations, Mick, that was the best red light I've seen in a long time,' Sponge said.

'It wasn't fucking red, it was green,' replied Mick from the driving seat.

'No, it wasn't, it was bloody red. I told you to slow down,' said his wife.

'Oh shut up, you stupid tart,' Mick said.

'Does he normally speak to you like this?' Sponge asked the landlady.

'Only when he's shit-faced,' she replied.

'Would you like to take the knife out of my bloody back?' said Mick in disbelief.

'How much have you had to drink, Mick?'

'About eight pints of Guinness and five shots of whisky.'

'In that case, I'm going to have to ask you to do a breathalyser,' Sponge said.

'Why? Don't you believe me?' said Mick apprehensively.

'Oh, come on, Sponge,' said the landlady. 'You know us too well to do that.'

'Well, I can't let him drive in this fucking state,' replied Sponge. He hesitated. 'Can you drive the car home?' he asked the landlady.

'I haven't got a licence,' she replied.

'Both of you hop in the back of the car and we'll run you home,' Sponge said finally. 'You can pick your car up tomorrow.'

Bubba felt a tug at his ankles as he lay on the sofa in Sponge's living room on Friday afternoon. He woke from his doze and opened his eyes to see Saddam standing before him holding a black bin liner.

Saddam dropped the bag down in front of Bubba. 'Here's your cash, big fella,' he said with a smile.

Bubba sat up as Saddam stooped down to reveal its contents. 'I hope I don't regret this,' said Bubba, rubbing his eyes.

'Listen, Bubba, there are only winners and losers in life,

no in-betweens. You have just decided to be a winner. I'll leave you with your loot: one hundred and seventy-five grand.'

'One seven five?' asked Bubba. 'I thought it was only one twenty.'

'Well, life is full of fucking surprises, isn't it?'

'Yes, it is,' said Bubba, smiling. He would be able to afford the restaurant after all.

It was 11 p.m. on Friday and Saddam had not turned up for work.

'I'm getting fed up with this!' shouted Slippery. 'Jesus Christ on a bicycle! This team is fucking falling apart. First I lose Lionel, now Saddam can't turn up on fucking time. Bubba's wife's just left him and Rigsby's a pain in the fucking arse. Gordon bloody Bennett, it's like captaining the *Titanic*.'

'Well, whatever you do, don't send me out with Rigsby without a prescription,' said Speedy.

Slippery assigned the duties and concluded parade. Just as they were leaving, the telephone rang. Slippery whipped it up. 'Saddam, is that you?' he asked.

'Round the corner, sarge. I'll be in soon.'

'Jump into the Irv when you come in,' said Slippery. 'You're out with Jazz.'

He put the phone down and they went for their coffees. The area-car crew had returned and was waiting patiently in the canteen.

By 11.10 p.m., Saddam had still not turned up. Sponge's mobile phone rang. It was Saddam and, from the background noise, Sponge could tell he was calling from a busy pub. He got up to speak to him outside.

'Where the hell are you? Slippery's been tearing his hair out,' Sponge asked.

'Shouldn't take him long,' replied Saddam.

'When are you coming in, mate?'

'I don't bloody know. I'm beginning to wonder why I should bother working anyway.'

'Listen, just come in tonight,' urged Sponge.

'Yeah, I'll be there soon. I'm just finishing a quick one with my missus. Tell Slippery I'm round the corner,' said Saddam.

'See you in a short while then,' said Sponge, concluding the call. He went back inside.

'That was Saddam, wasn't it? Where the hell is he?' steamed Slippery.

'He told me to tell you he was round the corner, sarge,' answered Sponge.

'Round the corner,' Slippery echoed. 'It's a very long corner he's been coming round. I don't know what's fucking happening. Trying to run this fucking team is like trying to bottle smoke.'

The canteen intercom bleeped twice and the controller's voice came on. *'Slippery, you've got a phone call. Shall I transfer it to the canteen?'*

'Who is it?' asked Slippery.

'Your ex-wife.'

'All I fucking need,' muttered Slippery. *'Put her on hold for a few minutes then put it through to the canteen. I think I'll make myself a strong black coffee before I speak to her.'*

*

Bubba was out with Rigsby in the van. Slippery had issued orders that he wanted the probationers to arrest more suspects; the monthly arrest figures had come out that day and their team was bottom of the divisional league table.

Rigsby was slowly drifting off to sleep.

'Hey, Rigsby, fancy playing a game of Name That Tune?' asked Bubba, breaking wind suddenly. 'Wind down the window, it might smell a bit,' he continued, not bothering to apologize.

Just in front of the King's Arms pub a man was lying propped up against the bus shelter.

'Bollocks! We can't ignore this,' said Bubba, swinging the van into the opposite lane and pulling up beside the man.

They got out to speak to him and noticed he reeked of alcohol.

'I think he's had a bit to drink,' said Rigsby.

'Well, nick him, don't wait to be told,' said Bubba.

They lifted him into the vehicle.

'That's one for the figures,' said Bubba, shutting the van door.

'What's this? "Unsteady on his feet"? How did you come up with that?' asked Slippery angrily.

'At training school we were told to put it down as evidence of drunkenness,' replied Rigsby.

'"Unsteady on his feet,"' ranted Slippery, rereading Rigsby's report book. 'He hasn't walked since he was three, when he had polio. If you'd bothered to look round the corner, you'd have seen his fucking wheelchair. You change that "feet" to "seat". That's about the only way I can think of squaring this one up.'

'But you wanted us to keep up the arrest rate, sarge. Bubba told me to arrest him,' protested Rigsby. 'He was lying by the bus shelter, we couldn't have left him there.'

'I said I wanted figures not cripples,' said Slippery.

Bubba phoned Vinny on Saturday afternoon to make sure that he'd received part of the cash paid into his bank account. The remainder had been transferred into traveller's cheques. When the right moment arrived, he would make his move. Once he had settled in, he would return to collect his wife and children.

They met up in the pub before the Saturday-night shift began. It was already busy; most of the seats were occupied.

'Hello, Joe,' said Bubba. 'Do you do anything other than sit in the pub and get pissed all day?'

'Aye, get pissed all day. What else can I do?'

'Too young to feed the pigeons and too old to chase the birds?' said Bubba.

'I'm off for a leak, before you two start,' said Jazz.

Saddam waited a short while, then followed him to the lavatory. He stood beside Jazz at the urinals. 'Why do blokes always look up when they're having a piss?' he asked.

'Probably from boredom,' replied Jazz.

Saddam hesitated before asking him the next question. 'Have you given more thought to our conversation earlier on?'

'You don't bloody give up, do you?' answered Jazz. 'I've told you, I'm not a criminal.'

'If you've got the cash, you're master. No one asks you how come, but how much?' said Saddam.

'Well, I've told you to leave it. I'm not interested,' said Jazz, doing up his zip and making for the door.

'It's not about black or white any more. It's about rich and poor,' said Saddam.

'I don't care,' retorted Jazz.

'Aren't you going to wash your hands?' Saddam shouted after him.

'What's the point? I stand a better chance of catching something from London tap water than I do from my own piss,' said Jazz, letting the door slam shut.

They had just walked into the canteen when the first call came out. *'All units, an "I" call, a fight, the Broadway outside Scandalous nightclub. One male injured, LAS called, and the suspect believed to be nearby,'* transmitted the controller.

Before the announcement was over, the yard was alive with revving engines and car doors slamming shut as everyone made their way to the call.

By the time the first Northwick car got there, two Newpark units and the ambulance had already arrived. It was not long before the entire Broadway was a fairground of blue lights, with units near and far coming in to cash in on the action.

It was a typical Saturday night, with nightclub- and pubgoers, loiterers, commuters, town-bound traffic, alcohol and high weekend spirits combining to form a cocktail of confusion. Speedy and Rigsby went over to the ambulance to find out what was going on.

'This bloke says he was beaten up by that bloke over there,' explained one of the ambulance crew.

The man got out of the ambulance. He had a bandaged head and had bled so much that one side of it was soaked with blood. 'It was that fucking geezer,' he shouted at Speedy. 'I want him fucking nicked!'

'Any idea what happened?' Speedy asked the ambulance driver, ignoring the man who had just stepped out.

'He went straight fucking for me, I want him fucking nicked,' the man screamed at Speedy a second time. He was pointing to a man who, though drunk, seemed quite relaxed as he chatted to some other police officers who had arrived on the scene.

'Yeah, all right, mate, I heard you the first time. There's no need to fucking spit on me,' Speedy replied.

At that point a bystander came up to Speedy. 'I saw it all and I'm willing to give you a statement. I don't know why those police officers are still talking to him; he should be arrested,' he said, indicating the man speaking with the police officers.

'What happened?' Rigsby asked the witness.

'They got into some sort of argument over a cab and that bloke just started to beat the shit out of him. If it wasn't for us, he would have killed him. He's bloody mad! He shouldn't be on the streets.'

'Go on then, fucking nick him! What are you waiting for?' screamed the assaulted man, pushing Speedy in the back.

'I know you're a victim, mate, but if you push me again I'll smack you in the gob so bloody hard you'll have to stick your toothbrush up your arse to brush your teeth,' Speedy threatened. He walked over to the suspect, who was still standing by the area car talking to the police officers.

'Here, lads! Diet Coke break! On your left!' said Sponge from within the group of officers as some skimpily clad girls walked past. 'Look at the fucking knockers on that Jezebel!'

All heads turned.

'Can you lads give us a ride back?' asked one of the girls.

'Why, can't you get back to the fucking kennels on your own?' the suspect said.

'Like to explain what happened, mate?' Speedy asked.

'The bloke is a wanker,' replied the suspect. He was so drunk he had to lean against the railings to stay upright.

'According to a few witnesses, you went straight for him and if they hadn't stopped you you'd have killed him.'

'And you fucking believe that, do you?' asked the suspect.

'I'm not saying that,' said Speedy. 'Get into the car, will you?' He opened the area-car door.

'Will I fuck!' retorted the suspect.

'You don't have much of a choice. If you don't, I'll fucking force you in,' replied Speedy.

Rigsby grabbed hold of the man's arm. In an instant, he swung round and threw a drunken punch which Rigsby effortlessly evaded. Moments later, the suspect was bundled into the area car.

'Aren't we going to put handcuffs on him?' asked Rigsby.

Speedy ignored him and started up the engine.

'I hope they lock you up and throw away the key,' someone shouted from the crowd of spectators as they drove off.

Rigsby was bemused by the fact that they were heading away from Northwick police station rather than towards it. Without warning, they turned into a residential road and pulled up. Sponge got out and knocked on the front door of one of the houses.

'I thought we were taking him into custody for assault?' asked Rigsby.

Again Speedy ignored him.

Sponge came back to the area car accompanied by a woman. She opened the rear door and, helped by Sponge, pulled the suspect out.

'He's on earlies tomorrow,' said the woman. 'I'm getting fed up with this. He's got a serious drink problem that he won't get help for.'

'It's a good job your kids are asleep,' said Sponge as he helped her carry the man up the steps and into the house.

'Is that bloke a copper?' asked Rigsby.

'You're fucking quick off the mark,' replied Speedy. 'He's a skipper from Kilburn.'

'He assaulted somebody!'

'Look! There are enough bloody people in this job who want to piss on you and fuck up your career, don't I know it,' said Speedy. 'I'm not in the business of doing it to my own fucking colleagues. If you want to survive in this job, you want to make friends not enemies,' he continued. 'That bloke is now going to owe you for the rest of his service and, when you need it, you call in the favour.'

'I won't need a favour from somebody like him,' said Rigsby.

'You've got to be careful about which feet you tread on in this job because they might go with the arse you've got to kiss the next day,' said Speedy.

Sponge walked back and got into the car. 'Twenty-four years in the fucking job and he's more worn out than a whore's toothbrush,' he said sympathetically as they set off back to the station.

'Have you changed your mind yet?' Saddam asked Jazz quietly as they walked into the locker room at the end of the shift.

'Listen, don't bring that stuff up again, OK? I'm not that sort of fucking copper. I joined to uphold the law and serve the community, not destroy it,' replied Jazz.

'Oh, don't be a martyr,' Saddam said. 'There's no such thing as a community, only a group of people who live in a particular locality, who hope that one day they'll strike it lucky and get rich. They couldn't give a shit about you or your ideals.'

'That doesn't mean I should become a criminal, does it?'

'There's no such thing as a criminal, only those that get caught and those that don't. All those concepts are for poor people. Money is God in action! When you've got it to give, nobody gives a shit about what's morally right or wrong,' Saddam whispered. 'Tell me,' he continued. 'If you're on such a moral crusade, why are you so keen to befriend a self-confessed drugs baron?'

'That's different,' answered Jazz.

'I know it is. Other people might not see it like that, though.'

'That's different, and you know it.'

'I said I know. But, you see, it's all a question of interpretation,' said Saddam.

CHAPTER 15

Speedy and Sponge came in to man the area car on Monday afternoon. They left the yard without wasting any time.

'How did you get rid of the gear?' Speedy asked.

'We flushed most of it down the public loos at Kingsbury shopping centre. They're normally quiet in the early hours of the morning,' lied Sponge.

'Bit of a waste of money, eh?' said Speedy. 'Anyway, how are you getting on at home, with Bubba?'

'He's OK. He's very quiet, though,' replied Sponge. 'His woman's caused him a lot of grief.'

The rest of the team paraded at 2.45 p.m., except Saddam, who had not turned up.

'Bubba, I'm afraid I'm going to have to ask you to go into the control room. The controller's called in sick,' Slippery said.

'Fair enough,' replied Bubba indifferently. 'I might as well go now then, sarge.' He got up and left the room, no longer seeing any point in coming into work. His cousin had everything set up. He went down to the control room and settled into the chair. Normally he hated doing this duty, but today he really didn't care.

Before long the touch screen started indicating an incoming call.

'I'll get it,' Bubba said to the other control-room operator. He put on the headset and pressed for the call. *'Police Northwick,'* he answered.

'It's about my scalp, it's in an awful state,' said the caller. *'I can't believe he could do this to me.'*

'Do you want the police, sir?' Bubba asked nonchalantly.

'I want an emergency hairdresser, my scalp's been destroyed.'

'Do you need the ambulance service, sir?' Bubba suggested.

'Why? Can they do a curly perm? I've got to have dinner with my boyfriend's mother tonight and I just don't know –'

'You're having a laugh, aren't you?' interrupted Bubba. Then he recognized the muffled sniggering down the phone. *'Lionel, that's you, isn't it?'*

'Had you going for a bit, didn't I?' said Lionel.

'How are you?'

'Not bad, mate. I can't speak long; I'm not allowed to communicate with you at all. I just thought I'd phone up to find out how you're all doing.'

'Not too bad. I'll be leaving the job soon,' said Bubba casually.

'Why?'

'Long story, but I'll be off really soon. I've had enough.'

'Don't you think you're overreacting?' asked Lionel.

'Trust me, there's been a lot going on. I'll get in touch with you soon,' said Bubba, concluding the call.

The other control-room operator came in with the coffees. Bubba sat up, clearing a small space on his desk.

'Cheers,' he said as the cup was placed in front of him.

Rigsby came into the custody suite to speak to Slippery. 'Can I have a word with you, please, sarge?' he asked.

'Yes, what's the problem?' replied Slippery.

'I'm not comfortable with the way the rest of the team want me to work. I just feel it's wrong, it's not what I joined to do.'

'I remember when I was a detective in the flying squad and we nicked an armed robber. We knew he'd done a bank job but we just couldn't piece together the bits,' said Slippery. 'So one of the chaps brought in a pink bunny-rabbit's outfit. Every thirty minutes he went into his cell, bounced around and kicked the shit out of him. When we next interviewed him he confessed. When he got to court he said to the judge he'd only confessed because a big pink bunny bounced into his cell and kicked the fuck out of him. Of course nobody believed him. So, you see, it's really the end that justifies the means. We make the job work.'

'I can't work like that, I'm afraid, sarge,' said Rigsby.

'You think because you've got a university degree you're better than the rest of us, do you?'

'No, I don't, sarge.'

'Your problem is that you can't do the job and you're looking for somebody else to blame. Speedy's told me how you have to be pushed to do stops; you can't use your initiative.'

'It's got nothing to do with initiative,' replied Rigsby.

'You don't want to upset me. I'm your sergeant; I do your reports. When I was a probby, I was so far up my sergeant's arse, if he suddenly stopped walking I wouldn't have seen daylight for a week.'

'I can't do it, sarge.'

'Just fuck off before I lose my temper!' exploded Slippery.

Rigsby turned and left the custody suite.

*

Jazz was still asleep at midday on Tuesday when there was a knock on his door. His mother normally knocked twice, so he knew it wouldn't be her; his father believed it was his house, so he needed no authority to knock on any door. He got out of bed and put on a pair of jeans. Unlocking the door, he was surprised to see Bubba standing there. Bubba only ever turned up on Sundays for some of his mother's cooking.

'Bubba,' exclaimed Jazz, 'what's the matter?'

'Can I come in?' Bubba asked.

'Yeah,' said Jazz, inviting him in.

'I'm leaving the job,' Bubba announced.

'We've all been leaving the job since we fucking joined,' replied Jazz.

'This is real,' said Bubba.

'When are you leaving?'

'Next week.'

'Why?'

'There's been a fuck-up.'

'Who's done the fucking? And up what?' asked Jazz.

Bubba sat on Jazz's bed and explained everything, beginning with the Sunday night duty, the money they had come across, how it had been shared and how Sponge had become a problem.

'I knew it all along,' Jazz said when Bubba had finished. 'It doesn't take a fucking rocket scientist to know that when Sponge suddenly comes into money and everyone else is fretting when he spends it, you've either all won the lottery or done something dodgy.'

'When did you start to suspect?'

'The night we went to Watford and Sponge handed that fifty-pound note to the receptionist. I saw your faces. What are you going to do?'

'There's a restaurant in Dublin that I'm buying with my cousin,' replied Bubba. 'I've got to bail out while I can.'

'Just one question,' said Jazz. 'Why was I left out?'

'Because you're too much of a straight copper,' answered Bubba. 'Not because you're black.'

'Not because I couldn't be trusted,' said Jazz sarcastically.

'Don't start that. Listen, if you need money –'

'No, mate, I'm OK,' said Jazz, cutting him short. 'Listen, thanks for telling me.'

'Yeah, mate,' said Bubba, getting up. 'I'd better go. I've got to put my things in order before I leave. I just thought you needed to know.'

Jazz kept quiet about Sponge and Saddam trying to use his contact to sell the drugs. He was going to make his own plans and have the last laugh, he'd make sure of that.

Jazz was the last to arrive for the late turn on Tuesday. As he drove in, he remembered he had to ask the station officer whether his cap and baton had been found and handed in. Not yet changed into full uniform, he wore a three-quarter-length leather jacket over his white shirt and blue trousers. He walked across the yard towards the station office and began to press the entry combination of the digital lock.

Just then a marked Leyland DAF police personnel carrier containing eight uniformed officers and a sergeant entered the yard. They were members of the Territorial Support

Group, the TSG, an itinerant squad that operated within 2 Area of the Metropolitan Police district. Having no permanent base, they used police-station facilities at their convenience.

The vehicle suddenly stopped. Jazz ignored it and twisted the door handle. As he moved to enter the passage, the driver called out to him. 'Excuse me, mate.'

Jazz looked round, waiting for the man to ask where the canteen was. Instead the side door of the vehicle slid open. Resisting the temptation to make them come to him, he walked down the ramp of the custody suite towards the van. Two officers got out and met him halfway down the ramp. Smiling and raising his eyebrows enquiringly, he asked politely, 'Yes, how can I help you, mate?'

'Who are you, mate?' the first of the two asked in an east London accent.

'What?' Jazz asked, not quite sure that he'd heard the question properly.

'Who are you, mate?' the officer repeated.

Uncertain whether they were serious, he answered. 'Tiger fucking Woods!'

'We're not fucking about, mate! Answer the question,' the second officer said caustically.

From his tone, Jazz realized he was not joking. Another officer emerged from the van, which remained where it was with the engine humming. Bewildered, Jazz produced his warrant card and handed it to the officers.

He watched them hold it up to the light and compare the likeness of his picture with his face. Satisfied, they gave it back to him.

'Sorry, mate,' one of the officers apologized.

Suddenly it clicked. They could only have apprehended him for a single reason.

'Who the fuck do you think you are, coming into this yard and embarrassing me like this?' Jazz exclaimed.

'I'm sorry, mate, I've already apologized. Besides, how was I to know who you were?' said the officer.

'You're not interested in who I am. It's what I am that's the problem,' Jazz said angrily.

The third officer moved forward to stand beside the other two. Jazz noticed the chevrons above his shoulder numbers, indicating his sergeant's rank. He ignored this and continued speaking.

'I've been in the job five years and never worked anywhere other than this nick. I come in every shift with a hundred and twenty other coppers who work at this fucking nick and no one's ever stopped them. You don't even fucking work here, so what makes you think you can drive in off the street and stop me?'

'Calm down, mate,' the sergeant said soothingly. 'We didn't know who you were. My officers haven't done anything wrong in asking you who you are; after all, you're not in uniform.'

'I'm in half fucking blues,' said Jazz.

'Yes, but I can't really tell those are police trousers and a police shirt from that distance. You're walking into a police station and you're not in full uniform,' replied the sergeant.

'Neither is anybody else who walks in for a tour of duty. I don't see you stopping them! Do you honestly think if I was a burglar I'd burgle a police station? Besides, you sat there and watched me punch in the lock combination,' Jazz objected.

'You could have been a terrorist,' suggested one of the officers.

'What?' said Jazz. 'How many black fucking IRA terrorists have you seen before? What fucking planet are you on?'

'I think you're overreacting. You've got an attitude problem and I won't have you having a go at my officers,' the sergeant retorted.

'I don't like people dictating to me how I should feel when they treat me this way, sergeant,' Jazz said.

'You've obviously joined this job with a chip on your shoulder. I suggest you shed it before it becomes a log,' the sergeant advised.

'Insult me but don't patronize me,' Jazz replied.

He turned and walked back up the ramp. Tapping the combination in again, he went into the station office.

The area car was still sitting in the yard at 3.45 p.m. Its driver, Saddam, had not turned up for work. The early-turn controller had sent a message to Saddam's local police station and they had sent a sergeant and inspector round to call at his address. Saddam opened the door still in casual clothes. He had spent the whole morning pottering around and had no inclination to go to work. The sole reason why he had worked the unsocial hours was for the money, and that reason no longer existed. He had taken the phone off the hook because he knew the control room would be trying to get in touch with him.

'PC 135 November X-ray?' the sergeant asked him.

'He's not here at the moment,' lied Saddam. The last thing he wanted was for them to radio their control room saying he was still at home.

'Any idea where he is?' asked the inspector.

'He left for work about an hour ago.'

'Well, he hasn't arrived because we've been asked by the Northwick control room to find out why he's not there,' said the sergeant.

'Well, I don't fucking know,' said Saddam. 'I'll let him know you fucking called.'

'Who are you, sir?' asked the inspector.

'A mate of his.'

'What's your name, sir?'

'Why do you want to know that?' asked Saddam apprehensively.

'Just to prove we've been round,' answered the inspector.

'I can't tell you that,' replied Saddam.

'Why not?' asked the inspector.

'I'm round here shagging his missus,' answered Saddam, just to see the expression on their faces.

'May we speak to his wife?'

'No, you can't,' said Saddam. 'Look, why don't you come back later? Can't you see I'm busy?'

'Listen, we need to speak to somebody,' said the sergeant earnestly.

'I'll give him the message,' said Saddam.

'If you could, please,' said the inspector.

'OK, I'll give him the message. I've got to go now.'

'Who's at the door?' His wife shouted from the bedroom.

'The fucking filth,' Saddam shouted back. With that, he closed the door and went into the bedroom.

'What did they want?' his wife asked as he walked in.

'Some blokes from work. Get some sleep, you've got a long way to travel,' he replied.

The rest of the team had paraded on time. Since Saddam wasn't there to drive the area car, Sponge, the area-car operator, joined them in the team office.

'Can you get us some tubes for the breathalyser?' Slippery asked Sonia. She bent down to open the cupboard. 'Stay like that, I want to remember you just like that,' he said.

'Bit slow, isn't she?' remarked Sponge.

'You dozy tart, you still haven't got it. You'll probably come in every day and entertain us all when Slippery asks you to bend over to get something,' said Speedy.

'Anyway, I need to start parade,' said Slippery, drawing the duties binder towards him. 'The probationers can walk today,' he announced. 'They've been carried about in vehicles for too fucking long. Rigsby, you can walk the Broadway.'

'Can somebody drop me off?' asked Rigsby.

'We don't drive over any bridges on the way there,' said Speedy.

'Who said you were driving?' Slippery asked Speedy. 'Someone's going to have to go into the station office; the station officer has phoned up sick. Any volunteers?'

'Can't one of the probationers do it?' protested Speedy.

'It's a bit too complicated; they haven't had the training yet,' answered Slippery.

'Who said you needed to be trained? When I was a probationer, I was slung into the station office and told to get the fuck on with it,' said Speedy.

Rigsby had been summonsed to see the superintendent and was escorted there by his reporting sergeant, Slippery.

Slippery took a deep breath as they stood outside the office door before knocking. 'Come in,' the superintendent's voice rang out from inside. Slippery pushed the door slowly, then took a step into the large, sparsely furnished office. Without getting up, the superintendent ushered them to two chairs in front of his desk.

'From what I hear, you've spent the few weeks you've been at this nick being a complete nuisance. What's really surprising is how successful you've been at it,' the superintendent began.

'I've only challenged what I've felt was wrong, sir,' said Rigsby uncomfortably.

'Why do you want to pick a fight here?' the superintendent replied. 'There's a whole world out there that wants one; why don't you fight with it?'

'That isn't why I joined the job, sir,' Rigsby said.

'Tell me something, did you join with any ambitions or do you intend to be a wanker for the next thirty years of service?' asked the superintendent, leaning forward with his elbows on the desk.

'I just point out things some officers don't want to hear,' said Rigsby.

'If you've got ambitions, you've got to learn that telling people what they want to hear is always better than telling them what you think,' advised the superintendent. 'If you can't learn that, then you've got an ice cube's hope in hell of getting anywhere in this job.'

Bubba took off his blue police jumper and tie, placed them in his locker, took out his newspaper and went out into the station office. He had volunteered to do the shift.

The early-turn station officer was still dealing with some customers when Bubba walked in. 'Are you taking over?' he asked.

'Yes,' replied Bubba.

'I'll be with you in a minute.'

After the out-going station officer had handed over, Bubba ushered in his first customer. The caller had come in to report an accident. It took thirty minutes to fill in the report booklet. The foyer was already beginning to fill up with other callers and it was getting busier and busier. By 6.30 p.m. Bubba had filled out two accident report booklets and two crime reports, and three people had reported on bail. By the time he got a phone call from the control room informing him that there was nobody to relieve him for refreshments, the strain was building up.

The next customer came in. 'I want to make a complaint,' she said.

'What about?' asked Bubba.

'The way I was treated yesterday when an officer gave me a parking ticket. I didn't like his attitude,' she explained. 'He could have told me to move first.'

Suddenly, Bubba could take no more. 'So you want to complain about the fact that he didn't give you a warning?' he asked sarcastically.

'Yes,' she replied.

'Do you think perhaps you've got a bit too much spare time on your hands?' said Bubba.

'And I don't like your attitude either, officer,' she began. 'I demand to see someone more senior.'

Bubba lost his cool. 'I've been working non-stop since I came in here; my life's in turmoil and nobody cares. My missus has just flipped lesbo on me and doesn't know whether she's Arthur or Martha. I could lose my marriage and my kids, and you're here talking to me about parking tickets. Why don't I give you something to really fucking complain about?' said Bubba, unzipping his trousers. He took out his penis and placed it on the front counter. 'Fucking complain about that!' he shouted.

The woman leapt back in horror. Bubba replaced his penis and, leaving her standing there, walked straight into the custody suite and put his warrant card on the desk in front of Slippery. 'I'm going home, I've had enough,' he said.

'What?' asked Slippery.

'Fuck this! I resign!' said Bubba.

Speedy came rushing into the locker room as Bubba was packing his belongings into his bag. 'What the fuck's going on?' he asked. 'Slippery came into the canteen and told us you'd just packed the job in.'

'Yeah, I've packed the job in,' Bubba sighed in contentment.

'That wasn't part of the agreement,' said Speedy. 'I hate the job just as much as you do, but we all agreed to stay in for six months. We're starting to bring attention to the team: Lionel's resigned, Saddam won't come into work on time, Sponge is always pissed and now you're leaving.'

'Bringing attention to the team?' asked Bubba. 'What do you mean? All you're worried about is you and your pension. My marriage has fallen apart, I stand to lose my wife and my kids, and all you can think about is me keeping up a front to protect you. Well, I'm thinking about myself and my family. I'm doing something I've been wanting to do for years but haven't been able to because I didn't have the money: packing the job in.'

'You've got to admit things are beginning to look a bit . . . sepulchral,' said Speedy.

'Fucking sepulchral?' exclaimed Bubba.

'Yeah, sepulchral,' replied Speedy defensively.

'I can see Rigsby's beginning to fucking rub off on you,' said Bubba. 'I'll be over the road in the pub if you lads want a celebratory drink.' He slammed his locker door shut and walked out.

They found Bubba playing on the fruit machine, pint in hand. 'Grab a table, I'll be over once I finish this,' he shouted.

Saddam, who'd turned up for work eventually, bought the drinks while Sponge went to watch Bubba play.

'I don't know whether to collect or play on,' said Bubba, his eyes on the button flash.

'Play on,' suggested Sponge.

'If you're telling me to play on, it must be time to stop,' replied Bubba, pressing the collect button.

Jazz joined Saddam at the bar. 'How much gear have you got to flog?' he asked.

Saddam looked at him uncertainly. 'A suitcaseful,' he said.

'We'll take a sample round to his place this evening,' said Jazz.

'What? You mean you've changed your mind?'

'I said we'll take a sample of the gear over there this evening.'

'Don't you think we should take the whole thing over there? That way, we won't have to worry about it any more.'

'You do that and he'll see you as an amateur straight away. Nobody takes their entire merchandise over to negotiate. Two things,' said Jazz.

'What?'

'First, you're my clients, not coppers. Second, I'm only taking one of you with me and that's Sponge, mainly because, between the two of you, he looks least like a copper.'

'Anything you say,' replied Saddam. He looked round to make sure that Sponge was out of earshot.

'You know we could go half and half on this. We don't have to include Sponge; all we have to do is tell him we got ripped off.'

'If I get involved in this, nobody gets double-crossed,' replied Jazz.

'Only a suggestion, just bear it in mind,' said Saddam.

'Tell me something, why have you suddenly changed your mind?'

'I got stopped by the TSG in the back yard of the nick. I don't know why, but it's taken me all this time to realize I'll never be one of you. I'm just the wrong fucking colour.'

Jazz and Sponge made their excuses and left the pub. There was no persuading Bubba, but they did arrange to go out for another leaving drink for him. They rang Dylan's bell and, after a short interval, he buzzed them up. As usual, he was rolling a joint. A cocktail of cocaine and other drugs lay in the centre of the living-room table.

'You shouldn't smoke that stuff so often; it fucks up your memory,' Jazz said.

'What did you just say?' Dylan joked.

'Listen, Dylan. I've brought you some business, no questions asked. Are you interested?'

'You know any business is business to me. Fire away, baby, I'm all ears.'

Jazz gestured to Sponge to hand him over a packet of the cocaine, then threw it at Dylan.

'What's this?' Dylan asked.

'Cocaine,' replied Jazz. 'That's a sample. There's a warehouse full of it and this gentleman and his associates would like to see if you can act as an agent. They'll try you out with a suitcase of the stuff.'

'This is a bit of a shock,' said Dylan.

'You're a fucking drug dealer, aren't you?' Jazz asked him.

'Not exactly. I like to think of myself as an uncertificated pharmacist,' Dylan replied. 'I can't bloody think; I need some stronger stuff. I'll just pop to the bedroom for my stash.'

When he came back and settled down into his chair, they could see from his actions that he was both nervous and excited. They set about smoking a few joints before returning to the business in hand.

'Can you do it?' Jazz asked Dylan.

'Yeah, I think so,' he replied.

'You're not as big-time as you made out, are you? Just full of shit, Dylan.'

'Give me a break!'

'Tell you what, I'll do even better: you cross me and I'll break your fucking neck,' said Jazz. 'I'll bring you the case tomorrow.'

As they walked down the steps of Dylan's flat, Sponge grabbed Jazz by the arm. 'Why don't we just do this together? Fuck Saddam, fuck the Met, fuck everybody; let's just get the money and bail.'

'I thought Saddam was your mate?' said Jazz.

'He is, but that doesn't mean we have to include him in this deal. He isn't here now.'

'You guys make me sick,' said Jazz.

'Fuck you!' said Sponge. 'Don't think you're any better than the rest of us.'

Wednesday was a rest day. Bubba spent the time buying a plane ticket and making preparations to go. He went back to Sponge's place to pick up a few of his things.

Sponge came into the living room as Bubba was putting

the ticket in the side pocket of his travelling bag. 'So you're going to fuck off and leave us then? There'll be no one left on the team, you know,' he said, sitting on the sofa and opening a can of beer.

'You'll just have to grin and bear it,' said Bubba.

As he spoke, the doorbell rang. Sponge got up to answer it.

It was Jazz. 'Are you packing up already?' he asked Bubba, finding himself a seat.

'Yeah, I'm not hanging about; I've got business to take care of.'

'Are you going to miss the job?'

'For me, becoming a policeman was the end of all small fuck ups and the start of one long fucking stupidity,' replied Bubba. 'I'm not going to miss it.'

'Are you coming down the pub?' asked Jazz.

'I've got to have lunch with the wife. I'll meet you lot later,' said Bubba.

Jazz and Sponge waited for him to leave before proceeding with their business. On Saddam's instructions, Sponge had taken care to withhold a quarter of the merchandise.

Jazz rang the bell and Dylan buzzed them up. They dragged the case up the stairs and into the living room. Dylan stood there in stunned silence when they'd unzipped the suitcase. 'I can't shift this bloody lot,' he protested.

'Bollocks,' said Jazz. 'You're a fucking pusher; how long will it take?'

'A while,' replied Dylan.

'Good, because they've got a warehouse full of the stuff,' said Jazz.

'What the hell are you doing involved in this sort of racket?' Dylan asked.

'I told you, Dylan, no questions asked. Your main concern is that you get paid. You're going to continue to make thousands of pounds, and the less you know the better for you.'

'That sounds good enough for me. Let's do business,' said Dylan.

'It's that pissing-in-the-wind feeling you have about the job and the people in it,' said Speedy as he stood with Bubba at the bar. 'But we had an agreement, and now you're leaving, everything is falling apart.'

'Come on, Speedy,' said Bubba. 'You didn't fucking believe that with that sort of money anybody would stick to a spur-of-the-moment agreement?'

The landlady put their pints down in front of them. 'Seventeen pounds fifty, please, gentlemen,' she said.

'I'll give you an extra twenty quid for ten minutes in the back yard,' said Bubba, handing her a twenty-pound note.

She shot him a dirty glance.

'I can't help myself; your husband's a lucky man,' said Bubba.

'You're just randy because your wife has left you. Haven't had it in ages?' joked the landlady.

'Sponge said he walked into his living room the other night and caught Bubba doing things to himself he'd never known a bloke be generous enough to do to a woman,' said Speedy.

'Well, I'm a married woman,' said the landlady.

Mick rang the bell. 'Any last orders, lads?' he asked the group.

'Yes,' shouted Bubba. 'I leave my kidneys to medical science.'

'I hear you're leaving for Ireland,' Mick said to Bubba.

'Yeah, in a week's time.'

'In that case, why don't you blokes stay behind and have a drink?' said Mick. 'I'd like to thank you for not nicking me the other night.'

'Cheers,' answered Bubba.

Saddam phoned Sponge on Thursday morning, curious to hear how things had gone.

'Not too bad,' said Sponge. 'The bloke's taken the gear and says he'll get in contact with us once he sells it.'

'You bloody what? Didn't he pay you any money?'

'No. Don't worry, Jazz took care of everything; he was fucking brilliant.'

'What happens if he decides to keep the fucking money?'

'Jazz said we had a warehouse of the stuff and he believed it.'

'Fair enough,' said Saddam.

'We haven't even discussed Jazz's cut yet.'

'Equal,' replied Saddam.

'Suppose he wants more?'

'We'll cross that fucking bridge when we get to it,' said Saddam. 'The only thing I'm worried about is Jazz crossing us.'

'Reckon he would?'

'You never know in this sort of business. IC3s turn on

other IC3s, talk less of us,' replied Saddam. 'Did you keep the amount I told you to aside?'

'Yeah, I left it in a sports bag in the shed.'

'Well, let's go to Jazz's tomorrow and find out when he expects the money to come through. I'm fucking fed up with this waiting around. Now Bubba's left, working on the team'll be like rowing a sinking boat.'

CHAPTER 16

Speedy and Jazz were manning the area car on Friday morning. The rest of the team paraded on time, except for Saddam, who had not come in by 7.20 a.m.

'This is really taking the fucking piss,' complained Slippery. 'I hate doing this, but I'm going to have to pull rank. When Saddam turns up, ask him to come and see me. We'll have to start parade without him and unfortunately we're another officer short.'

'Just don't send me out with Rigsby,' said Sponge. 'I've had shits that are more interesting than he is.'

Slippery ignored him and assigned them to their vehicles. 'I'm going to have to take Jazz off the area car and put Rigsby on it with Speedy. We're desperately short. We've got no officers on this team. I need a coffee,' he finally said, concluding parade.

After a cup of tea, Jazz and Sonia went out in the Irv for a short patrol. 'How are you finding the team?' he asked Sonia as they drove along.

'It's different to what I thought it would be,' she replied. 'You blokes spend so much time hanging around in the canteen that the dust in there hangs in the air.'

'Good to see you're getting the general idea,' said Jazz. 'Have you settled in OK?'

'I'm just beginning to realize there are three sexes: man, woman and policewoman.'

'It could be worse at other places. Working with coppers isn't that bad.'

'Coppers have one principle: if you can't fuck it or play football with it, piss all over it,' she retorted.

'Like I said to you before, you're working in a predominantly male environment,' said Jazz.

'What? Do I need to strap on a dildo when I come into work, just to fit in?' replied Sonia.

'They'll accept you eventually. Even if they don't, new officers will join the team and old ones will leave, pushing you up the hierarchy. Until then, you'll have to keep your head down.'

Soon they were back in the canteen for refreshments, sharing the table next to the CID officers.

'Oh, Jazz,' said one of them. 'Remember that IC3 burglar you nicked? Robinson, his name was.'

'Oh, yes,' recalled Jazz.

'He was found guilty, got five years. He went not guilty, but we had enough evidence against him to sink a battleship.'

'How did he take it?'

'Badly, he was absolutely gutted. He was sobbing like a baby, saying he couldn't do five years in prison again. I just told him to do the best he could,' said the detective, laughing.

'Five years is a little too harsh for one burglary,' Jazz said, failing to see the humorous side.

'Some other news for you. Apparently, according to the autopsy report on that bloke Lionel hit, his brain haemorrhage came from his head hitting the ground, not from a blow. Some witnesses say they saw him slip, so it looks like Lionel's in the clear.'

After work Saddam and Sponge met Jazz by his car. They wanted to speak to him.

'How are things going?' Saddam asked.

'I don't know; I'll speak to him in a week,' replied Jazz.

'We were just worried he might cross us,' said Saddam.

'Well, it's a risk we've got to take. He doesn't know who you blokes are, so my guess is that he won't. We've just got to sit tight and wait.'

'Just fucking remember we're in this together,' said Saddam.

'What's that supposed to fucking mean?' Jazz asked. 'I get the feeling you don't trust me.'

'I just want to get paid,' replied Sponge. 'I wouldn't trust my own mother with a suitcase full of cocaine, let alone you.'

'I'll give you a ring tonight after you've spoken to him,' said Saddam. 'We need to keep track of him.'

'Wait a minute, who said I was going to speak to him tonight?' objected Jazz.

'I'm telling you to,' replied Saddam.

'Get this straight: nobody tells me what to do,' said Jazz. 'Who the hell do you think you are?'

'Now listen up, guys,' said Sponge, defusing the situation. 'Let's calm down. There's a lot of fucking money involved here, and I'm not going to let petty squabbling get in the way of my share. If you blokes want to kill each other afterwards, you can.'

Jazz got into his car. Without another word, he started the engine and drove off.

'I don't trust that black bastard,' said Saddam, watching him go. 'We've already been ripped off by his kind; I'm not going to let it happen again.'

'You're letting this whole fucking thing get to you; just loosen up,' said Sponge. 'Come on, let's go for a drink.'

Rigsby had handed in his resignation at the end of the shift on Friday and was now using up the remainder of his annual leave. The team cheered when Slippery announced the news in the canteen after parade on Saturday morning.

'They might as well have sent us a box of laxatives; that bloke Rigsby irritated the fucking shit out of everybody,' said Speedy.

'Good riddance to bad rubbish,' said Saddam. 'Who picked him up, Onyx?'

'He wasn't that bad,' said Jazz in Rigsby's defence.

'He was a fucking jackass in an anorak with a university degree,' said Speedy.

'Are we going to buy him a leaving present?' asked Sonia.

'I'd be happy to fill up a specimen bottle for him as my contribution,' said Speedy.

'We've got a few blokes coming in to keep up the numbers; we're fucking ridiculously short at the moment,' said Slippery. 'In the meantime, I've passed my Special Branch board and I'm waiting for a date.'

'Who's going to take over?' asked Sponge.

'I don't know, but there's talk of Jazz acting up until they can find a skipper,' replied Slippery. 'The sooner I can get away from you lot the better.'

After the shift, Saddam, Jazz and Sponge met up in the pub. Joe was sitting on a bar stool as they walked in.

'How are you doing, Joe?' Sponge asked as they approached the bar.

'Not bad. I've spent the last few days moving,' said Joe.

'Where? To the cemetery?' Sponge joked.

'No, into your sister's flat, or didn't she tell you she'd kicked her boyfriend out?'

'My sister's sexually active. What you going to do, stick your dick in the freezer to get it hard?'

The landlady came round to serve them and Saddam ordered the drinks. When they arrived, they seated themselves on a bench in the beer garden.

'I can't wait to get my hands on the cash. I've had enough of working understrength. Now Rigsby's bloody gone, things are going to get bloody worse,' said Saddam.

'He was a waste of fucking uniform,' said Sponge. 'He should be done for wasting police time.'

'If we'd encouraged him rather than taking the piss out of him, I'm sure he wouldn't be jacking it in,' said Jazz.

'Like I've always said: if you can't take a joke, you shouldn't be in the job,' replied Sponge.

'He was never really given a chance, though, was he?' said Jazz.

'The sooner I get out of the job the better. I can see in less than five years' time, all they'll end up with is a brigade of short-haired dikes and long-haired faggots,' said Saddam.

'I'm sure people would rather have a bent copper who's straight than a straight copper who's bent,' replied Jazz. 'I don't think any one of us is in a position to criticize other coppers, do you? Anyway, I've got to go,' he said, finishing his pint.

After Jazz had left, Saddam turned to Sponge. 'I don't trust that bloke. Now you see why I told you to keep some of the gear,' he said.

'You're just getting paranoid,' said Sponge.

'We'll see if we can flog the rest of the gear,' said Saddam. 'Try and kill two birds with one stone. All I need is a couple more thousand and I'll be ready to leave the job straight away.'

'Fancy a game of pool?' Sponge asked.

The next morning Jazz was woken by a knock on the door. He got up and dressed before opening up to find Saddam and Sponge waiting outside. 'What the fuck do you want?' he asked.

'We just popped round to find out if there's any joy,' answered Sponge.

'Fucking joy? I spoke to you on Friday about this,' said Jazz.

'We're stressed out fucking waiting,' replied Saddam.

Jazz let them in and they sat down on the bed. 'If you two want this deal to go through, then the one thing you don't want to do is look desperate. He'll pick up on it. I want to give him time to flog the stuff,' he said.

'How long?' asked Saddam.

'A few weeks,' said Jazz.

'That's far too fucking long,' replied Saddam. 'Don't you think about fucking crossing us, Jazz!'

'Listen, don't come to my house and start threatening me. You think I don't know about the car you stopped and the money you all shared, leaving me out?'

There was a stunned silence.

'Who told you that?' asked Saddam. 'Bubba, wasn't it?'

'Don't worry about that. What matters is that you only decided to tell me when you couldn't flog the drugs and apparently you're the only ones running this enterprise. The others don't know,' said Jazz.

Jazz's mother put her head round the door. 'Why don't you put up the toilet seat when you go to the loo?' she shouted at him. 'How many times am I going to have to tell you and your father?'

'Mum, how many times have I told you to knock?' replied Jazz. 'I'll clean it later; stop embarrassing me.' He turned back to Sponge and Saddam. 'I'll speak to him in a few weeks and that's all there is to say,' he said resolutely.

'Fair enough,' said Saddam, getting up. 'We'll speak to you soon.'

They walked to Sponge's car in silence until Saddam said, 'I don't like Jazz being totally in control. I'm not fucking waiting.'

'What are you going to do?' asked Sponge.

'We're not going to wait for him,' said Saddam. 'I'll work something out.'

*

Jazz went round to see Dylan. He wasn't sure about the deal any more and wanted to see what he could do to call it off.

Dylan was smoking a joint. 'Easy, geezer! What's good?' he greeted Jazz.

'I'm sweet. How's the deal coming along?' Jazz asked without wasting any time.

'I've put the word out; I'll be able to flog it soon. I've put a lot of effort into this,' said Dylan, looking complacent.

'Could you call it off?' Jazz asked. 'Something's gone wrong.'

'Call it off?' echoed Dylan.

'Yeah.'

'Sorry, mate. I've got a reputation to keep and money to make. We go back a long way, Jazz, and I'd do a lot for you, but I'm afraid I can't do that,' said Dylan. 'Besides, what are you worried about? Once this first deal goes through, we're all going to be rich men!'

Monday was a rest day.

'There's nothing in the fucking fridge,' shouted Sponge from the kitchen, slamming the fridge door shut.

'I just put eighty quid's worth of fucking shopping in there,' Bubba shouted back.

'I can see that, but there's no fucking booze,' replied Sponge, coming out of the kitchen. 'Out of hash and out of booze: this is bloody hell on earth!'

The phone began to ring and Sponge ran into his bedroom to answer it. 'Hello?'

'Get the bag and pick me up at Finchley Central tube station. I've got a lead,' said Saddam in an urgent voice.

'What is it?' asked Sponge.

'I'll tell you on the way there,' replied Saddam. 'Just meet me there in forty-five minutes.'

'OK, see you there,' said Sponge, putting down the phone. He felt a rush of excitement as he went into the bathroom and got dressed.

'Where are you off to?' Bubba asked.

'Somewhere with Saddam,' replied Sponge.

'You're still going to be around to take me to the airport tomorrow, aren't you?' asked Bubba.

'I'll be back before then,' replied Sponge as he opened the door.

'If you're not back by five in the morning, I'll take a cab,' said Bubba.

'I'll be back before then,' shouted Sponge, slamming the door behind him.

'Where are we going?' Sponge asked as Saddam jumped into the car.

'Brixton,' said Saddam. 'Pick up Minty on the way.'

'Minty?' asked Sponge. 'Why's Minty coming with us?'

'He's the lead,' replied Saddam.

'So why the fuck are we going to Brixton?' asked Sponge as they drove along. 'It's really rough.'

'Exactly. It's the easiest place to flog a load of gear if you've got it. Minty's got contacts there.'

'This is giving me a bad vibe.'

'Trust me,' said Saddam. 'This can't go wrong.'

*

Jazz picked up the phone in the living room. It was Dylan.

'All right, geezer?' Dylan said.

'Yeah, what's up?' Jazz asked.

'So much bloody money, geezer! They want more! More gear!' Dylan said excitedly.

'What do you mean?'

'I went to this amazing house! The bloke is loaded, real big fishhead. They bought the gear but they want more! When can you bring it over?'

'I'll need to pick up the money first,' replied Jazz.

'Well, come over then, what are you waiting for? I've got the money here,' said Dylan.

Jazz put on a pair of trainers and picked up a suitcase. He ran up his road on to Burnt Oak Broadway and down Watling Avenue.

Saddam, Sponge and Minty sat in the Brixton Café at one of the tables facing the toilets. Minty was a short, scruffy-looking middle-aged man and a compulsive swearer with a pronounced stammer. The Brixton Café was a small, trendy bar just behind the tube station.

'I thought you said you had a contact?' Sponge probed Minty.

'I-I-I-I d-d-do. Just f-f-fucking chill,' replied Minty.

'So where is he?' asked Sponge.

'I-i-it's not a h-h-he! It's here,' said Minty. 'A-a-all we h-have to do is wait around and then p-p-p-pop to the bogs from t-time to t-t-time. N-normally a f-f-few dealers h-hang around there.'

'Once we make a contact, we'll flog the gear and get out,' explained Saddam. 'Minty's done it before, haven't you, Minty?'

Minty nodded.

They sat there for a while, taking turns to go to the toilet. Apart from the odd dubious-looking petty pedlar hanging about in the corridor, there was nothing. Eventually they decided to try later, Minty having suggested that they might have come too early.

As they walked out of the bar, a Rastafarian riding a mountain bike along the pavement came up to them. 'Yeah, white boy! You looking to buy something?' he asked, a distinctive slur to his voice.

Anxious that they might be watched, Minty invited the man to call Sponge's mobile phone number from the nearest telephone booth. Three minutes later, the phone rang; Sponge handed it to Minty.

'I'll fucking speak to him,' said Saddam, taking the phone from Minty, 'otherwise we might be here all fucking night.'

'Yeah, do you want something, rude-boy?' the man asked with the same recognizable slur.

'We've got a sports bag full of coke to sell,' said Saddam.

'Cocaine?' asked the man rhetorically.

'That's right.'

'How much you want for it, white boy?'

'About two hundred and fifty grand.'

'Well, I ain't got that sort of money. I'll make a few enquiries and discuss money with you later. All I want is commission.'

'When are you going to phone us?' asked Saddam. 'We're not from round here.'

'Give me one hour.'

'What, to find someone who can afford it?' asked Saddam.

'This is Brixton, my friend, you get me! There's always someone willing to buy something for any price. Just give me an hour.'

'OK then, we'll hang around,' replied Saddam. He handed the phone back to Sponge. 'We're in business, my son! I bloody well told you, these blacks know their stuff when it comes to drugs; pity they don't know much about anything else,' he said triumphantly. 'I've got a good feeling about this one. The bloke might be a Rasta, but at least he's fucking white. So he'll be less likely to rip us off.'

'What I d-d-don't f-f-fucking under-s-s-stand is why he's f-f-fucking calling you white boy,' said Minty. 'T-t-t-thinks h-he's fucking black, does he?'

The moment the Rastafarian put down the phone, he rang another number. It was a long time before it was answered. 'Angel?' he asked down the line. 'I've got some white boys who come down with some cocaine say they want money.'

'How much?' asked Angel.

'Two hundred and fifty.'

'Pounds?'

'No, grand.'

'What you want to do?'

'Get Slim and Ninja, bring along the gun. I'll take them down to the side of Harry's nightclub.'

Forty minutes had elapsed. They sat in the Range Rover waiting for the phone to ring and sharing a joint to pass the time.

'What are you doing in the job nowadays?' Sponge asked Minty. 'Last time I heard of you, you were on long-term sick.'

'I got c-c-c-c-cast,' replied Minty. 'I had a m-m-m-moody f-f-fucking complaint hanging over me, s-s-so my fed rep got the job to s-s-sort out an early retirement.'

'What did you get cast with?' asked Sponge.

'A b-b-b-bad back,' said Minty.

'I thought you fucking worked for ANTS Removals now?' said Saddam.

'W-w-what's that g-g-got to f-f-fucking do with it?'

'What are the chances of us getting ripped off, Minty?' asked Sponge.

'N-n-n-none and f-f-f-fuck all.'

'Well, when's he going to ring us back?'

'In th-th-the n-next couple of min-n-n-nutes, t-t-t-touch wood,' Minty replied, tapping his groin. 'I've got a j-j-j-joke f-f-for you,' he said.

'Yeah, go on,' said Sponge.

'W-w-what d-d-do you c-c-call a Welshm-m-man with t-t-two sheep under his arm?'

'I don't know,' replied Saddam.

'A p-p-pimp!'

'Minty, I've just thought of a cure for that stammer of yours,' said Sponge.

'W-w-what?'

'Shutting the fuck up!'

'P-p-piss off, you Welsh git!'

Suddenly the phone rang.

'You'd better speak to him,' said Sponge, handing Saddam the phone.

'Hello,' said Saddam.

'Yeah, white boy,' said the Rastafarian. 'Where are you now?'

'Still around the High Street.'

'Well, you come down to Harry's. You know where it is?'

'Do you know where Harry's is?' Saddam asked Minty.

Minty shook his head.

'No, how do we get there?' answered Saddam.

'Just follow Streatham High Road, keep going straight.'

The Rastafarian gave them directions over the mobile as they made their way to Harry's. Sponge pulled up on the opposite side of the road, making the Rastafarian cross over towards them.

'Before we go any further, white boy, how me know you no be Babylon?' he asked.

'How do you know we're not the police?' asked Sponge. 'I see your point. No, we're not.'

'Let me see what you've got,' the Rastafarian said doubtfully.

'G-g-go on,' Minty enjoined Saddam, 'otherwise he's not going to go ahead with it.'

Reluctantly, Saddam leant over and unzipped the bag. The Rastafarian looked in the bag in amazement. 'All right, turn round. You see that small side road?' he said, pointing to a little service road leading to the car park behind the nightclub. He walked back across the road as Sponge started to turn his car round and follow him.

'I've got a bloody bad feeling about this! You shouldn't have shown him the drugs,' said Sponge, waiting for the traffic to subside before turning into the alley.

'D-d-don't worry about it, I've d-done this before,' Minty reassured him.

'Let's just get paid and get out of here! Don't drive down the alley, though,' said Saddam.

Sponge drove to the front of the nightclub and pulled up by the kerb. The Rastafarian came up to the car. Saddam pressed the electric window control, opening it a little way.

'They're waiting with the money round the back,' said the Rastafarian.

'Tell them to come out here so we can see them,' said Saddam.

'We can't do a deal in public,' the Rastafarian said.

'Fuck it! I'm not going down there,' answered Saddam.

'Listen, you can't do this on the street,' the man said. It was obvious that he was becoming frustrated.

'J-just d-d-do it,' said Minty.

'We could do it somewhere else,' suggested Sponge.

'There's nowhere else,' the man said.

'You sure about this, Minty?'

'Y-y-y-yeah!'

Sponge drove slowly down the alley and into the car park.

*

Jazz pressed the bell to Dylan's flat.

'Sam, is that you?' Dylan asked excitedly over the intercom.

'Yes, mate,' replied Jazz.

Dylan released the door and Jazz ran up the stairs. Dylan stood in the middle of the room, a look of elation on his face. 'I've been through hell and back, mate, but we've done it,' he exclaimed.

Jazz looked down at the floor. Inside three large sports bags were dozens of bundles of fifty-pound notes. A fourth sports bag was lying on Dylan's living-room table, more batches of notes surrounding it.

'Yardie connections, mate,' Dylan replied to Jazz's unspoken question.

'How much?' Jazz asked calmly.

'We've hit it big-time,' Dylan said.

'Yeah, how much?' Jazz asked again.

'I got nine hundred and fifty grand for the lot.'

'Really?' replied Jazz, knowing Dylan was not telling the truth and had pocketed some of the proceeds. He had no intention of haggling or levelling blame – the money in front of him was ample – but he knew Saddam would accuse him of conniving with Dylan. 'How much have you kept?' he asked.

'What's that supposed to mean?'

'This wasn't my gear, Dylan, neither is it my money. Those blokes are going to think I've plotted with you to pull a fast one.'

'What are you saying?'

'They know exactly how much you were supposed to get for it; those blokes are big fish,' said Jazz.

'Oh yeah? Then how come they couldn't shift it? Why did they have to come to you and then you come to me?'

Knowing he had lost the argument, Jazz looked enquiringly at Dylan. 'What's your commission?'

'For you, Sam, I'll take twenty per cent.'

'How much is that?'

'One hundred and ninety grand,' replied Dylan. 'It's on the centre table, I've counted it out already.'

'I'll take these then,' said Jazz, looking at the three bags on the floor.

'Do you need a hand?' Dylan offered.

'No, it's OK,' replied Jazz. 'I can manage.'

'What about the rest of the gear?' Dylan asked.

'What gear?'

'You know, the warehouse you said they had that was full of coke.'

'Oh yeah. It depends on whether they're pleased with the money you've given them for what you've sold.'

'Tell them I got the best deal for them. Tell them I'll be waiting to hear from them. I told my contacts we've got loads of the stuff,' Dylan said nervously.

'I'll speak to you soon,' said Jazz, putting the bags into his suitcase.

Two of the Rastafarian's cohorts stood by a blue Volkswagen Golf as Sponge pulled into the car park and turned the Range Rover to face the exit.

'Where's the money?' asked Saddam without getting out of the car. It was now patently obvious that the Rastafarian was desperate. Saddam immediately sensed they were being set up.

It was too late! The Rastafarian produced a revolver from beneath his jacket. 'Get out of the car,' he shouted.

Saddam got out slowly.

'Tell your friends to get out,' the man ordered.

'Get out! He's got a gun!' Saddam shouted to Sponge and Minty.

They got out too.

'I thought you said you'd done this before, Minty?' said Sponge.

'I have, I-I-I didn't f-f-fucking say I'd been r-r-ripped off before, though,' replied Minty.

Bubba's alarm clock went off at 5 a.m. on Tuesday morning. He got up and went into the bathroom. Just as he had suspected, Sponge had not come back: his bed lay empty. He phoned for a cab and wrote Sponge a note while waiting for the taxi to turn up.

It wasn't long before the doorbell rang. Bubba picked up his things. Leaving the spare keys to the flat on a side-table, he took one last look around and shut the door behind him. He got into the cab and began his journey to the airport. Ninety minutes later, he was on a flight bound for Ireland.

Jazz was in his room with the bags neatly stacked on top of the wardrobe. He lay there thinking. He'd had enough and wanted out. A fresh start! He wavered between feelings of loyalty, greed, guilt and pleasure at the acquisition of new wealth by such nefarious means.

He had come to the decision that neither Sponge nor Saddam deserved any money. He would quite simply tell them that the deal had fallen through and give Dylan a couple of thousand to feed them the same story. He had over three-quarters of a million pounds sitting in his bedroom and he did not know what to do with it.

He got up and walked downstairs into the living room. His father was asleep in a chair, a copy of the daily newspaper resting on his rising and falling chest. Such a gentle and kind man, Jazz thought to himself. He had toiled all these years to raise a family and had never been on holiday in his life. If anybody deserved to live in luxury, he did. Jazz shook him gently to rouse him.

'Two of your friends phoned,' his father said. 'I didn't want to wake you so I told them to call back later.'

'Thanks, Dad,' Jazz replied.

If he could talk to anybody, it was to his father.

It took Jazz thirty minutes to tell his father the whole story, and he felt better now that he had shared his secret.

'I just don't see why you had to get involved,' his father said.

'It's complicated but the damage has been done now, Dad, and I need to get rid of this money.'

'Simple things please prudent minds while bigger fools look on,' Jazz's father said. 'You could still have been very happy without this money. Have you thought of anything?'

'Yeah,' said Jazz. 'I want you and Mum to buy a small guesthouse in St Lucia and once in a while I can come out and visit you.'

'I can't do that,' said his father.

'Dad, just do it this once. If I could turn back the clock, I would never have got involved in this whole thing, but I have and the damage has been done. The best you can do is help me make something good of it.'

'What about Sponge and Saddam?'

'I wasn't going to give them anything at all, but I think I'll give them one hundred grand each to keep them quiet.'

'And what are you going to do?'

'What I always do: go to work,' replied Jazz. 'As long as I know you and Mum can live comfortably somewhere, it's all worth it to me. Besides, a guesthouse will be a good investment. If I change my mind, I can always come out and help you run it.'

'I've got some bad news for you,' Jazz said as Sponge opened the front door. Saddam was sitting in the living room looking forlorn and miserable.

'Bad news doesn't get better with waiting,' said Sponge as Jazz made himself comfortable.

'We didn't make as much as I thought we would,' began Jazz.

'You mean you got some cash?' asked Saddam, sitting up.

'Yeah, four hundred grand,' replied Jazz. 'A hundred went to Dylan, I keep a hundred and you get a hundred each.'

There was silence as Saddam and Sponge sat lost for words.

'So, what's the matter?' Jazz asked, unsure of the mood.

'Nothing . . . nothing,' replied Saddam. 'It's fucking great!'

'Yeah, fucking great,' added Sponge.

'I'll go and get it out of the car for you then,' said Jazz, standing up.

Jazz watched Sponge and Saddam counting the money like men whose souls were possessed by demons. 'Is it all there?' he asked. 'That's the fifth fucking time you've counted it.'

'Yeah,' replied Sponge. 'I'm just counting it again because it makes me feel good.'

'Well, in that case, I'll see you at work tomorrow,' said Jazz.

'What fucking work?' said Saddam, without looking up from his counting.

'You not coming in tomorrow?' asked Jazz.

'You've handed me a hundred grand on top of what I've already got,' said Saddam. 'It's enough to set me up outside the job doing anything I want. So why the fuck would I come in to do earlies, lates and nights, get treated like a fuckwit by senior officers and be sworn at by the public?'

'So you're not coming in?' said Jazz.

'Nope,' replied Saddam. 'I never fucking liked the job anyway. Besides, any copper in my position would be doing exactly the same. The job can get fucked as far as I'm concerned!'

'Sponge, are you coming in?' asked Jazz.

'Am I fuck!' said Sponge. 'I'm going abroad for a couple of months to decide what I want to do.'

'Well, questions are going to be asked if everybody starts resigning all of a sudden,' said Jazz.

'Put it down to morale: we resigned in disgust at the way Lionel was treated. That's your answer,' replied Saddam.

'Tell the governor our warrant cards are in the post,' said Sponge jocularly.

Jazz got a phone call from Sponge at 9 p.m. that evening. 'What do you want?' he asked.

'I think you need to come round to mine to find out,' Sponge said.

'Why, who's there?'

'Everybody,' Sponge replied nervously. 'Just get over here as soon as possible, all right?'

'All right, mate. I'll see you soon.'

'How soon?'

'Fucking soon, all right? Just get off my case, OK,' said Jazz.

He put down the phone and turned to his mother. 'Listen, Mum, I need to go over to Sponge's place. I'll be back soon.' He picked up his coat and left.

Jazz considered all the different scenarios that could have brought about this sudden urgency to meet. Arriving at nothing concrete, he decided to keep an open mind as he walked down the steps to Sponge's basement flat.

The first shock was Lionel opening the door after he rang the bell. 'It's about fucking time,' he heard Speedy shout as he entered.

In the living room sat the team, ashen-faced and agitated. He could tell something was seriously wrong the moment he caught a glimpse of their expressions. Sensing that the number of people in the room was not quite right, he began to count. When he saw who was on his left, his mind became a mental blank.

Sitting cross-legged and gazing up at him was Rigsby. He wore a pair of blue jeans, a white T-shirt and a leather flying jacket. It was the first time Jazz had seen him out of uniform.

'All right?' were the only words Jazz could muster. Then he looked around the room for an explanation. 'What the fuck's going on?' he asked.

Nobody said a word.

Finally Rigsby got up. 'Would you like a drink?' he asked.

'A fucking explanation would be better,' Jazz replied apprehensively. 'I thought you'd resigned.'

'I have,' said Rigsby, 'but you didn't think I was just going to silently evaporate?' There was a mixture of confidence and arrogance in the way he spoke and Jazz suddenly realized just who was moderating this gathering.

'This little fucker's trying to screw us,' said Speedy. 'He knows about the fucking money.'

'You shut the fuck up,' said Rigsby, pointing an angry finger at him.

'Yeah, shut the fuck up,' rejoined Sponge. 'I've had enough of you.'

'This was all your fucking fault,' Speedy said, directing his anger against Sponge. 'I ought to break your fucking neck right here, right now!'

'He wasn't the only one to blame,' interrupted Rigsby. 'It was obvious. Put it this way, with the exception of Jazz, even if the whole lot of you put your heads together and counted the sergeant's balls, none of you would give the same answer twice. And I was supposed to be the stupid one.'

'So what do you want?' asked Jazz.

'What do I want?' sniggered Rigsby. He shook his head, looked at the floor, then up at Jazz. 'You're the smartest of this bunch. What do you think I want?'

'You don't want to get involved in this,' said Jazz. 'This isn't you.'

'And I'd say it definitely wasn't you either, but look at you.'

'Does Sonia know about this as well?' Jazz asked.

'You'll have to ask her,' said Rigsby.

'What do you want?' asked Jazz again.

'Well, I finished university and joined the police because there weren't many jobs around for a young graduate. It wasn't what I wanted to do, but I didn't have much choice and I wanted to pay off my student loan. You've all deprived me of that and I'm not just going to slink away with nothing. I don't know how you blokes came across the money or how much you've got, but it's obviously substantial enough for you to be willing to take the risk.'

'How much do you want?' said Jazz.

'Two hundred thousand from each of you. I don't care how much you end up with; I don't even give a fuck if you end up broke. After the way you blokes have treated me, I don't think I should give a flying fuck about you.'

'We never got anything like that amount in the first place,' Jazz answered, trying to manoeuvre.

'Like I said, I really don't care,' said Rigsby. 'I'll give you till Friday. It's either that or prison.'

'You fucking arsehole, I'll fucking kill you!' said Speedy, jumping up, and rushing towards him. He grabbed Rigsby by the throat and began to throttle him.

Jazz stepped in and wrested Rigsby out of Speedy's grasp. 'We're in enough trouble as it is,' he shouted at Speedy. 'Don't complicate things further.'

'Till Friday,' gasped Rigsby, massaging his neck. 'Make sure you have the money.' He walked briskly out of the flat.

'You should have let me wring his fucking neck,' shouted Speedy as the door slammed behind Rigsby.

'Shut the fuck up, will you,' said Jazz.

Ten minutes later, they began to discuss what they were going to do.

'We're each just going to have to fork out,' said Lionel. 'It's either that or go to fucking prison.'

'How are you involved in this?' Speedy asked Jazz.

'I flogged some gear for Saddam and Sponge,' replied Jazz.

'You fucking wankers,' Speedy screamed at Sponge and Saddam. 'You sold the fucking drugs.'

'Oh shut up,' said Saddam. 'Drug money, drugs, they're all the same thing.'

'Let's just pay him off,' repeated Lionel.

'What about Sonia? What if she wants a cut?' asked Speedy.

'I'll speak to her and find out,' said Jazz.

'Don't go bloody asking her; she might not know,' said Saddam.

'I'm the smart one, remember,' replied Jazz. 'I'll find out one way or another. We'll meet here Friday afternoon and everybody should have their share of the money.'

'We're early turn Friday,' said Sponge.

'I thought you were resigning?' asked Jazz.

'Not any more. We can't fucking afford it now,' said Saddam.

'Are you blokes saying we're going to give that shit a million quid in three days' time?' asked Speedy in disbelief.

'We haven't got much of a fucking choice, have we?' said Jazz.

EPILOGUE

Jazz walked into the inspector's office. Three officers were seated around the table.

'Ah, here's your sergeant,' said the inspector when he saw Jazz. 'There are three new officers joining your team. This is DC Clarke, now PC Clarke – he's just been busted down to uniform by the discipline board for smacking his governor. PC Bennett, transferred from Kentish Town, come over under a bit of a cloud, something to do with a plonk. PC Hill, been kicked out of the Yard on tenure being up.'

'All right, lads? No need to look so shocked. I know I'm black,' said Jazz. 'I've just got a new probationer you'll have to show the ropes to. I know you'll all be bitter, but you're going to have to keep up appearances.'

'I know morale is really bad at the moment because of the way Lionel was suspended, and you've had one or two resignations, but hopefully you can make a fresh start with this lot,' said the inspector. 'It's the best we could do.'

'Cheers, sir,' replied Jazz ruefully.

'We don't know what to call you,' said Jazz as he and PC Bennett walked into the canteen. 'Did you have a nickname at Kentish Town nick?'

'Benny will do,' said PC Bennett.

'What did you do before you joined the job?' asked Jazz.

'I used to be a plumber,' he replied.

'Why did you leave that to join the Bill?'

'I got fed up of dealing with other people's shit all day,' said PC Bennett. 'I obviously chose the wrong fucking job.'

Speedy, Sponge, Saddam and Sonia were sitting with the two other new officers and the new probationer, Sean Adey. Sean already looked quite comfortable and was doing most of the talking as they sat languidly around the table. 'Canned it fucking massive yesterday, six hours' overtime,' he said.

'What were you dealing with?' asked Sonia.

'An off-the-pavement,' he replied. 'Some slag off the Prado estate walking his dog and giving it the biggen as we drove past. So I stopped and did his mangy little fucking mongrel on suspicion of being a pit bull terrier. You should have seen the cunt, he was in fucking tears. Ended up having to do tons of paperwork.'

'How can you tell a pit bull just by looking at it?' asked Sonia.

'I don't fucking know,' said Sean, 'he just fucking deserved it. Anyway, he got it back in the end.'

'Who's making the coffees then?' Jazz asked.

'Sonia is, sarge, she's the plonk,' replied Sean.

'What did you just call me?' Sonia asked.

'Plonk!' PC Bennett answered for him.

'You've got a right fucking gob on you! Just remember, you're younger in service than I am. You've only been on this team for five days. You call me a plonk again and I'll kick your arse into tomorrow,' Sonia said fiercely to Sean.

'I think you've lit the fuse in her Tampax, mate,' said PC Bennett.

'I can't have you speaking like that to officers with more service than you,' said Jazz, finally stamping his authority on the conversation.

'Why don't you both leave him alone? He's a good egg,' Speedy said to Jazz and Sonia. 'Unlike that prick Rigsby, he's settled in nicely and become one of the lads. That's what we want.'

PC Clarke, formerly DC Clarke, reeled in disbelief at seeing Jazz stick up for a female officer in preference to a male. 'This is the fucking Met, isn't it? I mean, I have got the right fucking building, haven't I?'

'You got the time on you?' Speedy asked PC Bennett.

'Yeah, it's four thirty,' said PC Bennett, looking at his watch. 'Only another four hours, three days, thirty-two weeks and fourteen years to go till retirement.'

'Nice to see you're bubbling with enthusiasm on your first day here,' Jazz said.

'Experience and enthusiasm are two words you don't find in the same sentence if you've just been kicked out of a squad and on to the street like I have. After all the effort I made to get there in the first place, they sling me out, telling me I've been there for long enough,' said PC Hill bitterly.

'I'm glad you lads have already settled in,' said Jazz, getting up. 'Can I have a word with you outside?' he asked Sonia. He turned to Sean. 'Make the coffees and bring mine over to the custody suite. And if you fucking spit in it, I'll kill you!' he added, remembering the many sordid things he had done to his own sergeant's coffee as a probationer.

Jazz waited until they reached the centre of the yard before he began to speak to Sonia. 'Have you spoken to Rigsby lately?'

'Why?' she asked.

'I'm just curious,' he replied.

'Yes, I have, actually. He told me to thank you for the money if you asked me about it.'

Jazz shifted uneasily.

'Don't worry,' she assured him, 'he thinks I'm stupid not to want to get involved, but I don't want anything to do with it. The only thing I want from you blokes is for you to cut me a bit of slack and leave me alone to do my job. Tell the others that as well.'

'Sounds fair enough,' replied Jazz.

'The inspector wants to see you,' Sean told Speedy.

'What the fuck does he want?' Speedy exclaimed, getting out of the area car. He straightened up and tucked his shirt into his trousers before walking across the yard to the inspector's office. As he knocked on the door, he could hear the inspector talking to somebody in a low tone.

The door opened and the inspector leaned out into the corridor to check that Speedy was unaccompanied. 'Are you on your own?' he asked.

'Yes, sir,' said Speedy.

'In that case, come in. There's somebody here who's very interested in speaking to you.'

Speedy did not at first recognize the man sitting in front

of the inspector's desk. It was only when the man got up that the penny dropped. For the first time in his long career, Speedy nearly died of fright.

It was the Greek-Cypriot they had taken the money and drugs from.

'I'd like you to meet an acquaintance of mine,' the inspector said. 'From what I understand, you two have already met, but in rather different circumstances.'